THE TEXT

JULANE FISHER

infinite teen

Atlanta

INFINITE TEEN
An imprint of Infinite Skies Publishing, LLC
infiniteteenpublishing.com

Cover design by Deranged Doctor Design.

Infinite Teen Publishing can bring authors to your live event. For more information or to book an event, go to infiniteteenpublishing.com

Printed in the United States of America. ISBN 979-8-9882409-6-9 (hardback) / ISBN 979-8-9882409-4-5 (paperback) / ISBN 979-8-9882409-5-2 (eBook)

Infinite Teen
An imprint of Infinite Skies Publishing, LLC
P.O. Box 566281
Atlanta, GA 31156

For Connor and Bryson. Never be afraid...

Part I

"Humanity is acquiring all the right technology for all the wrong reasons."

R. Buckminster Fuller

CHAPTER 1

THURSDAY, SEPTEMBER 21

Creating backdoor access to the most popular social media app, Allicio, proved more difficult than I imagined. Opening Allicio on my mobile phone wasn't an option. Too many spying eyes. I created a code that would provide a behind-the-scenes look at Allicio's users. *If* it worked. It wasn't exactly hacking, because any beginning coder like me could have written this sequence.

My phone pinged a series of text messages from my best guy friend, Finley. A verified tech genius, Finley could decrypt almost anything. But he would have to wait. First, I had to check in with the STaR health device mounted to my bedroom wall. Failure to register night and day alerted the Safety Division of a potential health threat. That was the last thing I needed.

I approached my health device and gazed into the camera. The size of a mini tablet, the scanner read my temperature, oxygen level, and blood pressure. If anything registered elevated, a report was sent to headquarters, although most people suspected they were never read.

"Star keeps us healthy. Star keeps us safe," I muttered under my breath, repeating the mantra I'd been taught since I was little.

The Department of Safety Threats and Reinforcement, which everyone called STaR, was America's solution to the global pandemic that struck years before I was born. Sometimes I wondered what life was like before the pandemic, before health check-ins and safety protocols. I moved closer, allowing facial recognition to respond.

"Star," I said. I expected her daily boring speech. *Rami Carlton. Your temperature is normal. You would benefit from additional sleep. Vitamin D is recommended.*

But nothing happened. I pressed the reset button and called her name again.

"Star? Are you there?" When she remained quiet, I rolled my eyes and walked back to the computer.

Our STaRs were only supposed to activate when we called them by name, but everyone knew STaR could listen to conversations if they wanted to. I nicknamed mine Rosemary so I could talk about her without waking her up.

My phone buzzed again, distracting me from my rambling thoughts. I didn't have to glance at the screen to know Finley was taunting me. He'd created this game to test my decryption skills after I'd proven a worthy opponent in freshman coding class.

We competed to see who could get the real name of the techies in our online chat group first. It was a harmless game, more of a coding exercise, really, to see if we could do it. We never revealed anyone's identity. Their online screen name remained a secret between Fin and me.

Bald Eagle joined our chat group last month and gave me a run for his money. He was good, I'd give him that, but I would find him. Once I discovered his growing Allicio account with close to

100,000 followers, I followed a trail of clues. I scrolled to one of his first posts. Social media users often made rookie mistakes in the first few posts, like forgetting to hide their IP address or using their phone. Bald Eagle posted hundreds of videos on Allicio, but never of himself. He loved watching people do stupid things, like street racing electric vehicles. I figured that was the reason he chose Bald Eagle as an online profile: eagle eyes spying from a distance.

"Come on, show me who you really are," I whispered to myself. My phone dinged. Finley again.

You in Whitetail? Yep, I see you. 3-2-1.

Finley's way of telling me he was three seconds away from winning. I laughed at how competitive we'd become.

Bald Eagle's second post showed a video of two kids drone racing at night far below the no-fly zone. But it was the building behind the drones that grabbed my attention. A familiar sight, one I'd seen thousands of times. Connect Mobile's headquarters in the Southeastern region where I lived. Only select IP addresses could access the secure campus. Ones with access to Connect's internal network. Bald Eagle had left breadcrumbs, as if he wanted to be found. It all seemed too easy.

Got him. Bald Eagle aka Dominic Bell.

Smile emoji. 1-3.

Finley had beaten me three times to my one slam dunk tonight. Still, a win was a win. I smiled and shot a series of emojis his way, gloating in my success before shutting down my laptop.

I climbed into bed, prepared to fight sleep rather than give in to the terrifying nightmare that had hijacked my sleep for the past two years, but my body had a mind of its own. My eyes flickered then gave in to the sleep I desperately needed.

Harsh winds pressed against tall trees, their fallen leaves swirling at my feet. Behind me, water crashed against rocks, cascaded hundreds of feet below. Something sinister encircled me, pressing me backward further toward the abyss with no hope of escape except to plummet to my death. I awoke seconds before hitting the ground, breathless.

This leap marked the third day in a row I'd overslept. I rolled over to check the numbers on the vintage radio alarm clock my mom insisted I put next to my bed. She swore up and down that battery-operated clocks were more reliable than my phone. I should've listened because I'd set two alarms on my mobile last night—one to startle me and the other to force me out of bed. I blinked to clear my vision, but the red numbers on the vintage clock didn't lie. If I didn't hurry, I'd be late for school.

Before jumping into the shower, I approached my STaR health device mounted to the wall and gazed into the camera. "Star?" I said, edging in close. No response. Just like last night. "Stupid Rosemary."

I couldn't wait any longer. One more tardy to school meant detention, which would bench me for this weekend's volleyball game. Just last week I'd earned my spot as a starter on varsity. No way was I going to be late. After taking the world's fastest freezing shower, I threw on a flannel button-down over my graphic t-shirt and tugged on a pair of ripped jeans.

My STaR-issued phone sat on the nightstand, still plugged into the charging cord. I snatched it and tapped the messages to alert my best friend, Lela Ferreira, that I'd overslept and would catch a ride with my mom. I was probably the only junior who couldn't drive yet. Totally embarrassing.

When the messages didn't open, I pressed harder. Still no response. I tried to dial her number, but the phone app seemed frozen, too. Blackouts had become more common since every household had EV charging stations and multiple STaR units. But the power outages had never taken down our mobile phones. *Weird*. Out of time, I slung my backpack over one shoulder and ran downstairs.

Our German shepherd, Nollie, barked like aliens had touched down on our lawn, but it was just my brother Zac chasing after the middle school bus. Nollie seemed to think her job was to protect Zac at all costs, while she tolerated me. Sort of. Once the bus stopped and Zac disappeared inside, Nollie shut up. That's when I noticed the blaring television coming from the family room.

I walked around the corner where Mom stood catatonic in front of the TV. How could she possibly ignore Nollie's barking? It gave me a total headache.

"Mom? What the—"

The TV aired UNN, our only news source, and I watched as images of Atlanta came into view. Minutes from downtown Atlanta, I lived in a section of Buckhead that had once been an equestrian community before Connect Mobile moved its headquarters to the Southeastern region and established the technology district.

The reporter gazed into the camera's lens. "This is Latricia Roberts, reporting for the United News Network. A power outage of epidemic proportions shut down millions of STaR health devices and mobile phones, leaving Connect Mobile baffled. We take you live to Connect Mobile's Southeastern headquarters in Atlanta where..."

She described the event like it was the apocalypse. Yet something appeared off. A power outage like the one she described would take out our TV. Our home ran on solar energy with no backup power source. It didn't make sense. But if STaR wanted to crash their own network, why should I care? Before I voiced this out loud, the scene switched to some so-called expert arguing the impossibility of all devices crashing simultaneously. I glanced at the battery-operated wall clock. I had more important things to worry about than a blackout. The first bell rang in twenty-five minutes.

I pulled out my phone just in case the UNN reporter was wrong. It flickered, then went dark. "STaR's only cellular provider crashed their own phones. Brilliant," I said.

Mom moved toward me with cat-like speed, clutching me close to her chest. She brushed her lips across my ear, her words barely audible. "You can't speak against the TD, Rami. It's dangerous."

Mom had made comments about the Threats Division before, so I knew she feared being overheard. What I didn't understand was why.

Twenty-five years ago, after an unknown virus unleashed on the world and killed over two billion people, America's president was ousted for his failure to control the spread of the virus. President Iris Young was ushered in after promising to keep citizens safe. She replaced America's three-branch government with a new and improved system to protect us from future bioterrorism. STaR ran the government as three divisions, but information rarely got shared across the divisions because they couldn't stand each other. Yet every year at the beginning of the school year, we were required to memorize our governmental system.

The Safety Division kept us safe and healthy by installing health monitors in every home, ensuring we remained disease free. The Reinforcement Division reestablished law and order, encapsulating the police department, federal law agencies, and the military.

But for some reason, Mom was more concerned about the Threats Division. I didn't know much about them other than they contained the spread of disinformation. Whatever that meant.

My parents were my age when the pandemic occurred, so their childhood memories included life before scanners. But I didn't know of a single person who had been punished for something they said in their own home. My mother's reaction was weird.

"There's fresh rosemary in the freezer," I reminded her, our secret language implying STaR was offline.

She released her grip and turned back to the TV as if I hadn't spoken. "It's happening." Her voice trembled.

My mother so rarely showed emotion that her response startled me. "What?"

Her green eyes filled with fear. She hit the off button on the remote control and ran her fingers through golden-blond curls, a trait I inherited. "No matter what happens, promise me you'll protect Zac."

"What are you talking about?"

She reached for my shoulders and almost clawed through my shirt. "Rami! Promise me!"

I swallowed hard. "Okay. I promise."

Protect Zac? What does that mean? I'd always looked out for Zac, and Mom knew it. When Dad skipped out on us, Mom couldn't get out of bed, much less care for Zac. I helped him get ready for school, packed his lunch, and walked him to the bus stop, sheltering him from rumors that spread faster than a kudzu vine.

"It's happening," she repeated, her voice shaky. She pulled the key fob from her purse and spun on her heels.

"Mom? You're scaring me." I felt I should call someone, but my phone was like a roadside animal. Dead. Besides, who would I call? Zac didn't have a phone, and I refused to tell Dad that Mom had lost her marbles, so I did the only thing I knew to do. I grabbed my backpack and followed her to the garage.

The instant I climbed into her electric car, she turned the radio to UNN, backed out of the garage, and sped down the two-lane road that led to my school. Her silence unnerved me. I stared out the window. A swarm of drones flew overhead in the direction of the technology district. Although drones were common, a swarm was never a good sign.

As one drone paused near the driver's side window, Mom stared straight ahead, clutching the steering wheel until her knuckles turned the color of snow. The drone ran parallel with our vehicle until we reached the turn for the high school. When the drone moved on, Mom exhaled with such force, I thought she'd pass out.

I muted the radio and raised my voice. "What's going on? The drones...it's happening? What does that even mean?"

Mom's eyes darted to the touchscreen, which housed STaR's safety features. I had no idea whether her car contained a listening device. I'd never given it a thought. Until her voice suddenly became chirpy. "I have a meeting tonight at church. I need you to stay home with Zac."

Although the Southeastern region permitted religion, I'd heard rumors that other regions had banned church attendance because gathering in crowds had the potential to spread illnesses. Still, her response angered me. "You're seriously worried about a meeting at church right now?"

"No..." Her fake cheery mood faded. She pulled up to the curb in front of the school and leaned over the seat.

A tear trickled down her cheek. She held up her thumb, index finger, and pinkie, and pushed her hand toward my heart. "Goodbye, Rami. I love you."

Mom taught Zac and me to communicate with sign language long before we could talk. And, although I hadn't thought about it in years, I used to sign with Zac when he was an infant. She'd even taught us to sign the alphabet. But why use sign language now? She was acting so weird.

I turned up my lip. "What is wrong with you?"

A horn honked behind us. "You better go," she said.

I climbed out of the car as a large drone flew overhead. Suddenly, I didn't care about being late. Something wasn't right. "Mom—"

But all I saw were taillights fading in the distance. I walked to the school's entrance and approached the health scanner. The lights flickered which meant the school had some sort of backup power source. When no one's temperature registered on the scanner, the assistant principal waved everyone inside.

The first bell rang as I entered the atrium, a popular spot for cheerleaders flipping hair over their shoulders and hiking their skirts up an extra inch for selfies. But instead of selfies, the girls stared into space barely speaking to each other. As I walked down the eleventh-grade hall, I made mental notes of other bizarre behaviors, like the absence of kids clustered together posting to social media. Instead, everyone's thumbs pounded against their phone as if that would make them work.

I thought about the reporter this morning and realized she had a point. My friends and I had grown up with phones in our hand. We'd never known life without it. Without phones, we acted a lot like zombies.

When I spotted Finley pulling a brown wooden box from his locker and chatting with some guy I didn't know, I let out a sigh of relief. They appeared to be the only ones unaffected by the zombie epidemic. If anyone had a logical explanation for today's events, it would be Fin. But once I overheard Finley say cyber-attack and EMP, I lost hope.

When I approached, the kid shifted backward, as if I carried a disease. *What's his problem*? I watched him dart off with amusement. "Fin? Is your phone working yet? Can I borrow it?"

Finley's eyes narrowed, giving me a once-over. "No one's phone works. Jack and I were discussing the power grids."

"But a power outage wouldn't have crashed our phones."

Finley shrugged. "Maybe, maybe not. If the power knocked out the cell towers, it could have taken down the network."

I leaned my head back and closed my eyes, envisioning my mother signing to me. The slamming of metal jolted me back to the present.

Finley ran his fingers through his wavy hair, making it stand on end. The shades of tan with flakes of gold and amber reminded me of a pile of oak leaves. His eyes, the color of pecan shells—creamy brown with specks of black sprinkled throughout—held my gaze a moment longer than necessary. "You okay, Rames?"

I let out an exaggerated groan and then described my morning, from oversleeping to Rosemary being offline. But it was Mom's odd behavior that gave me pause. "She didn't make any sense and wouldn't answer my questions. And she *totally* freaked out about me being home with Zac. If I could just call her—"

"They have computer-generated phones in the office, you know." Finley laughed at my dumbfounded expression.

STaR provided computer-generated phones in case of a widespread outage, like the one today, but only institutions had the power capacity to house them. While the solar energy in our homes worked to heat, cool, and cook, the mandated EV plugs and STaR monitors left little reserve.

"Oh, yeah. I always forget about those." I pointed to the wooden box in Finley's hand. "What's that?"

"Chess. Remember? I joined the club last month."

"Ah." I feigned interest. "You're hanging out with nerds." *As if being a techie didn't make me nerdy, too.*

"Chess is a game of strategy and intelligence." He puffed out his chest, making me snicker despite my mood. "And we have a chance of making it to the state finals this year."

"Isn't it an augmented reality simulation?" I motioned to the solar-powered headset hanging from his backpack.

"Yeah, so even with the power failure, we can still play in Coach Richards's homeroom, if everyone charged their headsets last night." He turned toward the gym. "You should see if you can use the school's phone."

"Will do." I wandered through the maze of students near the office and pushed my way inside.

The receptionist, Mrs. Bowling, held the receiver to her ear, shouting over the volume of chatter. Her glasses sat perched on the tip of her sharp nose and her thin lips were drawn into a tight scowl. "Yes, the students are just fine. No, we won't be closing school today. The students can learn using pen and paper without their electronic devices." She hung up, and it rang again. "If anyone is trying to go home because of STaR's outage, we deny your request. Please go to first period."

As the other students grumbled their way to the exit, I marched up to her desk, where her phone continued to ring. Above her head, a large TV screen aired UNN, with the caption, *Connect Mobile denies responsibility for network outage.*

Mrs. Bowling peered above her glasses. "Can I help you?"

"Oh, um, yes. I need to call my mom. We had a...an emergency in our house this morning. I...I want to be sure she's all right." A slight exaggeration but not a complete lie.

She nodded to the computer behind her desk. "One minute, then please get to class."

"Yes, ma'am." I slipped on the headset and punched Mom's work number into the keyboard.

After three rings, a lady answered. "Good morning. Griffin and Howell attorneys at law. How may I direct your call?"

"Hi. Is Annie Carlton there? This is her daughter, Rami."

"I'm sorry. Annie isn't in yet. Would you like her voicemail?"

Something vibrated against my leg, followed by a faint ping. I pulled my phone from the front pocket of my jeans. A text from a number I didn't recognize.

The voice on the other end of the computer line chirped. "Hello? Did you want her voicemail?"

“Yeah. I mean...” The words stuck to the roof of my mouth. My eyes darted about. Chills crept up my spine.

Mom’s voice echoed through the headphones. “This is Annie Carlton, legal assistant for Mark Griffin. Please leave a message and I’ll get back to you.”

I dropped the headset without leaving a message, desperate to make sense of the words that appeared on my phone.

STaR watches over you, Rami.

CHAPTER 2

Thursday, September 21

I grabbed the hall pass from Mrs. Bowling and fled to the nearest bathroom where two girls stood in front of the mirror applying black eyeliner. The one with the nose ring pulled a tube of mascara from her purse and plastered it to her lashes, totally ignoring me.

I initiated facial recognition, which suddenly worked, then scrolled to the Messages app. My sweaty palms shook.

Who is this?

I waited, my stomach in knots, as gray dots pulsed. An ellipsis popped up. *Someone is answering.*

Seconds passed, then the typing bubble, and the message disappeared. Connect Mobile's logo appeared—a red C swirling around a scarlet globe—then the screen turned black. I pushed the power button harder, harder. Nothing. The girls gawked at me, whispering to each other as they left, and I wondered for a split second if I had imagined the text message. But I knew I hadn't.

Why would I need a reminder about STaR looking out for me? It was totally creepy.

Unless I'd upset someone last night. *Could Bald Eagle have sent the text? And how could I even get a text during a network failure?* None of this made sense.

I clutched the white porcelain sink and peered into the mirror. Considering the morning I'd had, I half expected to see a green alien protrude from my body or my flesh decaying, but it was just me, with my hazel eyes that now simmered with fear. The black circles against my pale skin made the brown ring around the green iris appear darker. I pulled a light-beige concealer from the outer pocket of my backpack and dotted a bit on my skin, but it didn't help. Nothing hid my lack of sleep.

With homeroom over, I weaved through the crowded hallway to first period. Brannon Martinelli's unmistakable swag drew closer until I caught a whiff of his cologne—pine with a hint of spice. He laughed, the deep, throaty kind that made my skin tingle. His deep-set blue eyes twinkled, and I drew in a breath. He fiddled with his jet-black hair as if the gel he applied this morning hadn't done its job. But Brannon brushed past me, leaving me standing in the middle of the hall feeling totally stupid. He draped his arm around one of the cheerleaders I'd seen in the atrium this morning. I stared at the dingy tile floor and wished I could stuff myself in a locker.

As Brannon and the girl went to class, I watched my classmates scurry around each other, heads down, no eye contact. No one paid any attention to me, including Brannon. Almost as if I were invisible.

"What do all the girls see in him, anyway?" Finley said.

The loud humming in my ears made it impossible to hear Finley's approach. "Wha...what?"

Finley gave me a slight elbow jab. "Brannon. He's a total player."

"Yeah. Well, he hasn't always been like that," I countered, surprised I defended him.

Brannon and I had been friends freshman year. Not like "hang out after school" friends, but our teacher had paired us up for biology lab, and that became the highlight of my year. In a way, Brannon saved me.

My dad had left—moved out without an explanation—and I couldn't handle it. Brannon made me laugh without trying and joked about our crazy teacher, who resembled a cartoon character. Because of Brannon, I looked forward to going to school. That's when the crush started.

But everything changed when Brannon made the varsity lacrosse team. He spent every waking moment in the gym bulking up, and I swear his head swelled bigger than his biceps because after that, he only talked to the popular girls, and apparently, I didn't make the cut.

"It doesn't matter," I continued. "He doesn't know I exist, so I'm not too worried about getting caught up in his game."

Finley followed me to Algebra II. "Probably just as well."

I pretended not to care, but Brannon had hurt me. More than he knew. I needed to move on, to forget him and stop letting it affect me.

Annoyed with myself, I sat in the desk and quickly changed the subject. "Did you just send me a weird text?"

"What part of *everyone's* phone is dead did you miss?" Finley smirked, choosing the seat next to mine.

"I'm serious, Fin. If you're pulling a prank on me, it's not funny."

Finley shot me a sideways glance. "I'm not pranking you, Rames."

My skin tightened. *Was I the only one who received the bizzarre text*? "I got some crazy message about STaR watching out for me. I tried to respond, but my phone shut back down."

Finley's eyes darted about. He leaned in close and spoke just above a whisper. "That's not possible, Rames, not with a network failure and STaR offline."

I glanced at our teacher, Mr. Tarito. He was looking down at his laptop. If Finley could fix my phone before he caught me with it in class...

"I know it sounds crazy, but I'm not making this up," I said.

"There's no way you got a text. Connect Mobile hasn't had voice or text capability all morning." Finley's super-smart explanation made sense. But I didn't imagine the text. Of that, I was sure.

Before he could check me into a mental institution, Lela plopped down, her head buried in her phone. The phone she wasn't supposed to have in class. But who was I to judge?

"This is the worst day of my life." Lela's brown hair had new streaks of fuchsia mixed in, and her exaggerated pout made her lips look more puffy than normal. *Did she get fillers and forget to tell me*?

I loved my best friend, but seriously, her obsession with social media overwhelmed me. Especially her fascination with Allicio, which boasted over two billion users worldwide. Everything in Lela's world got posted. Every pic. Every event. Every video. Not being able to post today was equivalent to torture. With a huff, Lela flicked a strand of fuchsia behind her shoulder. I wondered whether pink signaled happy or distressed. Based on Lela's expression, I assumed the latter.

"I couldn't take a video of you drooling over Brannon. It would've been perfect for Allicio," she said, flicking her eyes upward.

Quince, Lela's boyfriend, lowered his six-foot-something frame into the tiny desk behind Lela. While smoothing his black curly hair, he let out a half laugh, half snort, and his chewing gum flew across the floor. He scrambled to grab his wad of gum and gestured to my messy hair and mismatched outfit before reaching for my chin. "Hey Blondie? There's some leftover drool right about here." His milk chocolate eyes held a hint of mischief.

I swatted at Quince's hand. "Lela, your phone doesn't work at all? Not even to send a text?"

"Uh, no. No phone, no camera, no selfies. I might as well die." Lela muttered something unintelligible in Portuguese.

Okay, so Lela was also a bit of a drama queen.

Mr. Tarito handed out worksheets on multiplying and dividing complex units. His nervous nose twitch seemed amplified this morning, as if the outage put him on edge, too. His tortoise-shelled glasses slid down his nose with each twitch and he stopped several times to shove them upward.

Without thinking, I stood up and walked to the open classroom door, peering into the empty hallway. When I returned to my seat, Mr. Tarito stood in front of the class with raised eyebrows.

"Miss Carlton? Find what you're looking for?"

I tugged at my silver dangle earring. "Um, not really."

When he turned away, I whispered to Lela, "Did you message me this morning? Like a prank or something?"

Before she answered, Mr. T whipped back around. "Want to share something with the class?"

My parents taught me to behave in school and never talk back to a teacher. The advice had served me well. Until today. "Sometimes there are more important things happening in the world than finding the values of x and y."

Red splotches crept up Mr. T's neck. His nose trembled like he couldn't stop the twitch. He cleared his throat and headed my way, no doubt with a detention slip in hand.

Finley intercepted his flight. "Um, Mr. Tarito? Rami ate way too much sugar before coming to class, and with the outage and all, she's not herself. I'm sure she'll contain her thoughts the rest of class. We're covering unit three today, right?"

If anyone else had spoken to Mr. T this way, he would have been furious. But Finley's a brainiac, and Mr. T loved him. Finley worked on Mr. Tarito's computer and even helped automate his lessons.

Mr. Tarito shot a look at Finley before giving me a stare-down. "Miss Carlton? You need to stay away from sugar. Are we clear?"

"Yes, sir." I bit my lower lip and grinned at Finley.

He just saved me from detention.

By the 3:30 dismissal bell, it took every ounce of energy I could muster to keep from bolting out of this building. A familiar hum stopped me in my tracks. Everyone stopped what they were doing as ringtones, songs, and message alerts on every mobile phone came to life at the exact same time, like something, or someone, had orchestrated the event. I stared as zombies rose from the dead—their cheers deafening—and tugged my phone from the back pocket of my jeans. When I swiped up, another message appeared.

A fatal error occurred. Software update not available. Go to Connect Mobile for assistance.

Then the red C swirled, and my mobile shut down.

Since blackouts had become more common, the school required everyone to keep an old-fashioned binder with lined paper in their assigned locker. It seemed stupid considering everything school related stored to our laptops. But today, everyone had their school-issued binders in hand and no one wanted to lug the thing home, especially since the network had been restored.

Lela rushed toward me, with Quince trailing behind. Before I reached my locker, she held up her phone and smashed her face against mine.

Something gave me pause, like a flutter in my stomach, only worse. "Where are you posting that?"

Lela's contagious grin returned. "Allicio. Duh."

"You know what Allicio means, right?" Quince chomped on his gum and didn't wait for an answer. "Lure, entice, attract. Just sayin'."

Lela scrunched up her nose. "And you know this how?"

"Two years of Latin." Quince shrugged, as if understanding Latin was totally normal.

"Whatever, Quince. Just because you're social media averse doesn't mean I have to be." Lela turned to me. "Does your phone work?"

"Sort of." I stuffed the bulky binger into my locker. "But I got an error message."

A concerned frown flashed across Lela's forehead, but with her precious social media account restored, it vanished quickly. "That's weird. I just have to download the update." She bobbed her eyebrows up and down. "Lure me in, Allicio. Lela is back in business."

I laughed and shut my locker. "Can I borrow your phone on the way home to message my mom? She acted really weird this morning."

"Yeah. Sure." Lela looped her arm through Quince and turned to go. When I didn't move, her brows crinkled together. "You coming?"

I groaned. "In a minute. Coach Sanchez wants to see me."

"That doesn't sound good," Quince said.

"No doubt." I cringed. "I'll meet you guys at the car."

In the gym, Coach Sanchez tossed basketballs from PE class into a large metal bin. Her perfectly tanned skin glowed under the gym's florescent lights and her long black ponytail fell across her chest. When she spotted me lingering in the doorway, she smiled. At least that was a good sign.

I fiddled with a loose hangnail. "You wanted to see me?"

"Yes. Thanks for stopping by." Coach Sanchez wiped her hands on her gym shorts. "You had a good practice yesterday. I liked your hustle and determination. I want you to start in tomorrow's game."

"Okay." I swallowed hard as she locked the bin.

"You earned it, Rami, but just so we're clear. Make sure you're on time to school from now on." She shot me a wicked grin.

She knows. "I will. I promise."

"If you ever need to talk, *estoy aquí para ti.*" After three years of Spanish, you'd think I'd understand. Confusion must have registered on my face, because she quickly translated. "I'm here for you."

Unsure what to say, I gave a slight nod. "Thank you, Coach."

"See you tomorrow." She turned and strolled toward her office.

I smiled at her words and raced to catch up with Lela. Coach Sanchez worked us hard, but she cared about her players. I wouldn't let her down.

When I reached the parking lot, a stupid mosquito landed on my leg, and all the pent-up frustration from the day unleashed on that annoying insect. Some moron had the bright idea of building a school near a mosquito-infested marshland we call the Swamp. It's been the endless source of pranks for years, especially at Halloween. Today's low-hanging fog gave it a ghostly appearance, like a graveyard scene in a horror film.

A creepy sensation, like being covered in spiders, crawled up my back. The same feeling I got earlier when the text message appeared. I glanced over my shoulder, but nothing seemed out of place.

Until I spotted him. Near the edge of the Swamp. A shadowy figure beneath an enormous birch tree. Something about his crooked smile made the hair on the back of my neck stand up.

He stared at me, motionless. Watching over me.

Just like the text.

CHAPTER 3

Thursday, September 21

Lela and Quince remained tangled against Lela's baby blue electric coupe, oblivious to my situation. I raced to the passenger seat, slammed the door, and honked the horn to get Lela's attention. My eyes scanned the parking lot, but the man I'd just seen in the Swamp disappeared.

Lela threw her head back in laughter, the kind that drew in a crowd, then pecked Quince on the cheek. She climbed in the car and handed me her phone, then without warning, tore out of the lot at high speed. She bounced to the beat of her playlist while strands of fuchsia hit the back of the seat. Behind us, a charcoal gray car followed, edging close enough to make out a male driver wearing a baseball hat, but the darkened windows shielded the driver's face.

I dialed Mom's mobile. It went straight to voicemail, so I called again and left a message. Then a text.

Mom? Are you okay?

Seconds felt like hours as I waited for the ellipsis to appear. But the dots didn't show up. Maybe she turned her phone off for a meeting, or maybe her phone hadn't come back on since the outage. My thumbs pounded on the keys.

Text me! I'm worried!

Where are you? Please answer.

The loud music made my head throb. I glanced in the side mirror again. "That car's been following us since we left school. It's creepy."

Lela glanced in her rearview mirror. "This whole day creeped me out. I mean, no one could take a selfie. That's a bad day."

I threw a glance at Lela, whose face held a smirk. She'd been my best friend since sixth grade when her family moved in three doors down. Everything about Lela exuded confidence, from the way she walked into a room of total strangers without a moment's hesitation to how she held her head high. Lela's carefree attitude reflected who I longed to be—bold and uninhibited.

"Just because the car drove down Horse Farm Road doesn't mean he's following us. Almost everybody goes home this way." Lela offered a slight smile.

Horse Farm Road marked the boundary between the old part of town and the technology district, with our high school smack in between like a referee. I watched out the window as we passed the historic horse farms, with their expansive fields, black fencing, and white barns that boarded horses more expensive than my house.

"The technology district was on the news this morning," I said.

"So?" Leila lifted a shoulder.

"I mean, it's weird, you know?"

I couldn't shake the uneasy feeling in the pit of my stomach, yet Lela continued bouncing to her playlist, seemingly uninterested. When the historic silos came into view, she made a quick right turn, then swerved left. The vehicle fell behind but stayed with us. Heavy-footed Lela slammed on the brakes to make the left-hand turn into our neighborhood, Paddock Springs, but this time, the pickup stayed straight, not bothering to turn. I exhaled and chastised myself for my continued paranoia.

When she pulled into her driveway, I grabbed my backpack from the floorboard. After tugging at the sticky door, I climbed out. Lela blocked my path. Her expression reminded me of my mom's signature *I'm-worried-about-you* look. At five-foot-nine, she was one of the few friends who can look me in the eye.

"Did the dreams start up again? Are you not sleeping?" Lela deserved the truth, but I didn't want to talk about it. I tried to move past her, and she held my arm. "Rames? If you think you're being followed, then I believe you. All I'm saying is you've been letting other people's actions affect you for a long time. Maybe it's time to stand up for what you want and stop letting others control your happiness."

Lela touched on a nerve, and I winced. I had allowed my dad's actions to control me for far too long. My emotions seeped into my dreams at night and trapped me in a web of fear.

I pulled Lela into a hug. "I'm a mess. Please don't give up on me."

"Never. That's what best friends are for." Lela squeezed so tight, she sucked the breath out of me. She dropped her arms to her sides and shot me a wry expression. "Call me when your phone works, okay? And get some sleep, girl."

Lela's familiar teasing lightened my mood as I fumbled with the front door key and opened the door. Nollie greeted me in her usual manner of barking first and asking questions later, as if she forgot

I lived here, too. I scratched her floppy ear until she dropped the tough girl act.

She followed me to our white kitchen where Zac sat on a wooden bar stool at the center island eating a bowl of ice cream. Chocolate oozed down his chin. I opened the white fridge, grabbed a bottle of water, and plopped onto the stool next to him.

"Has Mom left for church?"

"I guess." Zac swooshed his long, dark bangs off his forehead. "I haven't seen her."

I raised my eyebrows. "She didn't come home after work?"

He shrugged and set his bowl in the stainless-steel sink. "Maybe she did before I got here. I don't know. Why?"

"What about this morning? Did you talk to her before you got on the bus? Did she act normal?"

"Depends on your definition of normal. She insisted you stay with me...like I need a babysitter. I'm twelve, not two."

I gazed at Zac and marveled at how much he favored Dad, with his olive skin and dark, wavy hair. I inherited Mom's blond hair, pale skin, and the only characteristic Zac and I shared—hazel-green eyes with hints of amber. Zac's long lashes fluttered up and down in an eye roll.

I hopped up and tousled his hair. "I'll try to be a fun babysitter, okay? Want to build a fort?"

He punched me in the arm. "Not with you."

I smiled, then grew serious. "Mom is overprotective, but you can't blame her. She wants you to be safe."

"Safe from what?" Zac groaned. "Nothing ever happens in Atlanta. It's the most boring region in America."

Under normal circumstances, I would have agreed with Zac and laughed about Mom's overprotectiveness. But waves of doubt washed over me. STaR had stayed offline all morning. Millions of Connect Mobile phones had crashed. The phones mysteriously restored all at the same time. I got a text message that vanished into cyberspace. Then some dude watched me from the Swamp and followed Lela's car.

As if that wasn't enough, Mom always came home before Zac got off the bus. Her job allowed her the flexibility to be here for us. Something didn't add up. Mom said something about a meeting at church. Did she go there straight from work? My mind swirled like melted Neapolitan ice cream, the colors and flavors mixing in a pool of confusion. But I didn't want to scare him with my crazy thoughts, so I changed topics.

"Everyone's phone shut down today." I tried to sound indifferent and hoped Zac wouldn't catch the strain in my voice.

"I know. That's all everyone talked about. I'm sick of hearing about Dead Phone Day," he said.

I snickered. "That's what you guys named it?"

"Yep. DPD for short. Everyone's came back on at the end of school."

"Same, except mine still doesn't work. It's officially a DPD." I dropped my empty water bottle in the recycle bin and followed Zac to the family room. "I got a message to go to Connect Mobile for the update. A software failure or something."

He lifted his backpack off the sofa. "You don't need to go there. Plug it in and turn on Wi-Fi."

"The message said—"

"Let me look at it," Zac interrupted. Maybe all the time he spent on on augmented reality simulations would pay off. He fiddled with my phone for a couple of minutes before handing it back to me. "Not cool. Hard reset didn't work. Try looking it up on your laptop."

I sighed. "I wish Mom would let you have a phone."

"Tell me about it. I'm the only kid in middle school without one."

My lips curled into a playful grin. "Really? The *only* one?"

"Pretty much." He rolled his eyes again. "Mom left spaghetti for dinner. I'm getting on a game. Try charging your phone."

We marched upstairs and Zac shut his bedroom door in my face. I walked across the hall and plugged my mobile into the charger before jumping in the shower, staying under the hot water until it turned cold. Then I dressed in gray sweatpants and an oversized blue t-shirt.

I returned to the kitchen and heated the spaghetti in the microwave. Zac and I ate on the couch, watching a TV show about sharks sightings in the intercoastal waterways of the Southeastern region —a welcomed distraction from today's craziness. After the show, Zac retreated to his room to finish his simulation, which involved destroying the enemy before they destroyed you. The more he shouted into the headset, the more my head hurt. When I couldn't handle him yelling in the microphone a minute longer, I wandered to my room. I had procrastinated long enough. I opened my chemistry binder to today's lesson on nuclear reactions and fell asleep.

Stuck somewhere between consciousness and a coma-like state, my body became a corpse. Heat smothered me, making it impossible to breathe. My chest ached from the lack of oxygen to my lungs.

I sat up straight in bed, gasping for air. The nightmare again. Only this time, everything changed. From the patch of woods to the dark presence, something was all wrong.

My STaR device beeped, shaking me from my confusion. I'd fallen asleep and forgotten my nighttime check-in. The clock next to my bed blinked red numbers. Three-oh-five. Guess I hadn't been a fun babysitter after all.

I flipped my feet off the side of the bed and shuffled to the wall, calling STaR's name. Her familiar voice greeted me.

"Rami Carlton. Your temperature is normal. Your blood pressure is elevated. Sending a report to headquarters."

Of course my blood pressure is high. I was just fighting for my life, I wanted to scream. But I didn't dare voice this out loud. Mom's fear of being overheard came rushing back. What had spooked her? And why was she so worried about the Threats Division?

I crept across the hall to Mom's bedroom, where her STaR gave off a string of harsh beeps followed by a flashing red light. Only Mom's facial imprint could stop the noise and access the alert. But her door stood wide open, her bed untouched, with the edges of the bedding turned down and white pillows piled high, exactly the way she liked it.

Zac's door squeaked when I pushed it open. Blue light from the TV illuminated the room. Nollie opened one eye, then repositioned herself at the foot of Zac's bed. I turned off his video monitor and headed downstairs.

"Mom? Are you here?" I whispered, half expecting to see her asleep on the couch.

The only response came from a heavy gust of wind outside. I peered out the blinds to the empty driveway before rushing to the garage. No electric car plugged in. My mind raced to the worst scenario.

"Oh, God. Please let her be all right." The words caught in my throat.

My cry for help was more of a reaction than an actual prayer, since I wasn't sure how I felt about God. After Mom got sick and Dad abandoned her, I wondered if God could be trusted. And if he could, why wouldn't he have kept my family together?

I dashed upstairs and raced into Mom's bedroom, imagining her sprawled on the bathroom floor from food poisoning, or a thousand other possibilities. But there was no sign of her or any indication she'd come home. Across the hall, I yanked my phone from the charging cord and pounded on the power button. Nothing. I needed a working phone.

I pulled on a cream-colored sweater and sprinted out the front door, locking it behind me. The motion sensor light in the front yard triggered. The cold grass between my toes made me shiver. Tree branches swayed in the wind, casting eerie shadows on the lawn. The pecan trees that lined the long drive to the horse stables across the street gave off a human-like appearance as the repetitive rhythm of tree frogs filled the night silence.

The same sensation of being watched flooded over me again. My eyes darted in every direction, searching for signs of life. The breeze ceased, but the chill creeping up my spine remained. I quickened my pace across the damp grass before stepping onto Lela's porch. *There is nothing out here. You're safe.*

I rang the doorbell and glanced around, unable to shake the fear that rose to my throat. On the other side of the road, a shadow formed. A tall figure leaned against a pecan tree. There was no mistake this time.

Someone was watching me.

CHAPTER 4

Thursday, September 21

The Ferreiras' porch light flickered and Mrs. Ferreira's face appeared in the side window, her dyed blond hair piled on top of her head. She unlatched the door and stepped onto the porch. "Rami? Is everything all right?"

While the pecan trees stood steady, I shook like a leaf. "I'm sorry it's so late, Mrs. Ferreira. My mom. She, uh, she didn't come home." I peered over my shoulder and breathed a sigh of relief. The man had disappeared. Mrs. Ferreira ushered me inside, murmuring unintelligently in Portuguese. "Can I borrow your phone? Mine is..." I paused. "Doesn't work."

She checked the clock and spoke again in Portuguese, gesturing the sign of the cross against her forehead and chest. "*Graca de Deus*. May God's grace be upon your mother." She led me to the cozy family room where I'd spent hours hanging out with Lela.

I collapsed into my favorite suede chair where the TV above the fireplace aired President Young's speech from earlier today. The ticker at the bottom of the screen repeated what I'd seen earlier. *Connect Mobile denies any responsibility for the network outage.*

Which made no sense considering STaR controlled Connect Mobile.

Mrs. Ferreira turned the TV off and handed me her phone. "I did the update, so it should work fine."

I dialed Mom's number, but it went straight to voicemail. After I hung up, I called again. No answer. The third time, I left a message. "Mom? Um, I thought you'd be home by now. My phone's dead, so call me back. On Mrs. Ferreira's phone. Okay?" I hesitated before hanging up, then sent a text.

Mom? Where are you?

She'll see the three gray dots on her screen, right? Please answer. I watched the phone, willing it to come to life. But no dots appeared. No reply. No phone call. My heart raced so fast I could feel the pulse inside my ears. I sent another text and another.

Hello?

Call me. I'm scared.

Out of options, I called the last person I expected to help. My hands trembled as I dialed my father. I hadn't talked to him in weeks and questioned whether he'd even answer.

My parents' marriage fell apart when my mother was diagnosed with a chronic illness five years ago. Mom started a support group at church for those suffering from painful illnesses, but the more she talked about prayer and healing, the most resentful Dad became. Soon, rumors of multiple affairs surfaced, and Dad moved to a high-rise condo in downtown Atlanta with his assistant from work, a lady half his age. He might as well have moved to another region. We hadn't seen him for two years.

Then last month, Dad moved to the technology district, claiming he wanted to spend more time with his kids. It didn't take long to figure out he'd moved in with a different woman and wanted to portray the good dad image for her.

On the third ring, my father's raspy voice came on the line. My words gushed out in one breath. "Dad? Mom's not home. She left before I got home from school for a church meeting and isn't here. Do you know where she is? Has she called you?"

Dad cleared his throat and I could hear Olivia's muffled whispers in the background. "Rami? Slow down. It's after three in the morning."

A snarl leaked from my lips. *As if I don't know that.* "That's why I'm calling. Have you heard from her?"

"No. Wait, you said she's at church?"

"Yeah."

Dad let out an exaggerated sigh. "She's probably praying for the world and lost track of time. I guess someone has to pray for world peace."

Disgusted at his lack of concern, I yelled into the receiver. "Dad! She-isn't-home!"

His voice softened. "Are you and Zac all right?"

"Yeah, we're great." Sarcasm dripped with each syllable. "It's the middle of the night. My phone doesn't work, someone's following me, and Mom is missing."

"Rami, hang on." A loud clang followed, and he came back on the line, his voice clipped. "Who's following you?"

"I'm not sure." Tears streamed down my cheeks despite my efforts to remain strong. "Are you going to help me or not?"

"I'm calling the Reinforcement Division. Go home and lock all the doors until I get there." When I didn't respond, he raised his voice. "Rami? Don't open the door until Reinforcement Officers arrive, okay?"

"Yeah, okay." I hung up.

Mr. Ferreira had come downstairs, most likely to see who was yelling at three in the morning, and whispered with Mrs. Ferreira. When I stood, she rushed to my side. "Let me walk you home. I'll stay until the ROs arrive." She glanced at Mr. Ferreira. "And your father."

When we got home, I unlocked the front door and raced upstairs to Zac's room. I flipped on the light and Nollie's fur stood straight up on her back. A low growl escaped.

Zac rolled over and squinted. "What are you doing?"

"Mom's not home." A tear leaked from my eye. "I called her from Lela's, but she didn't answer. I left a ton of messages."

Zac rubbed his eyes and sat up. "What time is it?"

"Three-thirty." I paused and swallowed hard. "I called Dad."

"And?" Zac raised his eyebrows.

"And nothing." I shuffled my feet on the carpet. "I was nice. Sort of."

"Does he know where Mom is?"

"No, and he didn't seem worried about her."

I left out his comment about praying for world peace. Zac didn't feel the way I did about Dad, and I refused to poison him with my thoughts. Ever since Dad's latest girlfriend filled his closet with her belongings, he feigned interest in Zac's obsession with skateboarding. But I knew it wouldn't last. Dad's interest in us never did. Eventually, Dad would break Zac's heart. Like he did mine.

CHAPTER 5

Thursday, September 21

Flashing blue lights flickered through the thin, wispy curtains where I sat frozen on our worn, leather couch. My arms wrapped around Zac, as if protecting him from unforeseen forces. I pretended to be brave for Zac's sake, but I feared he could see right through me. Mrs. Ferreira adjusted her bleached blond ponytail, then tucked a plaid blanket around our legs before answering the door. When Nollie tried to charge at the intruder, Zac held her by the collar and whispered a down command.

"Please come in. I'm Gabriela Ferreira, Annie's neighbor." Mrs. Ferreira shifted backward.

A young officer peered at Zac and me clutched side by side on the couch, but kept his attention fixed on Nollie. He had bright red hair and enough freckles to reach around the globe. He seemed more nervous than me, as if he didn't know what to do or say.

Mrs. Ferreira broke the silence. "The children's father, Ian Carlton, will be here shortly. Would you like to sit down?"

"Oh, um, no thank you, ma'am. I'm Officer Gaits with Reinforcement Division," he said, as if remembering why he came. Red splotches crawled up his neck and merged with his endless freckles. He flashed his Reinforcement Officer badge before pulling a handheld reader and stylus pen from his chest pocket. "An RO from missing persons unit is on the way. He insisted on coming."

A knock on the door startled Nollie, and she barked. Zac gripped her collar and whispered in her ear to keep her from racing after the three ROs who stood in the open doorway. The one with thinning salt-and-pepper hair with bald spots on both sides of his forehead flashed a badge and moved closer. Nollie let out a low growl.

"That's an excellent guard dog you have there," he said, bobbing his chin toward Nollie. "Shepherds are the best. I'm Officer Sam Murray with the Reinforcement Division. This is Officer Gomez and Officer Burns." All three were dressed in identical navy Reinforcement Division uniforms. "You are Rami, I presume?" When I nodded, he continued. "Mind if the officers look around while I ask you a few questions?"

Every region's Reinforcement Division had local officers who could move up the chain to become National Agents. But it seemed strange that a regional officer would answer a call at three in the morning. My eyes darted to Mrs. Ferreira. "My dad's not here yet."

"Right. He's on the way?" Murray asked.

Officer Gaits cleared his throat again. "Um, yes. Mrs. Ferreira, the neighbor, stated he would be here shortly."

Mrs. Ferreira sat down next to me, her kind smile lifting the tension. "Rami. Maybe you could tell them what you told me?"

I watched as Gomez and Burns headed to the kitchen, where I could hear cabinet doors opening and closing. *What does our kitchen have to do with Mom's disappearance?*

"My mom said she had a church meeting after work, but she should have been home by now." My words came out in a whisper.

Gaits wrote something down on his pad. "Did you call her?"

"Yes."

"What time?" he asked.

I squirmed in my seat, wondering again if I should wait for my dad before answering questions. "Earlier. When the phones came back on. And again a few minutes ago. I used Mrs. Ferreira's phone because mine didn't come back on after the outage."

"If your phone isn't working, how did you call your mom earlier?" Gaits asked.

"I used my friend's phone."

Gaits nodded and wrote something on his handheld reader.

Officer Murray edged closer to the sofa. "You waited until 3 a.m. to call your mom when she didn't come home?"

"I fell asleep." My gaze swung between Murray and Gaits. "When I woke up, all the lights in the house were on, including my bedroom light. I checked in on Mom, but she wasn't in her room. I looked everywhere." Tears burned the insides of my eyes. The questions exhausted me, and I buried my face in my knees.

"Perhaps we should wait for Ian to arrive," Mrs. Ferreira said. "This is very upsetting for Rami."

Murray whispered something to Gaits, and Gaits moved to the front door, speaking in hushed tones into the microphone on his shoulder. Within minutes, Dad's car pulled into the driveway. He rushed in, his dark hair a tangled mess. Spotting multiple ROs, his olive cheeks deepened to shades of crimson.

Zac leaped off the couch. Nollie lurched at Dad, but Zac shouted a command, "Nollie. Down." Instantly, she lowered herself to a crouched position, looking more like a panther about to pounce than a shepherd. "Where have you been, Dad? Mom's still not here."

Dad's tall frame towered above everyone in the room as he pulled Zac into a side hug. "I got here as quickly as I could, son. Let me talk to the ROs. We'll get this misunderstanding straightened out." He reached down as if to hug me, but I remained as stiff as a statue. "Rami. Everything will work out."

"No, it won't," I shouted, angry and defiant. "You left us. You left *her*. Everything didn't work out."

"Rames, I didn't mean—"

"Mr. Carlton? I'm Reinforcement Division Officer Sam Murray with the missing persons unit. This is Officer Gaits. We'd like to ask you some questions about your wife."

"Ex-wife," Dad corrected. His complexion shifted to a dark purple. "And why was a missing persons officer assigned to this case already? We don't know if she's missing."

"May I call you Ian?" Murray didn't wait for an answer. "Sometimes, Ian, I'm called in to determine the priority of a case."

Dad grumbled, then jutted his chin toward the ROs. "Who are they?"

"Officers Gomez and Burns."

The uniformed officers surrounded Mom's computer room, a small enclave near the kitchen. I watched as they pulled Mom's laptop from the charging station and placed it in a box.

"What are they looking for?" Dad asked as the men headed upstairs.

Murray narrowed his gaze. "They're collecting data from everyone's STaR."

Zac and I exchanged looks, but neither of us spoke.

"Why are they taking her computer?" Dad asked.

Murray shrugged. "Just precautionary. The information should provide us with an accurate picture of what happened," Murray continued. "We know Annie told the kids she had a meeting at church. When your daughter called you, did you contact anyone from church?"

"No. I thought it was too late to call anyone."

"Did your wife make it to church?" Murray questioned.

"Ex-wife," Dad repeated. "And I have no idea."

Murray tilted his head sideways. "You're not sure if she made it there?"

"How would I know? I don't keep up with what Annie does and doesn't do." Dad's anger surged. "What is this? Are you accusing me of something?"

Gaits shook his head. "No one's accusing you, sir. Standard protocol." He gave Murray a sideways glance.

Murray scrutinized me next, hovering like a hawk stalking a chipmunk. His presence gave me the creeps. "Rami? Any chance that because the mobile phones crashed today, your mom changed her plans and couldn't call you?"

My face burned. "She wouldn't leave Zac and me."

Murray edged closer. "Perhaps she couldn't call—"

"She wouldn't leave us," I reiterated through clenched teeth. By now I was seething. The officers searching the house came downstairs, moving in and out of the family room where we'd gathered. Their presence felt like a violation of privacy, and I longed for Mom to sweep in and chase them away. "Don't you think if she planned on leaving, she would have taken some personal things, like her clothes and laptop?"

Gaits lowered himself to the chair facing us. "Okay, Rami. You have a valid point. Let's focus on something else. Do either of you remember what your mom wore to work this morning?"

"A white blouse with black dress pants," Zac said, speaking to the ROs for the first time. I shot him a puzzled look, and he shrugged. "I remember her putting on black heels and giving me instructions on how to heat dinner. She kissed the top of my head and said, 'Goodbye, sweetie,' then signed, *I love you*."

Gaits frowned. "Signed?"

Zac stuck out his thumb and raised his index finger and pinkie, keeping the other fingers tucked into his palm. "Yeah. Sign language."

Pinpricks trickled down my arms. Mom had signed to me this morning too, and I'd dismissed it as melodramatic, even odd, but now it had me second-guessing. Something tried to work its way to the forefront of my memory, something important.

"See ya later," I whispered, my voice barely audible.

Officer Gaits leaned forward. "What was that?"

"It's something Mom and I say to each other. Ever since kindergarten when I leave for school, Mom says, 'See ya later,' and I answer—"

"Alligator," Zac finished.

I stood up and faced Zac. "It doesn't make sense. Why would she say goodbye and sign 'I love you' to both of us?" The hair on my arms stood on end.

"It would be helpful if we had a printed picture of her." Gaits pointed to the frames lining the bookshelves. "Can I borrow one of those?"

"Oh, um, sure. I guess," I stammered, walking to the shelves. The most recent photo in a wooden frame stood in the center. We'd taken the selfie after Mom got her hair cut short. I handed Gaits the frame. "We took this a few weeks ago. She looks a lot like Aunt Kate." When Gaits frowned, I said, "My mom's identical twin sister."

Gaits nodded. "Oh. Thanks."

My mind swirled like Connect's logo on my phone. "This morning, her curls hung all over the place, messy, like she was in a rush. And she hadn't finished her makeup."

Murray frowned. "And that's unusual?"

"Um hum. She flat-irons her curls every day." I tugged at a handful of hair, demonstrating flat-ironing. "And she never leaves the house without makeup."

Gaits placed the tablet and stylus back in the pocket of his shirt. "The information you provided is helpful. We've pulled the data from her STaR, so we should be able to locate her within twenty-four hours if—"

"Twenty-four hours?" Dad shouted. "She could be dead by then."

"Dad!" Zac stormed out with tear-stained cheeks.

"Way to go, Dad. Haven't you been through sensitivity training like a thousand times?" I threw my arms up and raced after Zac.

Zac sat against the kitchen cabinets with his knees pulled to his chest and his head buried. Slowly, I slid to the floor. "He didn't mean it, you know," I said, surprised I would defend my father.

Zac kept his head low. "What if Dad's right? What if she's—"

"She's not. Don't even think it." I wrapped one arm around Zac.

Dad entered the kitchen and leaned against the refrigerator before squatting next to Zac. "I'm sorry, bud. I wasn't thinking. I'm angry. But not at you."

Zac leaned his head against Dad's chest. He forgave so easily. "Do you really think she's dead?"

Dad paused and let out a loud sigh. "No. I don't."

We huddled on the cold tile floor in silence, none of us making eye contact with each other. *What do you say when your mom is missing and the ROs are more interested in asking dumb questions than looking for her?*

Dad suddenly sat up straight. "Rami. The man following you. You need to tell the ROs. It may have something to do with your mom. I can't believe I forgot to mention it."

Zac shot me an expression that told me I'd made a fatal error. I hadn't told him about Crooked Smile Guy in the Swamp or that he'd been outside Lela's house earlier. In my efforts to protect him, I'd failed. *Again.* Zac followed Dad back to the couch, where he pulled the blanket to his chin.

"Zac?" My voice quivered.

"You should have told me. We don't keep secrets from each other. Remember?" He glanced between Dad and me, the implication obvious. I'd agreed to be honest with Zac after discovering years of secrets about our dad. I hadn't lied to Zac, but neither had I been honest. "You don't have to keep sheltering me, Rami. I know the world's a dangerous place. I'm not stupid."

My head hung low. "I'm sorry."

"Save it," Zac snapped. "Just do me a favor. At least be honest with the ROs. Mom's life depends on it."

Officer Murray gave me the creeps, and I doubted he believed my story anyway, so I directed my attention to Officer Gaits. "There was a guy in the Swamp today after school, like, just standing there, staring at me. It totally wigged me out, so I ran to Lela's car—"

"Lela?" Gaits interrupted.

"Yeah. Her daughter." I tilted my head toward Mrs. Ferreira. Mrs. Ferreira's hands flew to her mouth, and she muttered in Portuguese. Next to me, Zac trembled. I had kept so many secrets from him, telling myself I was protecting him. Now, I wondered if the person I'd been trying to protect was myself. "Lela brings me home from school."

"Did Lela get a good look at him?" Gaits asked.

"No. She said she didn't." I faced Zac. "You're right, I should have told you."

Murray moved in closer, analyzing me the way a scientist studied a lab rat. "Are you sure you didn't notice anything about this guy?"

"He wore a hat."

"What color?"

"Um, black. I think."

"Good. Now, what else do you remember?" Murray's firing squad wouldn't let up.

"A gray car. It looked like every other EV on the road, nothing special, but I noticed it because of the dark windshield and because it pulled out of the parking lot at the same time as us, like he was following us. When Lela turned into the neighborhood, the car kept going."

Gaits sat up straighter. "Did you see the license plate?"

"No," I said.

"All right." Gaits smiled. "Is there anything else you remember? Anything at all?"

I shivered. "The guy from the Swamp? I saw him here. Outside. At least I think it was him."

Murray flew across the room to the front windows, pulling the blinds back in a frenzy. "Here? Why are you just now telling us this?"

What right did he have to be mad at me? "I'm sorry," I snapped, "but it's four in the morning, my mom is missing, and maybe, just for a second, I forget about some crazy psychopath showing up at my house because I'm more worried about finding my mom." Sobs I'd stuffed poured out of me. I wailed, gasping between breaths. Mrs. Ferreira drew me into one of her motherly hugs, and I let the tears fall.

Murray pulled his handheld reader from his belt and typed in his badge number. Each home and most outdoor streetlamps came equipped with a camera, courtesy of STaR's Safety Division, which automatically synced to our TV monitor on the wall. Murray set the coordinates to date and time of the incident and played the video. I stared at myself moments before racing across the cold, wet grass to Lela's house. Officer Murray zoomed in on the streetlamp camera where I'd claimed my stalker lurched. The trees swayed in the harsh winds, and autumn leaves fell to the ground. But no one appeared on camera.

Murray narrowed his gaze. "Are you sure about the location?"

“Yes, I’m sure,” I snapped.

“Interesting. Because as you can see, there’s no one there.”

I squirmed on the sofa, causing it to squeak. “I didn’t make it up. He was there. Watching me.”

Gaits squatted down in front of me. “Hey...it’s been a long day. Why don’t y’all try to get some sleep? Come down to the local Reinforcement station in a few hours and Officer Murray and I will gather what information we can about the gray car.”

Dad nodded. “Call me the minute you uncover something.”

Murray stepped backward, his eyebrows shifting to a deep scowl. A lump formed in my throat, making it impossible to swallow. He didn’t say a word, but I could read between the lines.

Officer Murray didn’t believe a word I’d said.

CHAPTER 6

Thursday, September 21

When STaR took over the government, all law enforcement fell under the Reinforcement Division. Over time, each region ruled as they saw fit, leading to widespread corruption. Local ROs accepted bribes, if the price was right, and miraculously made cases go away.

Atlanta's RD precinct, in the center of the Southeastern region, had two entrances, both with scanners, cameras, and intercoms. A large white plaque on the entrance to the left said "ROs only." We walked into the door for visitors, which opened to a canary yellow waiting room. The space gave off a cheery glow, a stark contrast to my emotions, especially at nine in the morning. Whoever chose the paint color should have stuck with dull gray, as I doubted anyone felt cheerful inside an RD station. Zac and I sat on worn fabric chairs, the same canary yellow, while Dad approached the red-headed female officer behind a thick glass shield.

"Can I help y'all?" she asked. Her roots desperately needed a touchup, revealing shades of gray where red dye had worn off. She smacked her chewing gum and flapped her long eyelashes faster than I could think.

"We're here to see Officer Gaits," Dad said.

"Sure, doll." Smack, smack. *Who calls a grown man doll?* "He's expecting y'all. Go through them double doors. When I buzz y'all in, go through the second set of double doors. Once inside, take the second left."

Happy to leave the sunshine room, Zac and I followed Dad into a small, dimly lit space. A single light illuminated a set of stairs to the left with a large sign that read *holding* and pointed downstairs. The doors behind us slammed, locking us into the cramped space. A jolt of panic reached my chest. Zac crept close to my side. A monitor mounted to the wall to the right of the doors flashed green. A computer-generated voice echoed in the small space.

"Approach the scanner." Dad stepped forward. "Facial recognition successful. Identity confirmed."

Zac went next, followed by me. When our identities registered, the double door opened. The sharp ring of telephones and angry voices punctured the air. An officer at the first desk, with an empty bagel box and six coffee cups scattered between endless piles of papers, sipped from a large Styrofoam cup. Down the hall, Officer Gaits looked up. Leftover crumbs stuck to his freckled cheek, which he wiped with his sleeve. He grabbed his coffee cup and led us to a well-lit conference room with a large mahogany table and burgundy leather chairs. With cameras on every block, someone inside the RD must have seen something.

"Have a seat. Officer Murray will be here any minute."

"What have you learned about Annie?" Dad asked, taking the seat next to me.

Red patches appeared on Gaits's neck, and he tugged at his collar. "Oh uh, right. Well, I just hung up with one of our officers.

Topothesia's security called it in. Said a gray car with Annie's license plate sat near the electric charging station all night. There was no sign of Annie's purse or phone."

Topothesia Networks? That's where my dad worked. But why would Mom's car be there? It didn't make sense.

Topothesia meant location: fitting, considering they developed surveillance applications for STaR. Dad's latest project, Finder Seek, was the latest installment in mobile tracking software. Connect Mobile planned to test the software as a microchip inserted into the back of our hand and had actively been looking for volunteers.

Although Dad claimed Finder Seek was far more reliable than the current tracking apps, Mom strongly disapproved. Personally, I hated the idea of a tracker on my phone or in the back of my hand that could follow me anywhere. My friends and I agreed: it was a total invasion of privacy.

Gaits's nose twitched. "Any idea, Ian, why Annie would have been at your office yesterday?"

Dad squirmed in his chair, causing a high-pitched squeak. "No."

Gaits directed his attention to me. "Rami?"

I stifled a gasp and forced myself to swallow before answering. "No. She told me she was going to church."

"Did she make it? To church, I mean?" Dad rubbed the back of his neck.

The red splotches crept to Gaits's cheeks. "We made some calls. No one saw her. The lady in charge of the meeting said Annie never showed."

Suddenly unable to breathe, I clutched at my chest and bent forward. Rapid breaths squeezed in and out of my lungs. I glanced at Dad. Sweat beads formed on his forehead. *What is happening? And what is taking Murray so long?*

Gaits glanced toward the door. "Hey, Zac? You want a soda or something?"

"Yeah, sure." Zac shot a quick glance my way.

Mom would never allow Zac to have a soda for breakfast, and I started to object. Then again, what did it matter? Mom wasn't here. Emptiness filled me all over again.

"Sure thing. Follow me." Officer Gaits stepped out with Zac as Murray walked in. The timing appeared orchestrated, and I wondered if they'd planned it.

"Good morning, Ian." Murray and Dad shook hands. "I thought I'd take Rami and Zac down the hall to give us time to talk for a few minutes."

Dad rolled his shoulders. "I'm not sure that's necessary."

"Just standard protocol, Ian. Gives you a little privacy. Rami, if you'll follow me, we'll catch up to Zac."

It wasn't a question. I waited for Dad to refuse to let him take me, but he simply watched. Aren't fathers supposed to protect their kids? Murray led me to a dark room with a single, white cafeteria-style table and two chairs, one on either side of the table. Except for the table and chairs, the room was bare. No pictures on the walls. No magazines. No windows. Green paint peeled from the cinder block walls. The overhead light flickered.

"I'm just giving your dad a few minutes alone," Murray said.

"Where's Zac?"

"Getting a drink. Take a seat," he commanded.

While Murray fumbled with his handheld reader just inside the doorway, I stared at his puffy eyes—light blue—and uncombed salt and pepper hair. He looked like he'd just rolled out of bed. I pressed my shaking hands together inside my hoodie pocket, gouging my nails in the palms of my hands. "Do you have any information about my mom?"

Murray lifted his head. "We're looking into every potential lead. We're trying to figure out why she was at Topothesia and how—"
A loud knock behind him interrupted whatever he planned to say. Another officer whispered in his ear. "Excuse me, Rami. I'll be right back."

"Wait. Where's Zac?" But the only sound was the vibration of metal slamming in my ears. I paced the floor, desperate to leave this place.

CHAPTER 7

Friday, September 22

When the door opened, an enormous guy entered, encompassing all the space in the tiny room. From the black suit, black tie, dark hair, and cutting dark eyes, everything about this man terrified me. He sat across from me, holding an electronic device that resembled a STaR health monitor.

"You must be Rami." His booming voice ricocheted off the bare walls. My eyes darted to the closed door behind him, wondering what happened to Zac. "I'm National Agent Williams. I investigate homicides."

I bit my lower lip until I tasted blood. "Homicide?"

"Officer Murray filed the case as a missing person, but he brought me in," he paused, "as a safety measure."

I suppressed a sob. "You think my mom is...dead?"

He typed something into his screen before answering. "Often, what appears to be missing is a simple displacement. People are not where they said they'd be."

My body shivered. I placed my hands back into my hoodie pocket. My mind drifted to Zac's comment yesterday about how nothing bad ever happened in Atlanta. "What's that supposed to mean?"

Agent Williams placed the reader on the table. He intertwined his fingers together and leaned forward, resting his elbows on the table. "I'm hoping by digging a little deeper into her whereabouts, we can rule out the possibility of any accidental...injuries. I understand your mother has a sister?"

His question caught me off guard. "Yeah. Why?"

Williams pointed to the screen. "It says here she has an identical twin named Kate. Has Kate contacted you?"

Tears burned in my eyes, but I blinked them away. "No."

"Are you sure she didn't come to the house this morning? Or call?"

"I'm sure."

"Has your dad been in touch with Kate?"

Suddenly the room felt hot, and I tugged at my hoodie strings. "Where are you going with this?"

He sat back and crossed his massive arms across his chest. "When someone goes missing, it's our duty to explore every connection. We need to find Kate in case she has information that will help us locate your mom. Kate could lead us straight to her." When I didn't respond, he continued. "Think back to yesterday. Who was the last person to see your mom?"

I dug my nails in deeper. "Me, I guess."

His eyes seared through me like a predator seeking its prey. "Rami? Do you want to find your mom?"

Surprised, my eyelashes fluttered. "What kind of question is that? Yeah, of course."

"You received an alert instructing you to go to Connect Mobile for the software update." Williams said it like a statement, but I never mentioned it to Officer Murray. Or to Officer Gaits. The room felt smaller and the panic I'd experienced earlier returned with a vengeance. Williams shifted closer, his eyes as dark and desperate as I felt. "Why haven't you restored your phone?"

Every muscle in my body tensed. "I haven't exactly had time. I went home to watch my little brother when everything turned crazy. What does this have to do with finding my mom?"

Williams stood up, his towering frame overshadowing me. "I need your phone."

A tingling sensation trickled down my spine. "I don't have it."

He chuckled a deep and cynical laugh. "A sixteen-year-old without her phone? Not likely."

"I. Don't. Have. It." My chest tightened with each breath. "It hasn't worked since the outage, so I left it at home."

"Don't you want your phone to work again? Perhaps post to Allicio about your mom?"

"Sure. I guess." I rubbed my hands up and down my arms to ward off the chill I couldn't shake.

"Then we need to find Kate and get your mobile working again."

All the blood drained from my face. "Okay. I'll do it later."

"Not later, Rami. As soon as you leave." His lips curved into a slight smile, still holding my gaze.

Sweat formed under my arms. I swallowed hard, desperate to keep my voice calm. "Can I go now?"

"Sure, sure." He followed me to the door. "You're free to go. Don't forget, Rami. The update."

I flew out the door and rushed to the conference room. Zac and Dad sat across from Officer Gaits. Murray was nowhere to be found. I squatted next to Zac, draping an arm around his shoulder. "Where have you been?"

"I could ask you the same thing," he said, pulling away. "We've been waiting for you."

My jaw tightened. "Where is Officer Murray?"

Gaits's brows squeezed together. "With you."

"He was for a minute, but he left me alone with a National Agent."

"Agent?"

"Yeah. Williams. Tall, dark suit, dark eyes," I said.

Gaits crossed the room and shook his head. "National Agents report to the president, Miss Carlton. If they were called in, I would have been informed. Are you sure you got the name right?"

Paranoia gripped me. Suddenly, I didn't know who to believe. Maybe the rumors about the RD being corrupt were true after all.

Gaits snapped the handheld reader from his belt and entered the time and date. Scenes projected onto the wall monitor in real time, from facial recognition confirming our identity as we entered the precinct to sitting in this room. Gaits rewound the tape to a few minutes prior and entered *interrogation room* into the data search. The words *no results found* flashed onto the wall.

The cherry clusters on Gaits's cheeks deepened. "There's nothing here, Rami."

"Check again," I insisted. Dad sat up straighter and leaned across the table. Gaits entered different search words, but each data set turned up empty. "That's impossible. He was here." With every ounce of strength I had, I pulled Zac out of the chair. "We're leaving. Something isn't right."

Zac jerked his body from my grasp. "You're hurting my arm, Rami. What's your problem?"

Gaits looked like a spotted leopard trapped in a cage. "No one's holding you here."

I pushed Zac toward the first set of double doors and punched the green button. They swung open. "Let's go."

Zac watched Dad and Gaits deep in conversation. "No. I'm waiting for Dad."

"Zac, please follow me." My words were forceful, but my voice shook. What began as anger at the Reinforcement Division's lack of protection had fused into intense fear. Why would National Agents be in Atlanta investigating a disappearance?

By the time Dad caught up to us, Zac wouldn't look at me. He climbed into the back seat of Dad's car as I merged into the front. I wrapped my arms around my waist to hold myself together while Dad pummeled me with questions I refused to answer. He claimed to be worried about me. *Good. Let him worry.* It let me know he wasn't completely heartless. He had, after all, broken up our family, cheated on Mom, and abandoned Zac and me.

All I ever tried to do was protect Zac from the hurt and disappointment of Dad's failures. But clearly, I'd failed too. None of this was Zac's fault, and I hated myself for scaring him. I twisted in my seat. "Zac? I'm sorry. I overreacted."

Zac wiped tears with his sleeve. "What is *wrong* with you?"

Where do I begin?

CHAPTER 8

Friday, September 22

Zac couldn't stand the thought of being home without Mom, which meant we were stuck staying at Dad's place tonight. We needed to grab some clothes and personal items to take to Dad's, so he swung by our house. Zac bolted from the car and I followed him upstairs. My phone sat on the nightstand, still attached to the charging cord. I pressed the power button. But like before, it refused to respond. Despite my confusion about why the RD cared about my phone, if the update meant finding Mom, I'd do it. I slipped my phone into my jeans pocket, pulled the charger from the wall, and dropped the cord onto my bed.

Since I didn't know how long we'd have to stay with Dad, I unplugged my STaR health device and removed it from the mounted holder attached to the wall. STaR permitted travel between regions as long as you maintained access to your health device.

One of my friends in ninth grade got a simple cold and slept through several check-ins. Within forty-eight hours, a team in hazmat suits appeared at her door and stuck all kinds of anti-viral vaccines into her arm. No thank you.

From a clean pile of laundry, I grabbed my volleyball uniform and stuffed it into my gym bag so I'd be ready for tonight's game. Then I grabbed some clothes, makeup, and toiletries and set them next to the charging cord. I reached for a small duffle bag from the floor of my closet and packed everything inside. As I dropped in my flat iron, a photograph in the small zipper compartment made me stop. It wasn't there the last time I used this luggage. I would have seen it. Wiping dust from the image, I sunk onto the bed as the memory came flooding back.

Ever since I was seven years old, I wanted a horse more than anything in the world. On Saturdays, I rode my bike down the long path of pecan trees to help care for the horses in the stables. On my ninth birthday, my parents surprised me with Cinnamon, a beautiful chestnut mare. I took horseback riding lessons and joined the equestrian team. At twelve, I won first place in show and second place in the jump competition. A few weeks ago, Mom set my enormous trophy on the family room bookshelf. It towered above the tiny soccer trophies, its presence a constant reminder that my life wasn't always this way.

In the picture, I lifted the trophy over my head, but accidentally lost hold of it. Dad caught it mid-air, and Mom and I laughed at his cat-like reflexes. At that exact moment, the photographer snapped the picture. A joyful girl, full of life and possibilities, stared back at me in the photo. But I didn't recognize that girl anymore.

Something changed between my parents after that. Mom spent more time with her church support group than with my dad. Eventually, Dad stopped coming home at night, claiming work kept him away. In my naivety, I believed him. Why shouldn't I? In middle school, my interest in riding waned, and by the time Dad moved out, I'd quit all together.

My breath caught in my throat as I stared at my mother's smile. I couldn't believe we had to stay with Dad, the one who took away Mom's smile. I needed to feel my mom close to me, so I tossed the picture into the bag and tugged at the zipper. Before walking across the hall, I slung the two bags over one shoulder and my backpack over the other.

"Ready?" I called from Zac's doorway. He stuffed his skateboard pads and helmet in a sling backpack without answering. I dropped my bags in the hallway, stepped into his room, and plopped on his bed. "I'm sorry I scared you today."

He stopped packing and faced me. "What's *wrong* with you?" he asked again.

My heart broke. I longed to tell him everything. About the officer who cared more about my phone than Mom, and how I wasn't sure whether we could trust the ROs. But I didn't because he's so much like I was at his age—trusting, carefree, and happy—and I didn't want him to turn out like me.

"I had a terrible dream last night." I paused. It wasn't a total lie, just not the truth he wanted. "It scared me more than the others."

He turned up his lip. "That's why you're acting crazy?"

I snickered. "Dumb, huh?"

"And annoying." He tightened the strings on his backpack. "You better get it together soon. Dad thinks you're losing it."

"I don't care what Dad thinks."

Zac glared at me. "You should give him a break."

"Why?"

"Because right now, he's all we've got." He turned and walked out without another word.

Zac was right, but I wasn't ready to admit it. My feelings were complicated. How could I explain my ever-changing emotions to my twelve-year-old brother when I didn't understand it myself? I spotted his favorite Swiss Army knife on the dresser by the door and shoved it and the cordless headphones he forgot into my pocket. Then I descended the stairs.

Dad waited on the front porch, typing on his phone. "All done?"

"Almost." I left my bags at the front door and walked to the family room. From a bookshelf, I selected two photos and scanned them on my laptop. When the images appeared, tears stung my eyes.

Zac crept up behind me and pointed. "Use that one." His teacher had entered him in a math contest in fifth grade with students from our region. He made it to the regional championship and took second place. In the photograph, he held the certificate while Mom grinned ear to ear.

I cropped him out and loaded Mom's face on the template. Above her photo, I typed "Missing." Below the image, I typed her height, weight, and hair color, as well as what she was wearing the day she disappeared. After what happened at the Reinforcement precinct, I wanted actual proof of her existence.

Zac and I planned to hand out the flyers with Mom's picture and description, hoping someone would come forward with new information. While the flyers printed, he went to the kitchen to pack Nollie's food and toys. I set my phone on the desk, its blank screen taunting me.

"Hey, Zac? I grabbed a couple of things from your room." I pulled out his headphones and set them next to my computer. My laptop chimed. A chat message from Bald Eagle.

He appeared around the corner, holding Nollie on a leash. "Everything okay?"

I slammed the laptop closed. "Yeah sure." I'd deal with Bald Eagle later. Right now, I needed to stay calm for Zac.

He opened his mouth like he was about to say something, then picked up copies of the flyers that had fallen from the printer. He stacked them into a neat pile on the desk before handing some to me. I stared at Mom's picture, the word "Missing" in bold type, and wanted to vomit. Zac followed my gaze, paled, and shoved his flyers at me, bolting upstairs with Nollie in tow.

My legs felt like someone had strapped lead weights to my ankles as I climbed our staircase. I edged into his room, past Nollie, who let out a low growl as I approached.

I tapped on the bathroom door. "Zac? We'll find her. Okay?"

"You don't know that," he said from behind the closed door.

"Then we won't stop looking until we do."

After a long, painful moment, Zac opened the door. His hazel eyes held a shade of red around the rims and puffed out from the sockets. "Let's just go." Without another word, he grabbed Nollie's leash and led her to Dad's car.

CHAPTER 9

Friday, September 22

There were few things I dreaded more than staying in this condo with my dad and his girlfriend, but here I was. Everything about it screamed Olivia, from the white walls, white wispy curtains, and white furniture donning each room. After I scared Zac with my crazy outburst at the RD station this morning, I had to pretend to be okay with this setup. Still, I had no idea how I'd survive this.

Nollie followed Zac around as Dad gave us the quick tour. The knot in my stomach returned, and I excused myself, racing to the nearest bathroom. I splashed my face with water before rejoining the others.

Dad gave me a concerned look but didn't offer any comforting words. Instead, he pointed to the stairs. "Rami? You can sleep upstairs in the spare bedroom. Zac's going to stay on the couch."

Without a word, I trudged upstairs carrying my tote, volleyball gym bag, and backpack. Everything in this place screamed Olivia, from the white comforter to the matching lace curtains. Nothing made me feel welcome. I dropped my bags on the carpet and collapsed onto the bed. I needed to let Coach Sanchez know why I wasn't at school. After I earned my spot in the starting lineup, I didn't want to be benched. I promised I wouldn't let her down. My phone needed that update.

Dad could call the attendance office so I wouldn't be accused of skipping school if I could just muster the energy to go talk to him. But I'd been awake for hours. I needed a few minutes of rest. Just a few minutes. My eyelids fluttered like a bird's wings before I gave in.

Their breath is near. I feel it on my skin. They move in closer, surrounding me. I am the prey. The cliff. The pool of water hundreds of feet below. I am trapped. I glance back. Then I jump...

"Rami?" My heavy eyelids blinked. Dad stood in the doorway holding bath towels. The potent smell of fresh laundry soap filled the room. "I wasn't sure if I should wake you. Olivia washed these for you." He set them on the dresser and took a step back.

I massaged my temples and glanced at the clock on the nightstand. Three o'clock. I planned to pass out flyers, but now I wouldn't have time. "Why didn't you wake me sooner?"

He pushed his shoulders up. "You're exhausted. We all are. I thought you could use the sleep."

I threw my feet off the bed and slipped on shoes. "Have you heard anything about Mom?" Dad shook his head. My heart sank. "Can you take me to a Connect Mobile?"

"Now?"

I nodded. "My phone...it's...DPD."

"What does that mean?"

"Dead Phone Day. Something Zac said earlier. Anyway, my phone isn't working."

He rubbed his chin. "Zac wants to take Nollie to the skate park and pass out flyers. I think it's his way of dealing with everything. I can drop you off on the way."

I pulled my uniform from the duffle bag and laid it out on the bed. "My volleyball game is tonight at six. I'm starting."

Dad's face lit up. "That's great. I think we should all go. It would be a good distraction."

We stood inches from each other, neither knowing what to say. The silence between us felt deafening. I reached into the bag where I'd set the photograph of Mom and set it on the dresser. Her smile warmed the icy silence. Dad stared at the image but didn't comment, as if Mom's presence made him uncomfortable. He turned without a word and walked out of the room.

I opened my laptop from my backpack and sat down on the bed. The message from Bald Eagle appeared again.

Whitetail? You there?

I logged into our chat room, but something made my skin crawl. Ever since my mom disappeared, I'd been on edge. I'd discovered Bald Eagle's identity, but he didn't know that. Did he? Another message popped up.

Ghosting me Whitetail?

Nope. Whasup?

A series of letters and numbers scrolled onto the screen in rapid succession. I studied the code and waited as he continued to type.

Report due STAT.

Simple command not working.

He'd reversed a function at the end of sequence two. Nothing major, but enough to explain his problem. Why couldn't he see it?

He was way better at this than me. As if sensing my hesitation, he typed again.

No sleep since outage boss up my a missed something simple right?**

Although I wasn't certain, it seemed to be a simple mistake. I filled in the rest of the sequence for him, changing his function to a response data.

That it?

Genius Whitetail gotta get sleep caffeine for now signing off.

And with that, he was gone. I logged off, shut the laptop, and grabbed my STaR health device. Downstairs, I pulled Rosemary into a vacant plug near the kitchen table, powered her on, and walked outside to Dad's car. He unplugged his car from the electric charger mounted near the driveway, and we took over toward the city.

Dad dropped me off at the Connect Mobile headquarters building with the iconic logo overhead. A red C swirled around a scarlet globe as it spun round and round, a constant reminder that Connect Mobile would keep us connected to one another, yet safe from outside threats. Yet the Southeastern region, with dozens of technology companies, experienced a catastrophic power outage yesterday.

Drones buzzed around each building in the technology district as we approached. Their presence had never bothered me before. But now, I felt like they were watching me.

A bubbly twenty-something lady with strawberry-blond hair greeted me at the door. “Welcome to Connect. I’m Marissa. How can I help you?”

I fiddled with the straps on my backpack. “Um, I need to do a software update on my phone.”

“I’d be glad to help. Sign in here and we’ll get you all set up.” Marissa handed me a tablet and asked me to fill out the required information before ushering me to a charging station. She plugged in my phone and typed on her tablet. “We’ve had dozens of people in here asking for this update. You could have done this yourself. Next time connect to Wi-Fi, keep it plugged in overnight, and voilà. You wake up to a new update.”

Her perkiness grated on my nerves. If she knew the day I’d had, I doubt she would feel the need to ramble. “I got a text saying I *had* to come in.”

Marissa hesitated ever so slightly. “Oh. That’s highly unusual. Let me check with my supervisor.” She yanked the phone from the charging cord and paced to the back of the store.

A flurry of activity buzzed around me as dozens of employees stood at tables working on laptops, tablets, and phones. When Marissa returned, her face filled with the same cheerful smile. Rather than use facial recognition, she held the back of her right hand to her tablet and the apps came to life. While she worked on my phone, she babbled about who knows what. By now, I’d tuned her out. When the apps appeared on my home screen, I almost hugged her.

"Okey-dokey. Here we are. A few more clicks and voilà. You'll be all set."

How many times can one person say voilà? Looking away from Miss Southern Sunshine, I spotted an image in the glass as light reflected off the large windows that surrounded the store. My eyes darted about, searching for signs of the man I'd seen outside Lela's house, but he wasn't there.

Disgusted with my paranoia, I turned back to Marissa. "How many people were affected by the outage yesterday?"

Marissa frowned, the first sign that she wasn't always this perky. "Well, millions. Connect is the largest provider."

"It's STaR's only provider," I mumbled under my breath.

Marissa blinked several times. "No one can say what caused it. One minute I'm talking to my boyfriend. The next minute, the call dropped, and I'm like, what the...?" Her voice trailed off.

Either she hadn't heard my snide comment or chose to ignore it. Either way, I decided to play along. "Did your phone come back on right away?"

Marissa bobbed her head, her curls falling in her face. "Uh-huh. And I didn't need an update. Neither did my boyfriend. But several million customers reported needing a software update. They thought Connect Mobile sent out the update. But we didn't."

The day of the outage, Connect Mobile had denied any responsibility. But that didn't make sense because the text told me to come here.

My heart raced, and I held the desk with both hands. "Then who sent it out?"

Marissa glanced around the store, lowering her voice to a mere whisper. "Okay, so don't like, quote me or anything, but rumor has it Connect was involved in a merger. STaR purchased another technology company, but no one knows who." She placed her finger to her lips. "The info is top-secret. Everyone around here thinks the other company submitted an update before the merger was finalized."

Although her explanation made sense, it still didn't explain why I couldn't complete the update the same way as everyone else. While she fiddled with her tablet, I mustered the courage to ask her what really bothered me. "Um, Marissa? Has anyone else reported they had to come *here* to complete the update?"

"Nope. You're the first." She glanced at her screen. "Wait. This is so strange."

"What?" I peered over her shoulder.

"The update on your phone is different."

"Different, how?"

She frowned again. "Not sure. I'm initiating the same sequence I've been doing on everyone else's phone, only on yours, it's not working."

She stayed silent for so long, I wondered if I'd told her to be quiet or just thought it. She typed again on the tablet's keyboard. "I'll be right back," she said, leaving the tablet in place.

A shadow flashed across her screen. The silhouette moved to the wall, where it crawled to the ceiling. A man wearing a black baseball hat and gold sunglasses stood in the window. His mirrored rims reflected the sunlight. *Crooked Smile Guy. He's here.* He put a phone to his ear.

I glanced back at Marissa, who spoke in hushed tones to a gentleman in a suit and tie. She shook her head, then pointed at me. Almost as if on cue, two men approached, both speaking into microphones. They wore the standard navy Reinforcement Division uniform, but with three red stripes trailing down the front. *National Agents.*

And they headed straight for me.

With the front door blocked by Crooked Smile Guy, I felt like a hamster trapped inside a glass ball with no hope of escape. The hair on my arms stood upright. I ripped my phone from the cord, tore the white plastic seam, and breezed past Marissa.

She looked up, startled. "You're leaving? But the download isn't finished yet."

With my backpack still strapped on, I spotted a side exit and fled.

CHAPTER 10

Friday, September 22

I ran across the street to Little Cone Ice Cream Shoppe, the most popular spot in the technology district for those with money. Even though the Safety Division pushed healthy eating, ice cream and candy were permitted, but affordable only to the rich. Although Mom made a decent living as a paralegal, it was nothing compared to Dad's technology income. I hadn't been here since Dad moved out.

When I stepped inside, screaming kids dripping colored milk on the floor touched me from all sides. It gave me goosebumps. But I had no other choice. It was either sticky ice cream or Crooked Smile Guy and National Agents.

Behind the counter, a tall guy with dreadlocks scooped ice cream while some girl with straight jet-black hair and a fish tattoo worked the register. I searched the brightly lit room for a back entrance. An exit sign glowed in the dimly lit hallway. Then I heard my name.

My skin tingled. My mouth felt dry. He inched forward, closing the gap between us. Time stopped as I watched in slow motion. He mouthed my name and moved even closer. The exit was steps away. I could make it. Instead, I froze like an ice cream cone.

"What are you doing here?" I cringed the instant the words shot out, wishing I could reclaim them.

He pointed to the emblem on his baby blue t-shirt. "I work here. It pays for the gas in my car, so I can, ya know, go out."

Heat rose to my cheeks. For a moment, I forget about my stalker and the agents that had invaded our region as I gazed into Brannon's eyes, a perfect match to his shirt. The adorable dimple on his left cheek popped out, and I caught myself staring.

He shuffled his feet on the sticky floor and rubbed the back of his neck. "Are you okay? You seem upset or something." He touched my arm, sending shock waves through my body until I realized he was waiting for a response.

"I'm fine." I unzipped my backpack and pulled out a handful of flyers. "I wanted to put up some flyers of my mom in the businesses around town, but I'm running out of time. My volleyball game starts at six."

"I heard about your mom. I'm sorry." He brushed a strand of hair off my cheek. I became mute as my body tingled beneath his touch. "I can put one in our window and ask the other places in the shopping center to post it."

My spirits lifted. "You'd do that?"

"Sure." He grinned, making his dimple more pronounced. "And if you need someone to talk to, I mean like, maybe we could hang out one day after school or something?"

"Um, yeah. Sure. I guess so." *Did Brannon Martinelli just ask me out?*

"Is Monday good?"

"Yeah, okay." I fumbled with the flyers, then handed him a stack. His hand brushed against mine. I couldn't think straight with him touching me, so I blurted out the first thing that came to mind. "I gotta go."

His hand dropped. "Oh. All right."

"No, I mean, I gotta *go.*" I pointed to the ladies' bathroom.

Brannon turned a shade of pink. "Right. Well, see you Monday."

He walked behind the ice cream counter, and I raced to the bathroom. I slammed the door and clutched the sink. One minute, some lunatic chased me. The next, Brannon asked me out. At least, I think he did. He said "hang out." *Is that a date?*

I should be ecstatic. I mean, I've liked him for two years. But with Crooked Smile Guy on the loose, my mind roamed from my mother's disappearance to my paranoia, which was growing with each passing moment. A loud knock jolted me. I opened the door a crack where a little girl with curly red ringlets stood cross-legged in front of the door.

"Are you done yet?" she asked in a squeaky voice.

"Yep. Sorry you had to wait."

She dashed inside without another word, smashing the door in my face. Behind the counter, Brannon bent over the ice cream cooler, scooping rainbow flavor. I slipped out unnoticed.

CHAPTER 11

Friday, September 22

I weaved around large dumpsters, glancing over my shoulder at each turn before coming to an opening between the buildings. I pulled out my phone to call Dad. Would it even work since I fled Connect Mobile before the update completed? I only had one hour to change clothes and get back to school for the game.

The screen remained black and unresponsive to my touch. Frustrated and out of time, I headed back to Little Cone to borrow Brannon's phone when Officer Murray flew around the corner. He crashed into me, causing me to stumble backward. Bile rose to my throat, though whether from the stench of garbage or his breath, I couldn't determine.

"Rami. Stop, please. I'm trying to help you." Murray reached for my arm, then must have changed his mind about touching me. He dropped his hands to his sides. I fought the urge to punch him and run. As if he read my mind, he jolted backward. "Your dad said you were at Connect Mobile getting your phone fixed. I saw you fly out of the store and run here. What's going on? And why did you leave the RD precinct?"

I shoved my phone into my backpack. "Because you left me alone with a National Agent who told me to get the update."

Murray cocked his head to the side, his expression a mixture of confusion and annoyance. "National Agent?"

"Seriously? You can drop the act." I rolled my eyes.

Murray creased his eyebrows together, forcing the bags under his eyes to enlarge. "What act? What are you talking about?"

"Agent Williams. Investigates homicides?" I paused, expecting some semblance of recognition. But just like Officer Gaits, his face remained blank. "He said *you* asked him to talk to me, in case my mom is..." I couldn't bring myself to say the word. I refused to believe she was dead.

Murray ran his fingers through his salt and pepper hair, revealing bald spots at the temples. Sweat beads formed, even though the temperature outside was fifty degrees. He spun in circles, growing more agitated. "What *exactly* did he say?"

"What does it matter?"

"What did he *say*?" Murray's face reddened.

I had no idea why Murray would be mad at me, considering he left me in an interrogation room. "So, you believe me?"

"What?" Murray's frown deepened.

"That an Agent interrogated me? Officer Gaits said the cameras didn't pick up the interview."

Murray shook his head. "Listen, Rami. I didn't ask anyone to interrogate you. And I'd never purposely bring an Agent in *my* case. Come back down to the station with me. We'll figure this out together."

"No," I shouted, a bit too loud. "You wanna know why I left Connect? I went there to get the update. I mean, seriously, with all the cameras STaR has, you'd think the RD could find my mother. But no. Then these Agents showed up, and I freaked out." I fought back the tears that threatened to unleash.

Murray whipped his head around, his eyes darting in every direction. When no one appeared, he pulled his handheld from his belt. I glanced at the screen as he punched in our location. He moved the screen to Connect's entrance and zoomed in. The red C circling the globe appeared followed by a flurry of activity around the building. Murray looked above my head at a camera lodged on the roof of the brick building. A familiar hum hovered overhead. *Drones.*

Murray powered down his device and grabbed my shoulders. "We need to leave. Follow me."

But I had no intention of going anywhere with him. I filled my eyes with fake tears. Well, not completely fake, since pain shot down my left shoulder from his grip. I inhaled and exhaled like I was about to explode. "I want to go home."

Murray's face softened, and he dropped his arms. "Come on. I'll give you a ride."

He stepped toward the parking lot. I hesitated, planning to make a run for it, when a man smashed Officer Murray on the back of the head. Murray collapsed forward, but the assailant caught his fall and placed him against the brick building. I opened my mouth to scream when a hand clamped down hard. *Crooked Smile Guy.*

A blue tattoo slithered out the collar of his tight t-shirt. The image that coiled around his neck reminded me of a snake that caught its prey. His black baseball cap and gold mirrored sunglasses covered much of his face, but when he removed his sunglasses, his dark and menacing eyes glowed. He removed his hand from my lips.

"You...you killed him." I blinked to keep from passing out.

"He's not dead. He'll wake up with a nasty headache, though."

The pounding in my head intensified. "But...he's an RO."

"You think because he's a Reinforcement Officer that he's protecting you?" His thick Southern drawl stretched like a slow country song. He pulled a toothpick from his pocket and stuck it between his teeth. "Want to know what I think? He knows more than he's telling you. People don't just disappear unless they're running away."

"My mom wouldn't leave us," I said, bold and defiant.

"So, where is she?" He gripped me by the elbow, placing his other hand on the small of my back. He tilted his head toward the trash dumpsters. "Walk with me. This place stinks."

He let go, allowing my escape. I should have bolted, but I was curious about the questions that needed answers. How was Mom's disappearance tied to a mobile outage? And why did this man continue to follow me? The questions haunted me.

Against common sense, I willingly followed him beyond the dumpsters to an abandoned patch of woods without cameras. He leaned against a giant tree, moving the toothpick to the opposite side of his mouth. His eyes roamed over my body, taking in each section before settling on my face. I envisioned the tattooed snake choking me to death. The cool October air seared through my clothing and my body shuddered with chills.

"So listen, kid. I know you're scared, but I can't help you if you keep running."

"Why are you following me?"

His crooked smile returned. "Think of me as your guardian angel."

"I don't need a guardian or an angel," I said. "Who are you? Do the Agents work for you?"

A slight twitch made his brows crinkle. *Had I hit a nerve*? His expression faded as quickly as it came, and he swirled the toothpick between his teeth. "Here's what I think. Your mom's disappearance might be connected to the software update. The Reinforcement Division isn't helping, and you think they can't be trusted. You're probably right. They don't have the best reputation."

But could the RD make video footage disappear?

"You suspect I'm after you too," Crooked Smile Guy continued, "but I'm not. I'm trying to help you find your mom."

My stomach tightened. "That's the second time today someone told me they're trying to help me. Who do you work for?"

"I'm considered...an independent contractor. Williams asked me to help with this case."

"The National Agent? The ROs said he doesn't exist."

"But you don't believe them," he drawled. It was more of a statement than a question, and he was right. I was having a hard time understanding who to believe. "Here's the thing. Your phone has a glitch and Williams needs to get in touch with your Aunt Kate. He thinks she'll help us find your mom."

My thoughts spun out of control. Something wasn't adding up. "Why Kate?"

"She's your mom's twin sister, right? Twins have this connection to each other. One experiences pain or distress; the other feels it. We believe Kate is vital to finding your mom. Do you understand what I'm sayin'?"

I shrugged. "Um, I guess so."

"Let's have a look at that phone of yours." As if sensing my hesitation, he pointed to my backpack and held out his palm. "Phone?"

I clutched the straps of my backpack until my knuckles turned the color of snow. "Why is everyone obsessed with my stupid phone?"

His jaw tightened. "Agent Williams instructed you to download the update at Connect Mobile, correct?"

"Yeah. Then you and the other Agents showed up, so I left."

"Hand me your phone." His tone changed so drastically, morphing from attempting to connect with me to controlling, that I took a step back. Clearly, this guy wasn't used to being told no.

I dug in my heels. "What does my phone have to do with any of this?"

He spat the toothpick onto the ground and curled his lips into a menacing scowl. "We all protect those we love. I protect my family, my country. How about you? Who do you protect?" I felt his hot breath on my skin. "It'd be a shame if Zac disappeared, too. Wouldn't it? At the skateboard park, jumping, flipping, an innocent victim of a drive-by shooting. Blood squirts on your father as he holds his dying son."

I lunged and pounded my fists on his chest. "Leave Zac alone!"

He grabbed my wrists, winding them together in one fateful swoop. I tried to yell for help, but he pressed against me like a massive boulder, stifling my screams. I never should have evaded the cameras. *Stupid.* Where was a drone to record proof of this conversation when I needed it?

His lips brushed against my ear, and I squeezed my eyes shut, holding back a sob. "Let me be clear. If you talk to a single RO or breathe a word of our conversation to anyone, Zac won't make it to his thirteenth birthday."

He edged back and waited until my lids fluttered. Then he slashed his index finger across his throat.

My knees went weak. I gasped for air. Crooked Smile Guy ripped my backpack off my shoulders and unzipped every pocket until he found my phone. He pulled the phone apart, searching...searching. He placed my SIM card back into its holder and reinserted the battery.

With his free hand, he made a call with his own phone. A phone I didn't recognize. I'd heard about untraceable phones—burner phones—ones STaR couldn't track. But they were illegal and impossible to find since Connect Mobile took over. *Who is this guy?*

The vein in the center of his forehead bulged as he grew more agitated and spoke into his phone. "It's not here. Yeah, I checked there, too." He glanced at me, his face a mixture of anger and excitement.

He pulled the phone away from his ear as the person on the other line shouted, then hung up. The voice sounded muffled, computer-generated even, but two words were distinct. *Next phase.* I had no idea what that meant, but neither did I want to stick around to find out.

Panic swelled. I had to get to the park to warn Zac. But how? *The Swiss Army knife.* I'd slipped it into my pocket before we left for Dad's house and forgot to give it to Zac. If I could pull it out unnoticed, I might get away.

I slid my hand inside the front pocket of my jeans, breathing slowly and steadily. Easing the blade out of the handle, I held tight and waited. Crooked Smile Guy placed his phone up to his ear to make another call. Then his eyes widened as recognition set in.

Slash.

He cursed as sprays of blood spewed onto my gray sweatshirt. He dropped both phones and gripped his forearm. As the knife fell to the ground between us, he shouted a slew of obscenities. I lunged for my phone, not bothering to pick up the knife. He grabbed me, leaving a bloody handprint on my hoodie. I shoved my knee into his groin, releasing all the rage within me. He dropped forward, shrieking in pain, creating all the space I needed to snatch my backpack and phone. Without looking back, I ran for my life.

CHAPTER 12

Friday, September 22

My heart pounded as I zigzagged in and out of traffic in the direction of the skate park. After sprinting close to three miles, my legs ached with exhaustion. I dashed through each section of the park, searching for any sign of Zac. Flyers with my mom's picture were taped to light fixtures, and a few loose ones blew on the ground as if people had simply dropped them. A gust of wind blew the papers into the nearby grass. Zac had been here. Of that, I was sure. I picked up the loose flyers and tucked them into the mesh water bottle holder on the outside of my pack.

A kid around his age with shoulder length chestnut hair zipped past me on a skateboard, attempting a kickflip. He fell but popped back up and dove into the pipe hole, whizzing up the concrete structure to offer a high-five to his friend.

"Hey," I called after him. "Have you seen a kid named Zac? Seventh-grader, brown hair, hazel eyes?"

He rode his skateboard up to me, missing my toes by inches. "The kid with the shepherd dog that never leaves his side?" I nodded. "Yeah. He was here, and man, did he have a good run."

" *Was* here?" My eyes darted in every direction.

"Yeah. He left with some dude."

My mouth went dry. "What did the dude look like?"

The boy grunted. "Like I paid attention."

"How long ago did he leave?"

The kid fiddled with his helmet strap. "I don't know. Fifteen minutes maybe?" He whispered to his friend before dashing off. "Dropping," he shouted, skating into the steep hole and back up again, landing a perfect rail slide across the metal railing.

A group of teenage boys huddled near a small building housing the bathrooms and water fountains. I searched for the cameras, unsure whether I wanted this conversation recorded. Only one hung by the restroom doors. I crept behind the building and pulled up my hood, tucking strands of hair behind my ears. I needed a working phone.

When the boy and his buddy made their way to the building and rested against the concrete wall, I slipped behind him. I lowered my head and whispered, "Can I use your phone?" The boy whipped around and his brown eyes widened. I tugged at my hoodie strings. "Sorry. I didn't mean to scare you. I'm Zac's sister, Rami." I offered a half-smile, attempting to put him at ease before pulling out a flyer. "Zac said he came here to pass these out. I need to get in touch with my dad, but my phone doesn't work."

The boy glanced at the flyer, then opened his sling backpack. "Yeah. He passed them out to everyone. That stinks about your mom." He held the phone to his face, unlocking his code, then handed it to me.

"Thanks," I said, offering a half-smile.

I dialed Dad's number. It rang once before the scrape of metal followed by loud cursing made me look up. A skater around my age with long, scraggly hair lay sprawled out on the concrete.

"Dude. What the—" Skater Boy's words were cut off the instant he jumped up because the man slung him to the ground in one fatal swoop.

Bile filled my throat. Crooked Smile Guy had found me. Skater Boy cursed louder this time, and other skaters approached to defend their friend. I dropped the phone I'd borrowed and bolted to the stretch of woods that paralleled the interstate.

Exhaustion caught up with me within minutes. Since leaving Little Cone, I'd been running for over an hour. My legs collapsed, and I grabbed a pine tree filled with sticky sap to steady my fall. As I leaned against the tree with my backpack strapped on, sap oozed onto the cloth material.

In the distance, the sun sank, and I shivered in the cool night air. The wind picked up, forcing the pine trees to sway, dropping needles all around me. I watched the trees lean into a powerful gust of wind, realizing how one big storm could snap a pine tree's trunk in half. I sat helpless beneath the tree branches, much like a pine—shaky and unstable. Every snap of a tree branch felt like someone out to get me.

I'd spent my whole life with a phone in my hand, registering my identity to STaR. But now, I longed to stay in these woods, out of sight of cameras and drones. Away from the technology designed to keep me safe.

My cramped muscles begged me to rest, but I couldn't succumb to sleep until I knew Zac was safe. But where could I go? And, more importantly, who could I trust?

Finley.

I didn't know why his name popped into my head, and right now, I didn't care. I willed my body to head north with the highway traffic, staying hidden among low-hanging branches. My deafening breaths and the crunch of fallen leaves pounded in my ears, but I refused to stop.

A yellow restaurant sign rose above the forest to help me get my bearings. Once known for greasy hash browns and breakfast steak, the Safety Division's emphasis on health did away with all processed foods, replacing them with genetically modified vegetable grown in greenhouses.

When I reached Breakfast House, I fled behind the building and kept my head low. I didn't dare lift my eyes to the streetlamp cameras. A water spigot stuck out from the brick wall. The cool water poured onto the black asphalt, and I scrubbed the dried sap and blood from my hands before interlocking my fingers to drink. The back door swung open, startling me, and water sprayed on my shoes. A young guy with hair more blond than mine held a bag of trash, then looked me up and down, as if he couldn't decide what to say.

"We got free water inside if you wanna come in." His mouth twitched, reminding me of Mr. Tarito's quirky habit of crinkling his nose. The boy motioned toward my blood-stained sweatshirt with an imprint. "Might need to clean that up."

A faint buzzing drew near. The sound escalated my fear. A drone approaching. "I'm...I'm fine." I stammered, then sprinted out of sight, not bothering to look back.

CHAPTER 13

Friday, September 22

By the time I reached Finley's neighborhood, a crescent moon provided the only illumination. But the darkness provided the perfect cover as I weaved in and out of backyards. But the lack of light made it harder to spot his house, considering they all looked the same—two-story with two-car garages and six-foot wooden fences in the backyard. I took a chance and crept behind a light tan house with a tall, wooden privacy fence. A menacing snarl behind the fence grew in intensity as I climbed up. Below me, two glowing eyes met my gaze. The beast charged full speed ahead, barking as if I were an intruder.

"Ranger?" I whispered in a high-pitched squeal. He stopped barking, and I jumped down, scratching Finley's yellow Labrador retriever between the ears.

On the porch above me, a floodlight came on, illuminating the yard. Finley's voice called in the night. "Ranger? Here, boy." When Ranger didn't budge, Finley stepped onto the wooden deck above me. He spotted me crouched in the grass with his dog and tore down the stairs in a frenzy. "Rami? Where have you been? Everyone's looking for you. I called and sent you like a hundred texts." The words flew out of his mouth faster than I could think. "You missed your volleyball game. Lela's out of her mind."

My game. It completely slipped my mind.

When I remained quiet, Finley took a breath. "Your arm. There's blood all over your sweatshirt. What happened?"

"It's not my blood."

"Then whose is it?"

Fatigue set in, and I found myself unable to move. I'd been running for hours on little sleep and my legs cramped in response. I reached down to rub my calf, shoving my backpack to the side. "Some crazy dude has been chasing me all day."

Finley shuffled his fingers through his wavy hair. "Chasing you? Why?"

I thought about Zac. Did he make it home? I should have gone to my dad's place to be sure Zac was safe. But first, I needed answers from someone I trusted. Someone to help me figure this out.

If you breathe a word of our conversation to anyone... The man's words echoed in my head until it throbbed. Tears trailed down my cheeks. I couldn't follow Crooked Smile Guy's instructions. I needed help.

Slowly, I leaked every detail to Finley, starting from the moment I entered the RD precinct. "I told the Agent I didn't have my phone, and he flipped out. He demanded I get the software update." I steadied my breathing. "Then he asked about my Aunt Kate and said I needed to find her."

Finley interlocked his fingers atop his head. "What does all this have to do with finding your mom?"

"I don't know. He said I could post stuff to Allicio if my phone worked. Totally wigged me out. I got an error message that I had to go to Connect Mobile to get the update. Then Crooked Smile Guy shows up with two National Agents. The thing is, how did he and the Agent know I got an error message? I never told the ROs about it."

Finley narrowed his brows. "Wait. What message? I thought your phone didn't work."

I let out an exasperated sigh. "It doesn't. But the morning of the outage, I got a random text that STaR watches over me."

"That's weird. Who sent it?"

"I don't know. And when I tried to answer, my phone crashed. How is that possible?"

Finley shook his head. "It's not."

My body shuddered. "Yet it happened."

Finley let me talk without interruption as I described the horrific sight of Officer Murray's body propped up against the building, bleeding out alone and unconscious, and how I fled to the skate park to find Zac.

"Let me get this straight." Finley's voice was tight and controlled as he paced on the lawn, leaving a trail of smashed imprints in the grass. "You're interrogated by a National Agent investigating your mom's case as a homicide. He insists you give him your phone and when you don't have it, he tells you to get the software update. Then, some random dude hunts you down, hits Officer Murray in the head, and you don't know why?"

I pulled my sleeves over my hands and rocked my body in the cold, wet grass. The zipped pocket where I'd stored my phone at the skate park taunted me. "He wants my phone."

Finley's face contorted, making his high cheekbones appear thin. "That's crazy, Rami. What does your phone have to do with any of this?"

The tears I tried to suppress now flowed. "It must have something to do with my mom's disappearance."

Finley squatted next to me. "You need to report this."

Lowering my voice, I looked at Finley. "Report to who? I watched the tape at the RD. There was no sign of Agent Williams." My voice pleaded as I pulled my knees to my chest. "I wasn't supposed to tell you any of this."

Finley lowered his voice to match mine. "I don't understand. Why don't you want to report this guy?"

Images from yesterday flooded my thoughts. My mother's expression when I spoke out against STaR. Her warning about the Threats Division. Using sign language to communicate with me. The text that STaR watches me. I placed my finger to my lips and jutted my head toward his roof. I didn't know how many cameras the Drake family had, but the sudden fear of being recorded overshadowed any reasonable thought.

I swallowed the anguish that threatened to choke me and whispered, "Because if I report him to the RD, he'll kill Zac."

Finley placed his hands on top of his head, interlocking his fingers. He exhaled, then held out his hand. "Come inside. It's freezing out here and I can't think."

He pulled me up from the lawn and handed me my backpack. A few loose flyers fell out, and Finley snatched them up, staring at the picture of my missing mother. I watched as his mouth twitched, but he remained silent.

He tucked the poster into the back pocket of his jeans and fled to the stairs, taking them two by two. I followed him to the wooden deck, weaving around a black wrought iron table with four matching chairs. Behind the table sat an open grill, revealing dirty slats. My stomach suddenly growled. I hadn't eaten in hours.

As if reading my mind, Finley said, "You hungry?"

I bobbed my head. "Starving."

Finley opened the door, and Ranger raced past us, collapsing onto his bed in the family room. We entered a pale green kitchen with framed fruit baskets donning the walls. Finley pulled out a container of sliced ham, neatly wrapped in a deli bag, and two slices of American cheese. "Mayo? Mustard?"

"Just mustard."

He set everything on the brown granite countertop, then got sandwich bread from a nearby drawer. I flopped down on a bar stool and watched as he assembled the sandwiches. He set one on a paper plate in front of me. "Water?"

"Sure." The dried blood on my sleeve stared me in the face and suddenly I lost my appetite. "I better wash up first."

He nodded without a word. I walked down the hall to the bathroom and scrubbed my hands with soap until they were red and sore. I reentered the kitchen, where Finley slid two glasses of water across the counter. Then he sat on the stool next to me. He devoured his sandwich, and I wondered when he ate last. I moved mine around on the plate, taking a few bites so I wouldn't hurt his feelings. He grabbed my paper plate with his and tossed them into the trash can.

"Where's your mom?" I asked, noticing her absence.

“She picked up an extra shift at the hospital. They have a nursing shortage, so she gets called in a lot. But she left early to attend the...” Finley shuffled his feet on the kitchen floor. “Look, I really need to take you home, Rames.”

“I’m staying with my dad for a few days since my mom....” The thought of spending more time with Dad and Olivia filled me with dread.

“Fine. I’ll take you there.”

“What if the guy follows us? I can’t risk putting Zac in danger,” I said.

Finley threw his hands in the air. “What are you going to do, keep running? Let’s go to the RD precinct.”

My throat tightened. “Last time I tried that, they stuck me in an isolation room with a whacked-out Agent who’s obsessed with my phone. Some protection that is.”

Finley groaned. “RD stations have security cameras, Rami. Someone must have seen what happened.”

“Yeah, they have cameras everywhere. No one goes in or out without being scanned. The cameras followed me down the hall, but when I entered the interrogation room, the camera flickered. Gaits checked his handheld. There’s no footage of Williams and me talking.”

“So, let one of the other ROs help you. They can’t all be corrupt.”

My voice tightened to a soft whimper. “I’m not sure I trust the RD. Gaits said National Agents report directly to the President, so he’d know if they had been called in. And Murray claims he never ordered anyone to interrogate me.”

Finley gripped the edge of the counter and stuck his face inches from mine. "Do you understand how crazy you sound?"

Finley's trying to help. Why won't I let him help me? Fear strangled me as I lowered my voice to a mere whisper. "I'm not crazy, Fin. Crooked Smile Guy threatened to kill Zac."

"I need a minute to think." Without another word, Finley walked outside, leaving me all alone.

CHAPTER 14

Friday, September 22

Finley's mind worked like a computer. It needed time to process information and spit out a logical explanation. I watched him pacing the deck, stopping only to rub his palms together. Inside, the ticking of an old-fashioned clock echoed in the silent room as regret flooded my thoughts. Trust didn't come easy for me. It took a lot to earn it, and even more to keep it. But I wanted to trust Finley, even if I didn't fully understand why.

As the minutes passed, I moved to the family room to be with Ranger. He sat on a red and black plaid bed next to the fireplace, grabbed a tennis ball and dropped it at my feet. I reached down and tossed the ball across the room. He darted after it, each time returning it to me. For the first time in hours, I smiled. Ranger's life was so simple—throw the ball and he was happy. I sat on Ranger's bed and rubbed his yellow fur while he chased the ball like his life depended on it.

Fear, regret, guilt—they battled for control of my mind. After hours of running, my body could no longer move. Years of strenuous volleyball practices had taught me that the muscle cramps that now invaded my body resulted from lactic acid buildup. At last, I succumbed to the fatigue and closed my heavy eyelids, burying my face in Ranger's soft fur.

When the back door opened, I sat straight up, alarmed. How long had I slept? Seconds? Minutes? I scanned Finley's face for any sign of sympathy or understanding, but his expression remained unreadable. He slumped onto the brown leather couch across from me, resting his head against the sofa cushions. He interlaced his fingers, then placed them on his forehead. His silence unnerved me. Without a word, Finley slid onto the carpet, leaning in so close his scent filled the space between us.

"Rami?" My eyes rose to meet his. His soft brown eyes spoke volumes. "I want to help. Please let me drive you to your dad's. From there, we'll figure out what to do next."

"Okay." I bit my lower lip in defeat.

He lifted one eyebrow. "No more fighting me?"

"I need to be sure Zac's all right," I said, my voice hollow.

He bobbed his chin, then stood. I pushed myself upright and followed him toward the door.

"Fin? I'm sorry." The words lodged in my throat.

He frowned. "For what?"

"For involving you. I shouldn't have come here."

"Stop. I'm glad you came to me. That's what friends are for." He gave me a half-smile. "Come on. We need to get going."

He slipped his key ring off a hook near the front door and put his baseball cap on backward. The electric garage door sounded, and Mrs. Drake walked into the kitchen, clothed in a set of teal scrubs and multi-colored clogs. Her hair was pulled back into a tight ponytail at the top of her head. When she spotted me with Finley, she dropped her water bottle to the floor. The crash echoed in the silence. Her tanned face paled in the dim light, as if she'd seen a ghost.

"Rami? You're...you're here? You're safe?" Her response reminded me of Finley when he found me in the yard with Ranger.

"Hi, Mrs. Drake. Yes. I'm fine."

She gave Finley an odd look. "Everyone is searching for you, Rami. Your picture is being blasted on monitors across town."

My mouth twitched. "I'm so sorry to worry you. I came here because..." *Because I don't trust my dad. Because I don't trust the RD. Because a stalker threatened to kill my brother.* But I didn't say any of those things. "Because my phone hasn't worked since the outage, and I needed to borrow Finley's."

The lie sat between us in an uncomfortable stillness until Finley spoke up. "I'm taking her home, Mom. Be back in a few."

Mrs. Drake watched from the doorway as we walked down the driveway and climbed into Finley's midnight blue Jeep. Somehow, Finley had rewired his STaR electronic screen to glitch now and then so he could listen to whatever music he wanted. I didn't know how he got away with it and I didn't ask. Finley's familiar playlist, the one we created a few months ago, rang through the speakers. I clutched my pack to my chest and closed my eyes, listening to the lyrics of the band OneRepublic.

Before my dad moved out, he introduced me to some of his favorite childhood bands. Bands his dad listened to when he was a kid. Dad held onto some of the discs, and before STaR took over he would play them for me. I fell in love with the way the songwriters from bands like The Script, Imagine Dragons, and The Fray expressed themselves through music. My generation's music seemed so guarded, like musicians were afraid to say the wrong thing.

Once our CD player broke, we had no way of listening, so Dad boxed up the discs and stored them in our attic. When Finley and I started hanging out, I mentioned I liked oldies music. Rather than laugh, he found songs from the early 2000s and made matching playlists. When I asked how he found the music, he just said STaR had more important things to worry about than two kids playing oldies rock. I never questioned him.

As the song continued to play, I found myself able to relate to the artists' words about how we all run for something. I wanted to run back to my life, the one before my mom disappeared, before the mobile outage, before Crooked Smile Guy and his threats. A lump formed in my throat. How had my real world turn upside down so fast?

Finley dabbed at a tear on my cheek. The intimate gesture must have registered shock on my face because he quickly withdrew his hand. "I'm...I'm sorry," he stammered. "I don't have any tissues."

My stomach flipped at the unexpected display of affection. An unfamiliar sensation, although not entirely unwelcome, washed over my tired body. What was happening to me? A loud humming filled my ears as my thoughts spun like a spider's web, and I wondered if Fin was aware of the effect his touch had on me. I blinked to clear my thoughts.

"What did you say?" I asked.

"Which way to your dad's place?"

Still mystified by the abnormal exchange, I tugged at a hangnail to avoid eye contact. "Oh, um, left at the next street."

Pumpkin-lined streets and decorated scarecrows stood in every corner as Finley weaved through the technology district. I loved October, with its cool temperatures and colorful display of leaves falling from trees. If this had been any other day, I would have begged Finley to pull over and jump into the neatly raked pile of oak leaves that reminded me so much of his hair color. But how could I have fun when Mom and Zac were in danger?

When Finley pulled up to Dad's townhouse, he cut the Jeep's hybrid engine and turned to face me. "There's still one thing I don't get. Why is homicide involved? It seems too early to jump to that conclusion."

I lifted one shoulder. "I don't know." Fin nodded as if my answer pacified his curiosity. I reached across the gearshift and tapped his arm. "You can go, Fin. I'm good."

"Not until you're safe," he said.

Finley's presence alone made me feel safe, but I didn't dare admit that out loud. I took one slow step at a time, dreading my father's reaction.

The door flew open, and Dad raced to greet me, pulling me into a tight hug. "Rames! You had us worried sick. Zac is beside himself. Where have you been?" Dad ushered me inside. "Wait. You're bleeding."

"I'm okay, Dad," I said.

Finley lingered in the doorway with his thumbs wedged into the front pockets of his jeans. He cleared his throat and Dad turned, as if noticing Fin's presence for the first time. "Did you do this to her? You sick—"

"No, sir." Finley threw up his hands in surrender.

"Dad! He's helping me," I shouted. "This is Finley. My friend. You'd know if..." I rolled my eyes. "Never mind."

"Rami?" Zac appeared from around the corner and crashed into me, latching his arms around my waist. He squeezed tight, then dropped his hold. Before I could react, he reared back and punched me in the gut.

I bent over, gasping for air, and my backpack flew to the floor. "Why—"

"For scaring me. We went to your volleyball game, and you weren't there. We drove all around. Where were you?" Zac pleaded.

I let out a long overdue sigh. My hands trembled as I cupped his face. "At the skateboard park looking for you. I should have come here to make sure you made it home."

Zac fought back tears. "You're bleeding."

"I'm... I'm fine," I said between strained breaths.

"No, you're not. None of this is fine."

"Zac? I'm sorry," I repeated, tears welling in my eyes. He darted for the stairs. "Wait!" I lunged for the handrail, but Dad held me back.

"Let him go. He's been on edge since you weren't at the game," Dad said.

My body trembled. Dad opened his arms and, for once, I fell into them, burying my head deep into his chest. He held me until I stopped shaking.

Olivia handed me a warm, wet cloth. "Here, I thought you could use this."

My chin quivered. I wanted to hate her. She and the other women who took my father away. But I couldn't bring myself to be angry at Olivia because she reminded me so much of my mom with her dirty blond hair with streaks of gray beginning to show. The look she gave me, with her emerald eyes glowing with concern, almost made me want to reach out and hug her.

Instead, I glanced at my father. "Any word on Mom?"

He shook his head. "The RD doesn't have a single lead. She vanished into thin air."

"What about Aunt Kate? Have you heard from her?" I couldn't imagine why Crooked Smile Guy wanted to talk to Kate, but if I could find her, maybe he'd leave Zac and me alone.

"She hasn't returned my calls. I gave the RD her address. They're looking for her."

Kate lived in some fancy high-rise downtown with a successful job she didn't talk much about. But she and my mom were best friends. Why hadn't she come over, or at least called?

"Rami? Where were you?" Dad said, interrupting my thoughts.

I motioned to the blood on my sweatshirt. "Let me wash this off, then I promise I'll tell you everything."

I edged toward the stairs, clutching the handrail, when I remembered Finley. I whipped around, embarrassed that in all the chaos he'd slipped out unnoticed before I could thank him.

Upstairs, I tossed my backpack and phone onto the bed. The aroma of lavender soap filled the room as I headed straight for the shower, scrubbing my skin until it turned the color of cherries. Then I sank to the floor of the tub and sobbed.

CHAPTER 15

Friday, September 22

After showering, I wrapped my hair in a towel, dressed, and returned to my family. Two large square boxes sat on a white kitchen table, the aroma tantalizing. Olivia pulled out two slices of my favorite—pepperoni and mushroom—and handed them to me.

Most grocery markets had food shortages and high costs, yet restaurants thrived under STaR's leadership, as if all the genetically modified food STaR grew in greenhouses had been allocated for them. Things like pizza were harder to come by due to the Safety Division's push for healthy living. Dad's government job provided him with access to things most Americans could no longer afford.

Since we hadn't had cheese pizza for years, Zac stuffed two slices in his mouth by the time I sat down. "We would've eaten earlier, but we were all out looking for..." Zac didn't need to finish his thought. I read between the lines.

They were searching for *me*. Suddenly, the expensive pizza seemed nauseating, as guilt made my stomach churn. I slid the plate away, no longer hungry.

Dad took a bite, swallowed, then rested his elbows on the table. "You need to tell us what happened after I dropped you off at Connect Mobile. Officer Gaits spent the afternoon looking for you, and Officer Murray suffered a concussion. Zac and I drove around for hours, passing out flyers of your mom and looking for you."

My head hung in shame. "I'm really sorry for the trouble I caused. I didn't mean for you to worry."

"You think I don't worry about you?" Dad's voice rose an octave.

"I don't know. Do you?" My voice held an air of accusation.

"Of course I do." He paused, as if choosing his words carefully. "Rami? Olivia organized a search party for your mom, which almost turned into a desperate search for you, too. Talk to me, Rames. What's going on?"

Thoughts swirled in my brain. *Why would Dad's girlfriend organize a search for her boyfriend's ex-wife?* That didn't make sense. Then again, nothing about today made sense. Crooked Smile Guy's words came flooding back. "If you tell anyone, Zac won't make it to his thirteenth birthday." Bile traveled up my esophagus, burning as it went.

I had to protect Zac, even if it meant more lies, so I told them what they wanted to hear—that I'd imagined the whole thing, adding the part about my nightmare to make my story seem authentic. I let them believe I was paranoid. Perhaps I was. I couldn't tell anymore.

Dad's incessant questions wore me down until I forgot which version I'd told. My lies had grown as tall as the Connect Mobile building. I hated lying, but I had to keep Zac safe, and I didn't know who to trust. Plus, my STaR unit sat inches from us. If the rumors were true that STaR could listen anytime, my answers were being recorded. Unable to hold my eyes open, I begged Dad to let me sleep. I approached my health device for the nighttime check-in and called her name.

Her familiar voice filled the room. “Rami Carlton. Your temperature is normal. You would benefit from additional sleep. Vitamin D is recommended.”

Really, Rosemary? What a shocker. I rolled my eyes and turned toward the stairs.

“Rami?” Dad stopped me before I reached the first stair. “No more disappearing. Promise me.”

My eyes moved up to the right before answering. “Yeah. Okay.”

I grasped onto the railing and pulled my aching legs up the staircase. After brushing my teeth, I crawled under the covers, but each time I shut my eyes, I envisioned Mom lying in a ditch in the middle of a different region, out of sight from cameras and drones. The images haunted me until I drifted into a fitful sleep.

CHAPTER 16

Saturday, September 23

Sunlight streamed through the blinds, and the scent of fresh-roasted coffee seeped into my room. The alarm clock next to the bed registered 10:00. I'd slept for close to eleven hours. I rolled onto my side and attempted to stand up. Cramps shot through my legs like the broadhead of an arrow as I pulled on a pair of jeans and a blue long-sleeved t-shirt, wincing with each movement from all the running and no sleep.

In the kitchen, Zac sat at the table, bent over a bowl of cereal. I poured cereal into a similar sized bowl, splashed in a small amount of milk, and sat down. He downed a glass of milk before taking another bite and ignored my presence.

"I'm sorry again about yesterday," I said.

He dropped his spoon in the bowl. His lip trembled. "For which part? Disappearing for hours while we looked for you, or coming home covered in blood? Oh, wait. You're sorry you freaked out and bolted from the RD precinct."

He continued to list my inadequacies, and I let him vent. It was the least I could do considering I didn't keep my promise to Mom.

She'd instructed me to keep Zac safe no matter what. I'd failed. Miserably.

Tears flowed down his cheeks. "Or maybe you're sorry for leaving me, just like Dad and Mom."

My heart broke. I moved closer to Zac and held him, letting him cry it out. I wanted to reassure him, to tell him Mom was fine, but I couldn't bring myself to say the words. Perhaps because I too had my doubts.

Mom used to watch a TV show where police used advanced technology to locate missing persons within seventy-two hours. If they didn't find the person within the timeframe, the odds of survival weren't good. A lump formed in my throat at the thought. My mom had been missing for fifty-two hours.

Only twenty hours remained. Less than one day.

"I'm not leaving you, Zac, and neither did Mom. She would never leave you. Never in a million years."

He dabbed at his tears. "Then where is she?"

"We're going to find her, son," Dad said, startling both of us. He leaned against the counter, letting the weight of his words sink in, then poured a cup of coffee and joined us at the table. "Officer Murray is on the way to Aunt Kate's place right now." He gazed into the warm brown liquid.

When the doorbell chimed, Zac rushed to answer, but Olivia got there first. Lela barged past Olivia and Zac, leaving Quince standing on the doorstep.

"I'm so relieved to see you alive." Lela squeezed the life out of me. "You missed our game yesterday. Why didn't you call me? You had me worried sick. What happened?"

The firing squad had arrived. When I motioned for Quince to enter, Lela released her death grip. "Oh, my gosh. Please forgive my manners. I'm Lela Ferreira and this is my boyfriend, Quince Harris."

I motioned toward Olivia. "Guys, this is Olivia. My dad's, um, girlfriend."

Olivia raised one eyebrow. "Nice to meet you, Lela and Quince. I'll be in the other room if you need anything."

As Olivia stepped away, Lela pulled me close, whispering in my ear. "*She's* the one who organized today's search party?"

My shoulders lifted, as if to say, "Weird, huh," but I didn't dare voice it aloud.

"You girls gonna hug all day?" Quince said, stepping behind Lela. "Save some lovin' for the man of the house."

"You mean Zac?" Lela retorted.

Quince pumped his fist against his chest. "Ouch, girl. Way to sting a man's pride." He glanced at Zac. "There's some serious girl drama in this room."

Zac rolled his eyes. "You have no idea."

Lela's face filled with red splotches. "I was a nervous wreck yesterday. When you didn't come to the game and no one could find you, I about lost my mind. What's going on? Brannon texted me and—"

"Brannon?" I interrupted.

She threw up her hands and exhaled. "Yeah. He said he ran into you at Little Cone and you kept looking over your shoulder. He made it sound like you blew him off. That's when I knew something was up. There's no way my best friend would blow off Brannon Martinelli."

Quince patted at his hair to flatten it against his head. "Seriously, girl. You got it bad for him."

"Not now, Quince," Lela said.

"Just sayin'." Quince stuck his finger down his throat and Zac laughed.

I dragged Lela away from the others and lowered my voice. "Brannon asked me out. I mean, not a date or anything, but he offered to help."

Lela giggled. "Seriously? So cool. But why are you whispering?"

"We can't talk in front of Zac. He totally wigged out when I didn't show up for our game last night."

Lela's splotches moved to her neck. "That makes two of us."

"You asked why I didn't call you, but my phone hasn't worked since the outage. Remember?"

She threw her hands over her mouth as if I'd just uttered something offensive. "You *still* don't have a working phone? O-M-G." She opened Allicio and flashed a picture of teenagers standing outside with lit candles. "We held a candlelight vigil outside church last night for your mom. When you didn't show to our game, it turned into a vigil for you. Fin was there with his mom. We were all there. Are you going to tell me what's going on?"

All those people gathered for me, and Fin never mentioned it. No wonder his mom looked like she'd seen a ghost when she saw me. My chin quivered. "I didn't mean to freak you out. There's a lot I need to explain, but not now. We need to go."

Lela eyed me suspiciously. "But you will tell me everything. Right?"

"Yeah." Another lie. "Can Zac and I ride with you? Please?"

Lela flipped a strand of pink hair over her shoulder. "If your dad will let you out of his sight. He's totally freaked out. I tried to reassure him you're always this weird."

I snickered, despite my dark mood. "Thanks a lot."

During the drive, Quince cut up with Zac, easing the tension we struggled to cover up. Quince asked Zac about augmented reality gaming, and for the next ten minutes, the two of them talked nonstop about game characters, battles, and maps. Lela turned onto Technology Park Drive, then into a large office complex with multiple glass buildings. The buildings appeared lifeless, with their blinds closed and empty parking spaces.

We drove behind building three to Topothesia's headquarters, and suddenly dozens of cars came into view. I uttered a silent prayer as Lela parked. As I slipped out of her car, I stole a glance at the camera mounted on the building. A red light appeared and flashed several times. I blinked to clear my vision, and when I looked back, the red light was gone. Had I imagined it?

Lela pulled me toward the other volunteers. My eyes widened in astonishment at the number of people who gave up their Saturday to help find my mom. Tears flooded my eyes, staining my cheeks as I struggled to hold it together. Everyone gathered around Olivia as she broke us up into groups of ten and assigned each group an area around the building. It struck me as odd that Olivia would know how to organize a search party of volunteers without the RD's help. What Olivia didn't address and what no one dared to ask was why my mother's car had been found here where Dad worked. Mom was supposed to be at work and later at church, both of which were in the opposite direction. A slight chill crept up my spine.

As my group set out for the woods behind Topothesia, Zac stayed close to my side. Even with our friends around, I felt better with him nearby. When we reached an industrial park, we turned left while another group moved right. We continued in near silence, pacing back and forth between trees, in and out of parking lots, and behind industrial-sized dumpsters. When a horn blared, we returned to base.

Almost immediately, my hopes dashed as I watched Olivia's expression. Her lip twitched, and she gave a slight shake of the head, enough for me to understand the gravity of the situation. Three hours, over fifty volunteers, and not a single clue about what happened to Annie Carlton.

Dad insisted Zac and I ride home in his car, but the sight of him made me sick. The idea that he could somehow be involved created a deep canyon that could forever divide us. The anguish I felt was a hole so deep it needed stitches. I was no longer able to hold back tears, and they flowed down my cheeks as my thoughts spiraled downward.

CHAPTER 17

Saturday, September 23

I lay facedown on my bed, willing sleep to come, but it evaded me. Tears had dampened the pillowcase as images of Mom flashed before me like one of Zac's simulations. Why didn't we find a single clue? And why didn't the RD have a suspect? The room's lack of color—white walls, white sheets, and white bedspread—reminded me of my life as color oozed from my pores, leaving nothing but emptiness in its place. Lela sat with me, silently stroking my hair, giving me the space I needed to make sense of my upside down world.

"Rami?" Quince stood over me, his expression a mixture of pain and sadness. "Sorry to interrupt, but Finley wants to talk to you."

I nodded and took the phone. "Hey."

"How are you holding up?" Finley questioned.

My lips curved up. "Better now. Lela and Quince are here."

"Good. Keep them there," he said, his words clipped.

"Why? What's wrong?"

"I'm coming over. Have you been on your computer lately?"

"No. Why?"

"There's something you need to see. Something you'll have to help me decipher. I'll be there in ten minutes. Don't leave." Finley hung up before I could reply, and I handed the phone back.

"What was that about?" Quince said.

I glanced between Quince and Lela. "Finley said don't leave."

Less than ten minutes later, Finley climbed out of his Jeep and slung a brown leather bag across his chest. His wavy brown hair, normally fixed in place, sat disheveled across his forehead, and he kept glancing over his shoulder.

As I ushered him in, Dad stopped him. "About last night—"

"Forget about it," Finley interrupted. "Totally makes sense."

"Well, I never got to say thank you. I'm glad Rami has good friends at a time like..." He cleared his throat.

Finley bobbed his chin. "You're welcome, Mr. Carlton."

Finley followed me to my room, where Quince and Lela waited by a small wooden desk with a white fabric chair. Finley slipped off his bag and placed his laptop on the desk. He inserted a small square into the computer's drive.

"What's that?" Quince asked.

Finley shrugged. "Stealth IP."

Quince tipped his chin toward Finley. "A what?"

"An untraceable IP address. Whatever I search can't be traced back to me," Finley said.

Quince threw up his hands. "Man, what's going on?"

"The guy watching Rami—"

"Someone's following you?" Lela gasped and turned to me. "Why didn't you tell me?"

Because I spent the day searching for my mom's body, I wanted to scream. But instead, I recited the story I'd told the previous night. Lela interrupted with a million questions, making it hard to focus. Quince wore holes in the carpet as he paced back and forth.

As I explained untraceable IPs, Finley pulled up a satellite image and pointed to the screen. "Recognize him?"

The blurred image showed a man in a baseball hat and sunglasses with his head hung low. "Maybe. Who is he?"

"That's what I'm trying to figure out. You said he showed up at Connect Mobile. They have hundreds of cameras and drones flying around the building. All I had to do was hack—"

"You're a hacker?" Lela whispered.

Finley spun around in the small white chair. "No. Well, not really. I mean, I can. I just don't think it's a good idea." He hesitated. "Under normal circumstances."

"Well, that's a relief," Lela said, her tone sarcastic.

Finley glared at her. "Look, this situation is out of control. The RD is clueless about what happened to Rami's mom, and there's a crazy guy chasing Rami. I had to do *something*."

Lela raised her eyebrows. "So… you hacked Connect Mobile?"

My face paled. "Hacking STaR is a crime literally punishable by death, Fin. What were you thinking?"

"I *had* to do something," he repeated.

Guilt weighed heavy on my heart. This was my fault. I went to him for help. I just never dreamed he'd be so reckless. "Let me see the code you created."

Finley turned back to the computer and punched the keys, revealing an amazing sequence, one I never could have created. A smug expression filled his face. "If I can get a clear picture, I can run it through FR main which should tell us—"

"English, man," Quince protested.

"Sorry. Facial recognition mainframe. Every time you log into your phone or health device using facial recognition, it's stored as a digital profile. Like a permanent file on you. It tracks where you are, what apps you use, and what you've searched. The problem is, we don't know how much is stored in STaR's database. Or who's viewing it."

My skin tightened. "So, you're saying the Threats Division's cameras are constantly watching us?"

Finley turned to me. "It shouldn't come as a surprise, Rames. STaR has been watching us for years."

Only it did surprise me. STaR had been listening and watching all along. I often wondered why STaR never placed guards on the borders, considering their job was to keep us safe from outside threats. But borders equipped with cameras and drones don't need guards with guns.

At times, my mother mumbled under her breath about how things used to be. Now, as I stared at Finley's screen revealing hundreds of camera images, it struck me. Had I been naïve to never notice this level of surveillance? Even as the thought twisted around my brain, I knew the answer. I'd been living with the false belief that I was perfectly safe.

STaR kept a record on each of us, storing it in some warehouse without our knowledge. Am I the only sixteen-year-old that had no idea? As I glanced around the room, the shock on Lela and Quince's faces let me know we'd all been living under this pretense.

"What does the Threats Division want with *me*?"

Finley pointed to the image on the screen. "This guy wants your phone, so there must be something on it he wants...or needs." An alert on the screen pinged. Finley typed furiously.

I peered over Finley's shoulder as images came to life. He scrolled through the shots until a blurry face appeared. One with a distinguishable crooked smile.

"There. That's the guy," I said.

Lela and Quince stood next to me as Finley zoomed in closer. He stored the screenshot in a file folder, clicked more sites, entered a set of numbers, then waited. "The data exists, but I'm not sure if I can access it. Or whether I should."

"You've already hacked Connect Mobile. What's one more hack?" Lela's voice dripped with cynicism. Finley's expression turned solemn as the answer hung in the air between us. Lela let out a deep exasperation. "This makes no sense. Why don't you guys let the ROs on the case handle this?"

I shot Finley a sideways glance. "Reinforcement Officers are supposed to protect us, right? Yet they put me in an isolation room with a crazed Agent who brought this guy in to find my aunt." I motioned to the screen. "Then Agents started showing up around town. I mean, think about it. What if the RD is in on this? Whatever *this* is."

Quince whistled. "Girl? What have you gotten yourself into?" The question didn't warrant an answer.

"I've got something," Finley interrupted. He typed on the keyboard, then sat back. He rubbed his chin before facing me.

"What is it?"

"Last night, your dad mentioned your Aunt Kate, so I did a little digging. Turns out, Kate Evans works for a technology company called Centurion. Ever heard of it?"

I shook my head. "No. Kate doesn't talk about work. What do they do?"

"I'm not sure. There's very little information about them." Finley blew out a loud puff of air. "No, no, no. I hoped I was wrong."

When Finley didn't elaborate, I pressed him. "Wrong about what?"

He stood and tucked his hands in his pockets before clearing his throat. "The guy that's been chasing you, Rami, is Dominic Bell."

The blood drained from my face as the realization settled. *Bald Eagle*. I'd discovered his true identity after entering his Allicio account through backdoor channels. He'd been after me ever since. But why? It was just a harmless game Finley and I played. What had I unknowingly uncovered?

Finley shifted closer. "That's not all, Rames." I braced myself for more bad news. "Dominic Bell works for Centurion Technologies. He works with Kate."

CHAPTER 18

Saturday, September 23

Air leaked from my lungs. I pressed the palm of my hand against the wall before collapsing to the edge of the bed. There had to be another explanation. Kate and Mom were best friends. Identical twins. They told each other everything. *Didn't they?* How could Kate work with the guy that threatened to kill Zac? I didn't know how I felt. Confused? Deceived? The throbbing pulse in my head intensified.

"I...I don't understand. Do you think Kate had something to do with my mom's disappearance?"

The crease between Finley's eyebrows deepened. "I think Auntie Katie has some explaining to do."

Quince spun in circles, wearing another path in the carpet while muttering under his breath, "Whoa, whoa."

"Bald Eagle contacted me yesterday," I said, unable to comprehend how the guy I knew from the chat room and the man who threatened to murder my brother were the same person. "Said he needed help writing a code."

Finley sat next to me. "Code for what?"

"I don't know. And it wasn't that complicated. Like he should have seen his error," I said.

"What did you tell him?" asked Quince.

I looked up at Quince, who had stopped pacing. "I fixed it for him and that was it. He thanked me and logged off." I turned to face Finley. "Remember the night we identified him I said it seemed too easy? That's what this felt like, too. Like he's testing me."

Lela's eyes widened. "Testing you for what?"

I shook my head and bit my lower lip. Muffled voices from below traveled to the quiet room. I'd forgotten Officer Gaits was coming here today. I stood and peered out the curtains. "Finley? You need to leave. The RD is on the move."

Lela and Quince raced to the door while I grabbed my phone and stuck it in my pocket. Finley threw the computer into his bag and followed me down the stairs and out the patio door. Although I hoped Gaits had not spotted them, I wasn't sure.

In the kitchen, I took deep breaths in and out to gather my composure and filled a glass with ice water. The cold liquid trailed down my throat, calming my nerves. But when I heard Officer Murray's voice from the other room, I nearly lost my lunch. Dad hadn't mentioned Murray would be here too.

I placed my glass in the sink and stared out the window. A figure moved in the backyard. Why were Finley, Lela, and Quince still hanging around? They needed to leave. My phone buzzed once. No twice. Three times. I pulled it out.

A picture of me seconds ago drinking the cup of ice water appeared on my screen. A second photo loaded. A jagged, bloody wound. The gash I'd inflicted on Dominic's forearm with the

Swiss Army knife after he'd threatened to kill my brother. He'd let a sixteen-year-old girl get a jump on him and I doubted he forgave easily. The message was obvious. Dominic was out for blood. My blood. And he wouldn't stop until he got what he wanted.

I dropped the phone to the counter and gasped. My body shook and breaths caught in my throat.

"Rami?" Officer Murray appeared behind me. The look on his face told me he knew something was up. "Everything all right?" He edged closer and my gaze shifted to my phone, face-up on the counter. Murray followed my gaze and stepped to the counter. The red C swirled, and the images disappeared, leaving only a blank screen.

My eyes darted back to Murray. I couldn't see the back of his head, but I assumed the blow left him with a large knot. The memory unnerved me. I grabbed the phone and stuffed it in my shirt, landing it inside my bra. "I'm fine."

Out of breath, I dashed into the family room where Officer Gaits stood in the corner. Dad and Olivia sat side by side on the white couch with bright green pillows. Olivia rested her head against the matching emerald blanket that hung loosely over the back of the sofa. My dad's computer sat opened in front of them, but spotting me, he slammed it shut.

Did the ROs know Kate worked with Dominic? Zac's life depended on how much I revealed. Should I stick to the same version I'd told my family last night? Or the version I'd told my friends? I'd told so many lies, I wasn't sure I could keep my story straight.

Officer Gaits cleared his throat. "I'm pretty new to the RD, so I need my reports to be, um, more complete." That explained the nervous spots that donned his face every time he came around. The red dots from his neck rose to his freckled cheeks. Gaits was more nervous than me. “Officer Murray allowed me to come here today to ask a few more questions, but we’ve turned the investigation over to him and his team.”

“Have you located Kate yet?” Dad asked.

Gaits shuffled his feet. “No. Nothing so far.” He swallowed, and I watched his Adam’s apple bob up and down. His face flushed pink, making his never-ending freckles pop out. “We have a few follow-up questions. I didn’t quite get all the information I needed the other night.”

Dad turned to me. “Rami? He needs a statement about what happened to you yesterday. Officer Gaits looked for you for quite some time.”

Dad acted like I owed the RD. Last time I checked, it was their job to protect me, not the other way around.

Murray strolled into the room. The white bandage on the back of his head gave me pause. He reached into the pocket of his shirt and pulled out a photograph, holding it inches from my face as if I had poor vision. “Is this the man you saw outside Little Cone Ice Cream Shoppe?”

I stared at the photo of the man I now knew as Dominic Bell, who came to my school, watched me outside my home, pretended he wanted to help, then threatened to kill Zac. The same one I’d outed from our online chat group. The image inflicted terror as Dominic’s warning rang in my ear. I pulled my knees to my chest and wrapped my arms around them to steady my shaking body. “I’m not sure,” I lied.

Murray's eyes narrowed. "Look again. Are you *sure* you haven't seen this man?"

I gripped my knees tighter. "I didn't get a good look at his face. When you fell, I freaked out and ran." I needed him off my back.

Sticking to my original story, I described running to the skate park to find Zac. When he wasn't there, I asked Finley for help.

Officer Gaits interrupted. "When you couldn't find Zac, why didn't you come here to look for him? Why go to...?" He shuffled through his handheld reader. "Finley Drake's home?"

I kept my voice as steady as possible. "The whole thing scared me. Finley helped me realize my paranoia. With my mom missing, my imagination went into overdrive. And I haven't been sleeping well. Panic attacks. I've had them for..." I stopped. *Since you walked out on us, Dad*, I wanted to say. "I have them sometimes, like just now, Officer Murray, when you walked in on me. They come out of nowhere and take my breath away. Sounds crazy, right?"

Gaits nodded and smiled. I assumed he bought my phony story. But when I glanced at Murray, I sunk deeper into the floor. *He knows I'm lying.*

"The night your mom didn't come home, you said someone was outside watching you. Did you make that up?" Murray asked.

Gulp. Now what? My throat felt tight. "No. There was a man outside that night, but it was probably a neighbor letting their dog out to use the bathroom."

"At three in the morning?" Murray said.

I bristled at the implication. "Hard to say, but he wasn't after me."

"Yet the cameras didn't pick up anyone outside except you. Interesting." Murray stroked his bandage.

Behind Murray, Zac sat on the stairs, watching, listening. Dad appeared flustered, shifting in his seat. “Zac. Why don’t you go back upstairs and finish your game?”

Zac didn’t move. “I want to stay.”

Officer Gaits rubbed his red spotted cheeks. “Ian. We have a few more questions for you. Is there somewhere private we can talk?”

“Why is that necessary?” Dad said, exchanging troubled looks with Olivia. “The kids are worried about their mom. If you’ve found something, please tell us.”

“This relates more to, uh, your relationship with Annie,” Gaits stammered.

“What about it?” Dad said.

Gaits peered over his shoulder. “Ian? Perhaps we can go outside?”

“I have nothing to hide.” Dad clenched his jaw.

“All right,” Gaits said, sitting back in his chair. “Tell me again. When was the last time you spoke with Annie?”

Dad’s mouth twitched. “Wednesday. Or Thursday. I’m not sure. What does this have to do with finding her?”

Murray leaned forward. “Wednesday or Thursday. Which is it?”

Dad rubbed his hands together. “Um...Wednesday night.”

“What did you talk about?” Gaits asked.

“This wasn’t supposed to be my weekend with the kids. I asked about Zac staying with me so I could take him to the skate park.”

Gaits rested his elbows on his knees. “And what did she say?”

Dad crossed his arms over his chest. “She said no.”

Murray narrowed his brows, drawing them into a deep scowl. “Uh-huh. And how did that make you feel?”

"Irritated. She always tries to control my time with the kids. I wanted more time with Zac."

The absence of my name stung, though I couldn't blame him. Dad and I hadn't been on speaking terms since he moved to the technology district. But something else bothered me even more. *She always tries to control...* Was Dad angry enough to hurt Mom?

Murray sat back in his chair and tapped the tip of his chin with his pen. "With Annie missing, you got your wish, didn't you, Ian? Zac is with you all weekend. You took him to the park last night."

"It's not what you think. I didn't do anything to Annie." Dad's face reddened into a deep purple.

"But with Annie gone, you got more time with Zac," Murray stated.

Dad wrung his hands together again. "Look. Where is this going? You think I'm a suspect?"

"Are you?" A smug expression covered Murray's face.

"No!"

Gaits wrung his hands together. His Adam's apple grew as he choked on his words. "We're working on a timeline for what happened that day. You might have been the last person to talk to her, Ian."

Dad picked his phone up from the coffee table and scrolled. When he looked up, his face changed colors. "I texted her Wednesday, and we argued over text. I thought if we could talk on the phone, she'd be more understanding. I called her early Thursday morning. Sounded like I woke her up."

Murray glared silently at Dad, then reached for the phone, tilting his head to one side. "The day of the outage. The day she drove to your place of employment. Interesting. You see, Ian, I'm having a hard time understanding why you didn't mention any of this before. You didn't mention you'd had an altercation with your ex-wife the same day Rami reported her as missing. Then her car turns up in the parking lot where you work. Doesn't that seem strange to you?"

Dad flew out of his seat, puffing out his chest. "I'm not saying another word. I want a lawyer." Most lawyers worked for STaR, including the one Mom worked for, so I didn't see how they could protect Dad from STaR's Reinforcement Division.

Murray stood, his eyes never leaving Dad's. "I think that's all for now."

Olivia jumped between the men, squelching the faceoff. "I'll show you out."

My chest tightened. Every muscle tensed. I forced myself to go to Zac, who rocked back and forth on the stairs, panting for breath. I wrapped my arms around him, whispering his name. But my eyes were on Dad. *What had he done to Mom?*

After the ROs left, I escaped to my room, desperate to make sense of everything. Dad knocked on my door, begging me to talk, but I pretended to be asleep. First Kate, now my dad? The idea that Dad and Kate could be in on this together horrified me. Were Dad and Kate having an affair and needed Mom out of the way? Where did that leave Olivia? Either Dad was the best actor outside of the Northwestern region where actors filmed movies or I was reaching.

I pulled my laptop out of my backpack and began searching for the code I'd created to access Allicio. I must have unknowingly seen something the night before the outage. Something that Bald Eagle, aka Dominic Bell, didn't want me to see. But what?

I entered a sequence of letters and numbers and retraced my steps. The original code let me inside Bald Eagle's Allicio account. From his posts, I determined he worked for Connect Mobile, or had access to their security network. What should I have not seen? And why is he testing my coding capabilities? Unable to find anything out of the ordinary, I shut down my computer and drifted into a fitful sleep.

CHAPTER 19

SUNDAY, SEPTEMBER 24

I had to get away from here. Away from Dad. Away from the thoughts that spiraled out of control. My puffy eyes burned from the lack of sleep. I stayed up most of the night begging God to bring my mom home. I wasn't sure if God cared about me, but after hearing story after story of how she'd helped other people, didn't God care enough about Mom to help *her*?

I applied an extra coat of concealer to hide the dark spots, brushed powder and blush on my cheeks, and flat-ironed my hair. Three-quarter-length black leggings, a long pale pink sweater, and tan boots were perfect for today's cool temperatures. I zipped on the boots and slipped a cross-body purse around my neck, stuffing it with a tube of lip gloss. I left my non-working mobile in a dresser drawer, not caring whether a Safety Division team came after me threatening to stick me with anti-viral vaccines for not keeping my STaR-issued phone with me. It had only brought me bad luck and threatening messages, anyway.

In the kitchen, I checked in with my STaR health monitor as Rosemary rattled off her usual report that I needed more sleep. Keeping my back to Dad, I poured myself a glass of orange juice.

"Lela and Quince are on their way here to take me to church." My words were flippant, but I didn't care after learning he might be involved with Mom's disappearance.

Dad spewed coffee across the table. "Church? At a time like this?"

Many churches and support groups, like the one my mother led, had been moved outdoors in view of STaR's cameras. But church attendance in our region was still permitted, at least for now. Plus, it was the one place I could feel my mother's presence. My anger burned and all the frustration from the night before came flooding back.

"Yes, Dad. Church. These people you hate so much are praying for Mom. They showed up yesterday to search for her body. The least I can do is thank them." I suddenly felt an intense need to defend God, despite my own doubts about him.

Olivia rested her hand on Dad's. "Let her go, Ian. She'll be safe there."

Dad exhaled, glancing between Olivia and me. "There and back. Nowhere else. Understand?"

I understood all right. Dad pretended to care about me. I turned to leave when Olivia tapped me on the shoulder. She fiddled with her phone. "Rami? Take my phone so we can get in touch with you. I'm disabling facial ID so you can use it for a few hours before an alert sounds." She handed me a pale pink case.

I took it from her, knowing full well I'd never *need* Olivia, let alone my dad. But at least I could call Zac. I touched the screen and an image of Olivia and my dad appeared. My stomach curdled.

"Call me if you see anything suspicious," Dad warned.

On one level, I was grateful Dad was worried about me. But if he was in any way involved in Mom's disappearance… I shook away the thought and headed for the front door.

Zac burst into the hallway. "You're leaving? Again?"

"I'm going to church with Lela and Quince. I'll come straight here afterward. Olivia gave me her phone, so I'll call you as soon as church lets out."

His olive cheeks turned a slight shade of pink. "Whatever."

"I promise I'll call."

"Yeah, right." He turned his back and took the stairs two at a time.

I opened my mouth to reply, then changed my mind. What could I say to assure him after lying to his face last night? One more day, I told myself, then I'd come clean with everyone. Zac deserved the truth. In my efforts to keep my promise to Mom that I'd protect Zac, I'd made matters worse. My heart pierced with agony that I'd let her down. The last time I saw my mother, she told me she loved me, but I was too embarrassed to respond. I'd do anything to relive that day.

Lela's baby blue coupe sped into the driveway. Her fuchsia hair glowed in the morning sun as she jumped out to pull me into a tight hug. Quince climbed out, popped the seat forward, and squeezed his six-foot frame into the tiny backseat. His black curls stood upright on his head and his dark brown skin appeared more red than usual. With my seatbelt still unbuckled, Lela hit the gas, sending me crashing against the door.

"Next time I'm driving," Quince said. "I told her I should drive, but she insisted. I'm never sittin' in the back seat again. How can you ride home with her every day? You need to get your license, girl."

Most kids get their learner's permit on their fifteenth birthday, but I wasn't in a good place last September and Mom thought it was best if I waited. That put me at a six-month delay in getting my license. It sucked. "I know. I should have gotten my learner's on time."

"You think?" Quince's snarky response only added to my frustration.

Lela sighed. "Okay, Quince. Next time, you drive. But for now, can you be quiet so I can talk to Rami?"

Quince clutched his chest. "She wounds me again. Good thing I like you, Rami."

Lela ignored Quince and turned to me. "Spill, Rames. What's wrong?"

I stared out the side window. "Who says anything is wrong?"

"I'm your best friend. I know when you're upset."

Olivia's phone rested on my lap, and I tapped the screen. I knew I shouldn't spy on Olivia, but what did she expect when she handed me an unlocked phone? I'd have about two hours before it asked for Olivia's facial recognition. "It's complicated."

Quince leaned forward, smooshing his face against my seat. "It's not that complicated. You say, 'Brannon, you're hot, and I want to go out with you.'" Quince's high-pitched, girly voice made me laugh out loud.

"Not Brannon," I replied.

"Tryin' to help," Quince said.

Lela glanced between the road and me. "Rames, talk to me. Please."

I opened Olivia's Allicio account. Her profile image displayed Olivia and Dad squished together at some beach resort. The image made me gag. "Olivia let me borrow her phone, since mine doesn't work. I want to look around."

"You mean cyberstalk her," Quince said.

I raised my eyebrows. "What would you know about cyberstalking? You hate social media."

Quince nodded. "True, because it's a bunch of spoiled kids bragging 'bout who they're with, what they drive, what they wear. It's stupid."

"Lela doesn't think so," I said.

He turned up his lip. "Lela's obsessed."

"I'm not obsessed," Lela fired back. "I enjoy posting pictures."

Quince grunted. "And news and opinions—"

"And who's right and who's wrong," I added.

"Geez, guys. What is this? Pick on Lela Day?"

I turned around and Quince gave me a high-five. Then I grew serious. "Olivia's been nice to me since all this started. I mean, she organized a search party for her boyfriend's ex-wife. I mean, who does that?"

Quince let out a disgusted sound. "She likes your dad, right? So, if she's nice to you, it makes her look better."

Maybe Quince was right, but I wasn't convinced. "The thing is, she seems genuine."

Lela spun around the corner. "You seem surprised."

"I am. I hated her, or at least the idea of her. I figured I'd take all my frustrations with my dad out on her."

Lela took a shortcut through an abandoned shopping center, and I scrolled to Olivia's recent post. *Rami found safe. Very scary for all of us. Thanks for prayers. Ian's ex-wife still missing. Prayers appreciated.* The post last night before I showed up said, *Ian's daughter, Rami, now missing. If you have any information, contact RD. Please pray.*

More posts revealed requests for prayer. Olivia was into religion? I thought about her comment this morning, about how she encouraged Dad to let me go to church. Did Dad know about her posts? Pretty ironic considering he left my mom because she was too religious.

Lela stopped at the red light. *Screech! Bam!* Lela's car jolted forward. "Great. Just what I need."

"I told you I should drive." Quince grumbled and unbuckled his seatbelt.

"The light was red. Don't people pay attention when they're driving?" Lela shouted.

"Nope," Quince answered. "Everyone's on their phone."

Lela opened her door and climbed out. "I'm going to see how much damage it caused."

Quince flipped the seat forward and raced after her. Olivia's phone fell to the floorboard, so I reached down to pick it up, deciding whether I should call Dad. Since no one was hurt and it was a mere fender-bender, I decided to let it go.

I whipped around and spotted Lela and Quince knocking on the glass of the other car. My breath caught in my throat. *Charcoal gray car. Black hat.*

Sweat beads formed on my forehead as I tugged at the door handle. It always stuck, and I had begged Lela to get it fixed. When it didn't budge, I shoved it open with my foot and sprinted to

Lela's side. As if on cue, the driver lifted his head, mouthing my name.

Quince eased back to Lela's bumper, oblivious to my terror. "Hey, man. You smashed my girlfriend's car."

Dominic Bell slithered out of his electric vehicle, ignored Quince's rant, and headed straight for me. He had wrapped his forearm in several layers of white medical gauze. I must have cut deeper than I expected, and he didn't look happy about it. He peeled his gold sunglasses from his face.

"We meet again, Rami. You don't have any knives with you this time, do you?" He stroked his arm while keeping his eyes glued to me.

Quince turned around. "What's your problem, man?"

"You might want to ask your friend that question." Dominic's sinister expression made my blood run cold. "I thought I was perfectly clear. Get the update. Find Kate. It wasn't complicated." He shifted his gaze, his mouth curving into a menacing smile. "You must be Lela."

Lela's face drained of all color. "How does he..." Her voice trailed off.

"Leave her out of this," I pleaded.

"Who is this guy?" Quince edged closer to Dominic, but I put out my arm to stop him.

"Rami, Rami." Dominic's drawl sent prickles down my spine. "You shouldn't have brought your friends into this. I was quite clear. Now it's my turn to have a little fun." Dominic held my gaze, his eyes cold and deadly. Oxygen slowly leaked from my lungs. I stood frozen like I'd stepped on wet concrete.

"I'm calling the RD," Quince announced, pulling out his phone.

Tears burned my eyes. "Quince, wait." I pressed my cheek against Lela's, my voice almost inaudible. "Lela? Get in the car. Trust me. Please!"

Without warning, Lela let out a gut-wrenching scream and lunged at Quince, shoving him into the back seat of the car. I sprinted to the other side and plunged into the passenger seat as Lela punched the gas, tearing down the street like she lost her mind—zigzagging in and out of traffic, screeching her tires, and leaving skid marks on the road. As cars whizzed by, I searched for Dominic's car.

When Lela reached our neighborhood, she doubled back before pulling into her driveway. I took one last look around as she zoomed into the garage and shut the overhead door. She stumbled into her house, dropped her key fob in a small ceramic bowl, and bent over. Her breaths were fast and shallow.

I rushed to her side. "I shouldn't have involved either of you."

Quince shoved me aside and held Lela's shaking shoulders. "Yeah? Well, now you did. You've got a lot of explaining to do, girl. We could've been killed today and my afro's gone wild from the wind speed." He attempted to smooth his curls, but it only made matters worse.

I filled three glasses with filtered water from the refrigerator, handing the first one to Lela, which she downed in several gulps. She collapsed onto the brown leather couch in her family room with Quince on her heels. I crumpled into the oversized suede chair opposite the wall of windows that filled Lela's family room and slipped my purse over my neck, tucking it under my leg. Three days ago, I sat here with Mrs. Ferreira—the night my mom didn't come home. So much had happened since then.

I didn't know whether Dominic was toying with me or whether he'd follow through on his threats, but I couldn't take a chance. Dominic had threatened not only Zac but now my friends. They deserved the truth.

"Why did you stop me from calling the RD?" Quince asked.

I swallowed hard. "The guy that hit your car is Dominic Bell. The one Fin told us about. A few nights ago, Finley and I were searching for the true identify of a chatter named Bald Eagle. I got into his Allicio account and snagged his real name."

"Why?" Quince asked.

"It's a game Fin and I made up. A competition just for fun. But I must have seen something I wasn't supposed to that night because everything turned crazy after that."

Quince whistled. "Whoa. Okay, so think back to that night. What weren't you supposed to see?"

"I don't know. I got into his Allicio account, grabbed his real name, and logged off. That was it. But he chased me down and went through my phone like he was looking for something." I lowered my head to my cupped hands. "He told me if I talked to the RD or told anyone about him, he'd kill Zac."

"That's why you won't talk in front of Zac, and why you lied to your dad." Lela exhaled. "What does this guy want?"

I shuddered and lifted my head. Lela voiced the one question I couldn't answer. "I'm not sure."

Quince's big brown eyes bore into mine. "You're not sure, or you're not telling us?"

My jaw clenched. "I don't know. I swear."

Quince pulled a comb from his pocket and tugged again at his curls. "I don't care what this guy says. He's insane. We gotta alert the RD." He whispered something to Lela. She held up her phone and snapped the camera button before I could react.

Lela glanced at the image. "Not your best, but I don't have time to filter it."

I raised my voice. "Lela? Don't—"

"Too late. Quince said if you won't call the RD, maybe someone else will," Lela said.

Had she sealed Zac's fate? My blood ran cold. "Thanks a lot, Quince. So much for not liking social media."

He shot me a cynical expression. "It was the fastest way to get the word out."

Within seconds, Lela's phone buzzed. Quince was correct about it being fast. Someone had seen the post. *Finley*, Lela mouthed, holding the phone away from her ear as Finley's shouts soared across the quiet space. She held it out to me. "He wants to talk to you."

Before I uttered a word, Finley yelled, "I'm calling the RD. This has gone on long enough."

Tears trickled down my cheeks. My friends were in danger because of me. The magnitude hit me like a level ten earthquake. *Why do I try to control everything? I only make things worse.*

"Okay," I whimpered, too exhausted to argue.

Finley exhaled into the receiver. "No more fighting me?"

I shook my head, as if Finley could see my response. "Where are you?"

"I *was* on the way to meet you guys at church. But I turned around when I saw Lela's post. My mom's going to kill me if she finds out I didn't show up, but I'll deal with that later."

I handed the phone back to Lela, not bothering to respond. Suddenly, Lela's face paled, her eyes a mixture of confusion and terror as they traveled from my face to a bright red dot on my flesh-colored sweater. "Get down!" she screamed.

Before I could respond, the red dot laser moved to the adjacent wall, and a bullet shattered the small window beside me. I fell to the floor and covered my head with my purse. Quince and Lela raced toward the side door. I yelled for them to stay inside, but they couldn't hear me over Lela's frantic cries for help. In one swift movement, I slung my crossbody purse around my neck and scooted on my stomach toward the kitchen.

Once outside, I followed Lela and Quince to a patch of woods behind the horse stables. Thick brambles tore at my flesh, but I didn't dare stop until I was well past the barn. I bent over, out of breath, as blood oozed down my leg, puddling at the ankle.

Quince spun in circles, his hands on top of his head. "This is crazy. This is so crazy."

"We can't stay here. It's not safe," I said. Every sound magnified as we waited.

Lela shifted closer, her face full of terror and desperation. "Where can we go that *is* safe?"

As long as Lela stayed with me, she wasn't safe. I sprang forward, more determined to get her to safety. "Follow me."

We charged through an older neighborhood with swing sets, sandboxes, and riding toys in the yards. A lake appeared in the distance, and I motioned for Lela and Quince to follow. We risked too much exposure to waltz through the entrance of Grand Lakes.

As if reading my thoughts, Quince tipped his head in the opposite direction. "There's a dirt road that way, past the lake. It'll take us to the back side of the neighborhood."

Lela raised her eyebrows. "And you know this how?"

Quince shrugged. "Been fishing here a few times." He glanced between Lela and me. "What? You think I can't fish?"

"I didn't say anything," Lela remarked.

"Come on, guys. We have to keep going." My body rebelled, but I forced myself to keep moving.

The dirt road led us to Finley's street, just as Quince had said. I spotted his house and climbed over the wooden fence. As expected, Ranger charged at us. I jumped into the grass below and whispered his name in a high-pitched tone. Ranger wagged his tail and bounded into me, nearly knocking me to the ground. Finley stood in the open doorway to the basement, waving us in. Quince took Lela's hand and sprinted across the yard. But I stopped short. The hair on the back of my neck bristled.

Nothing appeared out of the ordinary—Ranger chased his ball, a lawnmower engine roared to life, children's laughter chirped in the distance—but the strange sensation that something wasn't right filled me with dread.

CHAPTER 20

Sunday, September 24

Finley raced outside and shoved me into his basement. He locked the deadbolt and dropped into a black leather chair tucked under a wooden desk. Dual monitors attached to a laptop sat side by side on an L-shaped desk. He typed furiously into the keyboard.

My fingers fumbled with the doorknob as I stood at a distance. "How did you know we would come here?"

"A hunch," Finley answered without looking away from the screens.

My eyes narrowed. "A hunch? You were expecting us." It wasn't a question.

Finley swiveled his chair to face me. His nostrils flared. "Are you kidding me right now? I was on the phone with you when Lela screamed 'get down.' I assumed you'd come here. What is this, Rami? You think I'm out to get you, too?"

He held my gaze, unwilling to look away. I had leaned heavily on Finley these past few days. He'd been the one constant in my life. The one I'd turned to for help, and his pained expression filled me with guilt. I longed to reclaim my accusation, but there was no way to get it back. "I'm sorry, Fin."

He spun his chair back around without a word. I stared at Lela, curled in a ball in the corner. Quince fastened his arms around her shaking shoulders. A tinge of jealousy hit me as I watched them. Quince would do anything to protect Lela, even if it meant putting himself in harm's way.

I slid down the wall. "You guys need to get away from me. I don't understand what's happening, but I need you safe."

Lela released the grip on her knees and rested her head on my shoulder. "Your fight is my fight, Rami."

"I can't ask that of you." The words lodged in my throat.

Finley stood and joined us on the floor, resting his head against the wall. "It's what friends do for each other, Rami. We'll figure this out. Together."

Slowly, I placed one hand on Finley's knee and the other on Lela's. "Thank you." The words felt shallow after the vow they'd taken.

Finley glanced at my hand on his knee. "You're a pawn in their game, Rames. We need a pawn chain."

"Say what?" Quince swiveled to meet Finley's gaze.

"A chess reference," Finley explained. "It means you align your pawns diagonally to protect each other." Quince gave him a blank stare, and I worked hard to understand where this was going. Finley went to his desk, pulled out the small brown box he had at school, and set it on the floor in front of us. He unfolded the board, lined the black pawns diagonally, then did the same with the white pawns. "It's much harder for your opponent to attack if your pawns work together as a team. We're Rami's protection."

Quince unlatched his arms from Lela. He sat forward and surveyed me carefully. After what felt like minutes, he whispered, "If Lela's with you, I'm with you. Pawn chain and all."

I leaned my head back and smiled. After all I'd done, my friends remained loyal and trusting. I would protect them at all costs.

Finley rubbed his finger across the dried blood from my shin to the ankle. "What happened?"

My skin tingled. "It's… I'm fine. Just a minor cut from a sticker bush."

"I'll get a towel for you." Finley returned with a warm cloth and placed it on my leg.

The water stung, and I winced as he applied gentle pressure. His affection shocked me after I'd just accused him of being a traitor. My stomach tightened, though from the pain or from Finley's touch, I couldn't say.

"I notified the RD. They're on the way to Lela's house. I need to alert them you're here." Finley jumped up, tossed the bloody washcloth aside, and dashed for his computer. "Did you see anyone? Hear anything?"

I replayed the moment the red dot laser landed on my chest and shuddered. "No, but it had to be Dominic."

Lela sighed. "I tried to be careful. I went down one-way streets and stayed off the main road. I don't see how he could have followed us—"

"He knows where you live," Finley interrupted. "He's been watching Rami, so he's got intel on her friends, too."

The truth seeped in like a slow-leaking gas tank waiting to explode. "He was outside your house, Lela, the night my mom disappeared. He knows where all of you live. We're not safe here."

I pounded my fist against my forehead. *Think.* I squeezed my eyes shut. Kate and Dominic both worked for Centurion. It had to mean something. "Finley? What does Centurion do?"

"Working on it."

His curt reply stung, though I didn't blame him after how I'd treated him. As he clicked one site after another, entering a series of letters and numbers, I reached into my crossbody purse for my phone, forgetting for an instant I'd left it at my dad's place. Olivia's phone stared back at me, a painful reminder that I never made it to church and hadn't called Zac. "I was supposed to check in with my dad, and I promised Zac I'd call him. Fin? I really need to go home."

As if he didn't hear me, Finley mumbled, "There's got to be more information on Centurion."

Quince pointed to the monitor on the left. "What is all this?"

"Different websites offer, uh, additional information on people. If you recognize what you're looking for."

Quince punched Finley in the arm. "Dude. They can trace everything back to your IP address."

"I have a stealth IP, but technically, I'm not hacking. These sites are, well, let's just say, more like black market."

"But if someone's watching the site?" Quince's voice trailed off.

"Then, yeah, STaR could find me." Finley lifted his shoulders like being tracked by the government was an everyday occurrence.

Quince spun in circles, placing his hands on his temples. "Geez, Finley. You can't screw around with STaR. This is serious stuff, man."

One corner of Finley's mouth curved up. "So is pointing an assault weapon in a residential home. If he can play ball, so can we. Look, there's no record of what Centurion really does. They're a tech company, but what they do remains a mystery. As to Dominic..." Finley pulled up additional text on the second monitor and opened several tabs. "There's no record of Dominic prior to Centurion. If I can just find...oh, no." He typed something into the keyboard and the monitor on the right lit up with code.

"What?" I jumped up and stood behind Finley's chair.

He read from the screen. "Dominic Bell. Former military special forces. Then he drops off the grid." Finley turned toward me, his face pale. "Rami? Dominic is a trained sniper."

My head reeled with confusion. The military disbanded once STaR took over the government, and all personnel fell under the Reinforcement Division's jurisdiction. If Dominic left the military, it meant either he went rogue or someone had hired him to be discreet. The room spun, and I reached for Finley's shoulder to steady myself.

Lela clutched me and led me to the couch. "If he wanted to kill you—"

"I'd be dead," I said, finishing her thought. I collapsed onto the sofa. "He's not trying to kill me. He's trying to scare me."

"Mission accomplished," Quince exhaled.

Finley burrowed his eyebrows together. "Okay, so Dominic wants to flush you out, but why?"

"I think it's a scare tactic. Scare me enough until I do what he wants." I shuddered.

"What does he want?" Lela asked.

My thoughts spun in circles. Williams insisted I restore my phone. When I didn't listen, Dominic threatened to murder Zac. He showed up outside my dad's townhome while the ROs were there. He sent a picture of me inside. *He's always there, watching me. How is that possible?*

"The software update. It must be the missing link." I took several deep breaths to keep the panic at bay. "Dominic threatened me, Zac, all of you. I have to go back to Connect Mobile to get the update on my phone. Everything points back to that. The outage, the texts, Dominic. I don't get why Dominic cares so much about it or what it has to do with Kate, but I think it's the only way Dominic will leave us alone."

"The update restored our phones, but not yours," Finley said, more to himself than to me. "Which means something, or someone, is blocking you from using your mobile without the update."

My lips trembled. "Whatever is in this update, it's worth killing for."

Ding, dong.

No one moved except Ranger, who barked and scratched at the door leading upstairs. Quince headed for the stairs, but Finley stopped him.

"Quince, wait." Finley ran his hands through his hair. "I… I didn't tell the RD you were here."

"You said—"

"I know what I said, but I never made the call." Finley fumbled with his laptop, closing tabs and erasing his history.

Quince's cheeks turned several shades of crimson. "Why not? You said we weren't safe here."

Finley slammed his laptop, shoved it into his shoulder bag, and stuffed his phone into his pocket. "I was waiting until the info about Dominic came through. Stupid, stupid."

Quince stormed toward Finley, his chocolate skin red and splotchy. "Which means—"

Pop!

The window behind me shattered, sending tiny glass fragments flying across the room. Finley threw me to the floor, covering my head with his body. Lela's screams sent chills down my spine. Ranger howled and clawed at the back door. When no other shots rang out, Finley grabbed my hand, and we sprinted to the unfinished section of his basement. The stench of mildew filled my lungs. Quince used his phone to call for help, and this time I didn't stop him.

CHAPTER 21

Sunday, September 24

I had become all too familiar with our local Reinforcement Division, with its canary-yellow walls and messy desks lined with coffee mugs and stale donuts. As I passed the room where I'd sat with Agent Williams two days earlier, the memory flooded my mind. I should have felt safe here. It was a Reinforcement precinct, after all. Yet my entire body shivered.

A female officer escorted me to a white room with windows and comfortable chairs, a stark contrast from the room with Williams. Dad's animated way of communicating echoed down the hall as he railed the RD for their lack of protection. When Zac appeared in the doorway, I jumped up and pulled him into my chest. When he complained he couldn't breathe, I released him and leaped backward, anticipating another punch in the gut. But Zac slumped into the chair next to mine, his eyes red and swollen.

"Are they protecting me or holding me hostage?" I asked, sliding my chair closer to his.

"Probably both." Zac choked back tears. "Why did someone shoot at you?"

If only I could tell him, but I couldn't. At least not yet. Not until I figured out the connection between Centurion, Mom, and Aunt Kate. I diverted his line of questioning and said, "Did they question Dad again? About Mom's disappearance?"

"Yeah. They cleared him."

Relief flowed through my veins like water washing a wound. *My father is innocent.* But there was no time for celebration. Because if Dad wasn't involved, that only left one person. Aunt Kate. This reality felt worse than Zac's punch in the stomach.

"Rami?" Zac swallowed hard. "I know you've been lying. About a lot of things. But why? And why lie to me?"

Once again, guilt plagued me, and I hung my head in shame. Zac was right. It was time to trust the ROs on the case and tell them the truth. Or at least part of it. A tear escaped, and I wiped it away. "I never meant for anyone to get hurt."

I set Olivia's phone on the table. After several deep breaths, I asked to speak to Officer Murray.

Murray placed his handheld reader on the table. I handed Olivia's phone over as Murray took out a photograph of Dominic. The same one I'd lied about yesterday.

Murray leaned forward, resting his elbows on the table, all the while eyeing me suspiciously. "This is Dominic Bell. But then, you knew that already, didn't you? We believe Dominic Bell fired an illegal military weapon at Finley Drake's home. He's part of a tech company called Centurion, although Centurion's executives deny any knowledge of his existence. So, what I need to know is why you lied about your relationship with Dominic Bell."

My skin tingled as I attempted to steady my breathing. I still didn't know whether Murray could be trusted...whether I could trust anyone in the RD. I'd accessed Connect Mobile's security network, a punishable crime, yet no one in the RD had mentioned it. Telling Officer Murray what I'd done would incriminate me and possibly put Zac in danger. Keeping Zac safe was the only thing that mattered right now.

I swallowed, my throat dry and cracked. "Dominic told me if I went to the RD, he'd kill Zac." Dad grabbed my shoulder to steady himself. "I was trying to protect Zac."

"Let us protect him," Murray said. "That's our job."

"Find my mom. That's your job, too." My words were forceful, but my body trembled.

Murray ignored my outburst. "Did your mom ever talk about Kate's job?"

The question caught me off guard. *Does he know Kate works for Centurion?* "No."

"You sure?" Murray creased his eyebrows, revealing a large vein up the center of his forehead.

"Kate never talks about work in front of me." That part was true.

"Interesting, because it appears your friend, Finley Drake, attempted to hack into Centurion's server. Why would he do that?" Officer Murray paused, making my heart race faster. "Hacking is a criminal offense, punishable by death. Finley is in serious trouble, Miss Carlton."

Finley said he blocked his IP address. But if Finley was right about STaR, then no matter how safe we thought we were, STaR saw everything. "Finley's trying to help," I shouted, my teary eyes pleading for mercy. "He did this for *me*."

"For you?" Murray repeated. "Well, I sure hope you're worth it." The truth of his words stung. He sat back in his seat. "If you want to help Finley, Miss Carlton, then cooperate with our investigation. Tell us everything you know. Every detail. And let us handle it. No more vigilante activity. No more lies. Go back to school. Go to volleyball practice. In other words, be a kid again. Are we clear?" Unable to form the right words, I gave a slight nod. Murray stood. "Any questions?"

I gritted my teeth. "Yeah. One. Why did you send National Agents after me when I tried to get the update at Connect Mobile?"

Officer Williams gave me a blank stare. "I already told you I didn't make that call. Local ROs and National Agents aren't exactly friends, Rami. It's like turf war."

"Then how did they know I was there?"

"Honestly, I don't know."

I rolled my eyes. "Fine. Two. Agent Williams." Murray and Dad exchanged puzzled looks. "You pretended he didn't exist, yet he questioned me right here, without a parent present, I might add. He instructed me to get the update. If you want my full cooperation, start by telling me the truth about him. Why does he care so much about my phone? And why is an Agent who investigates murder involved?"

Murray sat on the table and narrowed his gaze. "Rami. I've already told you. We checked the video feed. There's no one matching your description on any of the footage."

"That's impossible. He was here. I talked to him."

Murray leaned so close to my face I could smell his breath. "Is it possible you made that up to throw us off?"

"No," I yelled. "He was here. Check your cameras again."

"Rami, I'm sorry. There's no evidence of him being here."

I couldn't see straight. That wasn't possible. The questions Williams asked, the information he had about me, he couldn't have known that unless someone had told him. He had my mother's missing person's file. But no one in the local RD precinct seemed to know anything about National Agents being involved. Was Williams even an Agent? Or did he work for Dominic? Could Dominic have hacked the RD and deleted the footage?

I never believed in Finley's conspiracy theories, but I played along because Fin was my friend. Is this more than a simple case of a missing person? My chest tightened, boring down into my lungs until every breath seemed forced.

"Rami?" Murray stared at me, waiting for a response. "You told the officer dispatched to Finley's house that you received several text messages and some photos from an unknown contact, but you also said your phone hasn't worked since the outage."

I suppressed a scream. "That's what I'm trying to explain. Someone texted me the day of the outage, but when I tried to respond, it magically disappeared."

"Let's have a look at your phone," Murray said.

"I don't have it. I left it at home because—"

"I have it." Dad handed my mint green phone case to Murray. "I had Connect Mobile install the update because you kept saying it didn't work. They tested it and it works fine now."

Murray held the phone close to my eyes until facial recognition opened the device. He scrolled through my apps, looking for any evidence of the text messages and pictures I'd claimed to have received. I chewed my nails until they were near nubs.

When Murray looked up, I saw the doubt in his eyes. "There's nothing here. It's possible the update may have wiped it clean. I'll have our techs take a look and bring your phone to the house tomorrow morning." Murray handed my dad Olivia's phone, which sat on the table. "Ian, if you could follow me, we'll finish the paperwork, and you can be on your way."

As Murray and Dad left the room, I stared out the window, exhausted and desperate to leave the station. I had to find Kate. She might be the only person who could lead me to Mom. *If* I could trust her. One thing was certain. I needed to find her before Dominic did.

A sound caught my attention, and I turned. Mrs. Drake and Finley walked down the hall, past the room where I sat. Spotting me, Mrs. Drake turned around and stared at me through the glass window. Her bloodshot eyes matched her ruby scrubs, and strands of dark, loose hair fell around her face. She wiped a tear from her cheek, then continued down the hall, no doubt blaming me for her son's involvement in this disaster.

But Finley lingered in the doorway, his expression bearing defeat. "The RD called my mom at work. She's totally freaked out. And now my house is an active crime scene."

"Fin..." My words caught in my throat, and I pressed my lips together.

He shuffled his feet on the floor, keeping his head low. "Heard they know about Dominic. Did you tell them anything?"

"Very little," I said, my voice a mere whisper.

Finley swallowed hard, like he was trying to assemble his words. "I'm in deep trouble, Rames."

"They said if you worked with them, they'd go easy on you." I hesitated. "I'm sorry. You never would have done those things if I hadn't involved you."

He studied me, then turned without a word. For the first time, I wondered if Murray was right. Perhaps I wasn't worth it.

CHAPTER 22

MONDAY, SEPTEMBER 25

News in a small town traveled like tumbleweeds in the desert. Before Zac and I could get out the door for school, reporters camped on Dad's lawn, wanting an exclusive about yesterday's shooting. As I peered out the front curtains, I thought back to Zac's comment just four days earlier, how nothing bad ever happened in Atlanta. Neither of us could have imagined anything like this.

Three white vans with United News Network logos painted on the side sat parked in front of Dad's townhome. I had no idea why they needed three, considering America only had one network. A mobile outage linked to the Southeastern region's technology district was bad enough, but a shooting in a residential neighborhood created ratings for these hungry reporters.

Dad's phone call with the RD reverberated through the house, demanding to know who leaked our names to the press. I suspected when the uniformed officer dropped my phone off early this morning, someone from the press followed him because within thirty minutes, the vans showed up.

If we waited for an RO to escort us to school, Zac and I would be late. And considering I was supposed to "be a kid again," as Murray phrased it, being tardy drew attention. Attention I didn't need. When Dad hung up, he instructed Zac and me to keep our mouths shut and shield our faces from the cameras as we raced toward the car. I started to climb in when a young female UNN reporter shoved a microphone in my face.

"Does last night's shooting have to do with Annie's disappearance? Is Ian a suspect?"

Dad raced around the hood and knocked the lady's microphone to the ground. His face darkened to a deep purple as the vein in his forehead popped out. "Get off my property." He gritted his teeth and shoved me into the car. "Don't say a word."

I should have listened to him. I should have kept my mouth shut. But I didn't. Enough with staying silent. It hadn't protected me, anyway. I squared my jaw and faced the reporter, my stance angry and defiant. "You want a statement? Fine. I'll give you one. If you want something worth investigating, find my mom." Then I climbed in and Dad sped away.

It wasn't my best moment on camera, and I'd probably pay for it later when my friends saw the feed. My body shook, and I laced my fingers together.

Once we were away from the cameras, Dad let me have it. "Do you realize what you've done, Rami? I was quite clear. Don't talk to the reporters! Let the Reinforcement Division handle it."

"Whoa, Rames," Zac interrupted. "Check out this picture." Zac leaned forward in his seat and pulled up an image of me with the reporter. "You don't look so good."

My eyes were ablaze. "How did it load to Allicio that fast?"

Dad gripped the steering wheel. “You don’t get it. Everything you do, everything you say, has the potential to make its way onto social media instantly. Your life isn’t private.”

I bristled at his reprimand. “It should be private. I didn’t agree to have that photo on Allicio.”

Zac played the video of me yelling at the reporter, then held it up for me to view. But I didn’t want to watch. I turned to face him and eyed him suspiciously. “When did you get a phone?”

He grinned. “Yesterday. Dad took your phone to Connect to get the update and bought me one. I’m finally like everyone else on the planet.”

“Mom didn’t want him to have one,” I said.

“Well, she’s not here. He needs one in case of an emergency.” Dad glared at me. “You’re so consumed with yourself. I want to be sure what happened to you doesn’t happen to Zac.”

His words stung, but they held an element of truth. I had been consumed with my own problems. “You’re right. I’m sorry.”

Dad heaved a heavy sigh. “I just wish... I want you to trust me. Let me help you.”

I glanced at Zac, scrolling through his new device, oblivious to the tension in the car. Zac trusted everyone. I trusted no one.

Dad dropped me off first before taking Zac to middle school, and as soon as my feet hit the floors of Peachtree Park High, the whispers began. The girls hanging out in the atrium looked up from their phones when I entered. Their snickers and murmurs screamed disapproval. Quince stood at a distance with his basketball buddies, probably unsure whether associating with me was a good idea. I didn’t blame him. Nearly getting your friends killed tended to warp people’s opinion.

Before I reached the eleventh-grade hall, Lela looped her arm through mine and Finley swept in to cover the other side. The three of us marched down the hall arm in arm. Their continued friendship with me, the crazy girl, would likely increase the gossip on social media.

A concerned frown replaced Lela's usual jovial demeanor. "We're your pawn chain. Remember? How are you holding up?"

"Not too well, judging from my outburst this morning." I glanced at Finley. "Does everyone think the shooting is my fault?"

Finley shook his head. "Nah. Everyone wants a juicy story. I think we disappointed them."

My head dropped in shame. "You're the one everyone should be worried about, Fin. You can't even go home."

Finley jabbed me with his elbow. "I'm fine. The trusty RD put us up in a hotel for a few days until they complete their investigation. It's a swanky place with free Wi-Fi." He laughed. "Rames? We're going to figure this out. Okay?" When I nodded, he turned to go, calling over his shoulder, "Meet after school?"

My mouth twitched as I glanced between Fin and Lela. I hadn't told him about Brannon. "I can't. I'm... I'm going out with Brannon."

Finley stopped and swallowed hard. "Oh. Like a date?"

After everything he'd done for me, the hurt in his eyes made me feel horrible. "No. Just friends. He's like, you know, concerned. That's all."

He shrugged. "Whatever you say. See you around."

My body deflated like a balloon leaking air. Finley took off, and Lela wrapped her arm around me. "You stung his pride, that's all. He'll get over it. You'll see."

As Lela skipped to class, I crept to class, mulling over Officer Murray's words. *I hope you're worth it.* I tried to step into Finley's shoes, to understand what he must be feeling. He'd hacked Connect Mobile to find my stalker and protected me from being shot, and I repaid him by going out with a guy he can't stand. My tangled emotions felt like a rope choking me, and I hated myself for it.

I sat down and opened my laptop. When I glanced up, Theresa May, our school reporter, appeared behind my open screen. She wrote something in a spiral notebook pad of paper she carried with her all the time. I wondered why she didn't just get an electronic tablet to store her notes like everyone else. Theresa was probably forming a story in her mind on how to increase viewership because her auburn hair appeared brighter today, as if drumming up juicy stories for school news created glowing energy. But I dreaded seeing her, knowing she'd expect an exclusive for *The Grove*.

When Theresa took over the school news freshman year, the readership was down to exactly, well, no one. She asked Finley to create a school app for kids to keep up with real-time news. Theresa tried to keep *The Grove* newsworthy and gossip-free, but no one wanted good news. Occasionally, she threw in some juicy chatter to increase viewership. Like last spring when Reinforcement Officers showed up on the senior hallway, Theresa conveniently leaked that Colton Asbury, the center on the basketball team, was selling drugs. *The Grove* hit an all-time high as the story unfolded, revealing Colton sold illegal substances at school.

Although Theresa and I weren't exactly friends, it wasn't as though I didn't like her because I did. She was smart and a talented reporter. But the last thing I needed was to be featured in *The Grove*. Officer Murray would have a field day with that.

"Hey, Rami? Got a second?" Theresa smiled.

"Not really." I typed on my laptop, but she didn't leave.

She twirled a strand of hair around her finger until it formed a knot. "I was hoping you'd explain what happened."

"I have nothing to say," I answered, my voice tense with frustration.

"It will only take a sec—"

"I said no." I didn't mean to yell, but honestly, reporters could be so pushy.

Theresa took a step back, her mouth agape. "I didn't mean to upset you. I just...wanted to run a story about your mom in *The Grove*. If someone saw something that day, it might help find her."

Now, I felt terrible. "Sorry. I got bombarded by reporters this morning and ever since I got to school, everyone's staring at me like I'm diseased."

Her lips turned down. "No, I'm sorry. I shouldn't have come at you like that. Forget it. It was a stupid idea."

I stood and reached for her arm before she could get away. "Theresa, wait. Can we talk later?" I flashed her a knowing look. "Like not at school?"

She brightened. "Yeah, sure."

I lowered my voice to a mere whisper. "I have practice tomorrow, so come to my dad's house after. Say, six o'clock? I'll text you the address."

She beamed. "Great. Thanks, Rami."

The rest of the day dragged on in slow motion. I had done my best to lie low and stay out of everyone's way, and by the last bell, I was old news. Our school could compete with the top-rated reality show for best drama. I should have had t-shirts printed that said *I Survived Peachtree Park High* and sell them at school functions.

As I bolted out of chemistry, I smashed into the rock-solid chest of Brannon Martinelli. Embarrassed, my cheeks inflamed, but I didn't step away because he smelled amazing.

"I'm so sorry," I muttered. I wasn't sorry at all.

Brannon chuckled, and between his pouty lips and adorable dimple, I almost forgot to move my feet, until a group of guys bumped me from behind, propelling me forward.

His self-assured gaze landed on me. "You still want to hang? I mean, I heard about what happened yesterday."

Who hadn't heard by now? "I'd like that."

He swooshed his jet-black hair off his forehead, revealing piercing blue eyes. "Tru Coffee? I can drive you."

"Yes." The word flew out of my mouth before I could stop it. Either Brannon didn't notice or girls always fell for him this way.

"Cool. Let's go." He slid his hand to the small of my back and led the way.

CHAPTER 23

Monday, September 25

Brannon unlocked a vintage truck with a lift kit, and I tugged myself up using the handle on the ceiling. I wondered how he could keep a truck running with so few gasoline stations around, but I didn't ask.

Earlier in the day, I'd added an extra coat of mascara, blush, and lip gloss. I even flat-ironed my hair in the gym's locker room in record time. Now, sitting next to Brannon, I felt stupid for being a try-hard. Brannon and I were nothing alike. At least we weren't anymore. Brannon was cool, popular, and confident, while I remained anxious and distrustful. I wanted to feign a stomachache and jump out of the truck, but Brannon tapped my knee. He popped in a piece of chewing gum and offered me a piece, but I declined. My hands shook, and I'd probably miss my mouth. I set my backpack on the floorboard and pulled my phone from the pocket.

"Ready?" Before I could respond, he punched the gas pedal.

Less than a week ago, Brannon pretended I didn't exist, like we were never friends. Why the sudden change? *And how do I bring it up?*

“What kind of music do you like?” he said, interrupting my dilemma.

My mind drifted to the time Finley and I stayed on the phone until midnight, loading songs to our playlist. Songs Fin and I had in common. “Lots of different types,” I said, trying to play it cool.

Brannon raised a brow. “But what’s your favorite?”

I hesitated. “Probably not your style.”

He grinned, making his dimple more pronounced. “How do you know what my style is?”

Touché. All I really knew about Brannon Martinelli was when he smiled, I melted and lost myself in his presence. Seriously, those blue eyes were hard to ignore. Unable to hold his gaze, I searched out the passenger window. I could offer Brannon a safe answer and change the subject. But I was through pretending. “My dad had gotten me into rock bands from the early 2000s. Oldies rock like The Script, OneRepublic, and The Fray. Stuff like that.”

Brannon chomped on his gum. “Oh, cool. What’s your favorite OneRepublic song of all time?”

“‘Say All I Need,’” I said without hesitation.

Brannon shook his head, forcing his bangs to fall into his eyes. “No way. I hate ballads. ‘Counting Stars’ is far better.”

I crinkled my nose. “Totally overrated.”

Brannon laughed. “What is it you like about the ‘Say All I Need’ song?”

I hesitated, unsure whether I should admit the truth. “Do you remember in ninth grade when we were in biology together? My dad left that year, and well, I had a hard time accepting it. I listened to that song over and over because it reminded me to breathe and move on. To find the things that mattered to me." My throat constricted. "I just didn't understand what I did wrong."

Brannon's lighthearted expression grew solemn. "Probably nothing. Adults are...complicated. Their relationships don't always make sense."

He was right, but suddenly I felt embarrassed at my admission. I tugged at my collar and changed the subject. "Do you actually like oldies rock?"

He snickered. "Not really, to be honest. I just know a few of their songs. Stuff my parents think is good music." He put his fingers in the air and formed quotation marks, then laughed. "I'm more of a country music guy."

I stared in disbelief. "Country?"

"Surprised?"

"Kind of."

"Born and raised in Atlanta. Capital of the Southeastern region," he said, a distinct country accent popping out.

Our conversation stalled, so Brannon turned up the radio to some country song I'd never heard. He pulled up to Tru Coffee, and we got out. Brannon ordered a cold caramel latte while I chose a cold mocha. When the barista rang up the order, I moved closer to the payment scanner and looked into the camera. But Brannon brushed me aside, insisting on paying. The payment registered his facial ID, and we stepped to the pickup counter.

"You didn't have to do that. I didn't expect you to pay," I said, slipping my phone into my pants pocket.

One side of his mouth curled up. "I asked you out, remember?"

"So, this is a date?" I wanted to blurt out, but I kept my outburst to myself. I grabbed two straws and focused on breathing.

"Want to walk in Marble Park?" I asked, cocking my head toward the area across the street. "One of my favorite creatures emerges this time of year."

"Yeah? What's that?"

"The blue morpho butterfly. You'll see." I led him across the street to the entrance, where a large fountain gurgled water into a pool of rocks and cycled the water back up through underground pipes.

Because marble occurred naturally in our region, the historical society raised millions of dollars to restore Marble Park to its original beauty, unearthing miles of natural stone. Rocks and tropical gardens lined the pathways at every turn and forced even the most stressed individual to slow down.

Mom often came here to pray, something my dad believed was a waste of time. But Mom insisted prayer was her lifeline to God. Since I could use a life preserver, I uttered a silent prayer, again begging God to bring my mom home safely.

A small greenhouse greeted us at the Path of Serenity and I felt myself relax. Just inside the doorway, a blue morpho butterfly flashed its wings as it flew past our faces, hopping from one flower to another. Another swarm neared, close enough to touch. I reached for one and it landed on my finger, its natural curiosity causing it to hover inches from my nose. When I proved to be a non-sustainable resource, it dashed away as quickly as it had come.

"Curious creatures, aren't they?" I said, turning to Brannon. "Can you believe they only live for about two weeks? They spend their entire lives camouflaging their iridescent blue in order to survive predators."

"That's not much of an existence," Brannon said, sipping his latte through the paper straw.

"Yet it works for these little guys. The juice from the flowers provides everything they need. If you think about it, they're survivors." I watched the butterflies hop from one flower to another, seeking sustenance. Then I faced Brannon, my throat suddenly constricted. "There's, um, something I need to ask. At school, well, you've been blowing me off like you don't know me. Then, I run into you at Little Cone and, like, you ask me out. It's like, confusing, you know?" My words jumbled in my mouth, making me sound like a blond bimbo.

Brannon shot me one of his million-dollar smiles. "I don't blow you off. It's just that, well, we don't hang in the same circles. When we ran into each other, something made me want to help you. Like the time you saved me in freshman year."

I frowned. "I saved *you*?"

"Yeah. Biology with Mr. Waxletter." I giggled, remembering how we called him Waxcandle. "I was failing the class until he paired me up with you. You made everything so easy, and I passed the class. Because of you. With your mom missing, and the shooting, I just thought you might need a listening ear."

"Oh," I said, deflated as the realization hit. This wasn't a date.

He bumped his massive shoulder into my side. "I didn't mean it like that. I never thought you'd go out with me. You're wicked smart, talented, and pretty. You could do way better than me. I'm a dumb jock who is good at lacrosse."

He thinks I'm pretty? *Brannon thinks I am pretty.* I should have responded, but his compliment rendered me mute. I couldn't have formulated a decent response if I tried. Heat rose to my cheeks, so I gulped my iced drink, hoping the cold would keep me from flushing.

"Anyway," Brannon continued, "want to talk about what happened the other day? You seemed pretty upset."

Where do I begin? My world had turned upside down in just a few days. "There was a search party for my mom on Saturday. A ton of people showed up to help, which was cool, but..." My voice choked. "We searched for hours. No one found a single clue."

Brannon's expression softened. "I'm sorry. I can't imagine." We continued down the pebble path in silence. He sipped his coffee and cleared his throat. "Then someone shoots at you. What can I do to help?"

What kind of guy would offer to help a girl he barely knows? "Nothing. But thanks for offering."

"Does the RD know who shot at you?" Brannon asked, his voice meek.

"I think so. It's complicated."

Brannon touched my arm, rubbing his thumb across my skin. "Hey. You can talk to me."

Could Brannon be trusted? As distrustful of everyone as I'd become, I couldn't decipher whether my jitters were because Brannon's hand warmed my skin or because I needed to keep my mouth shut. How do I explain the connection between the guy chasing me and my mom's disappearance when I don't understand it myself? The questions gnawed at me, begging for a response.

As we turned onto the Path of Least Resistance, making our way around the circular park, another butterfly whizzed past us. I longed to be more like the amazing blue butterflies—flit floating without fear. Lela was right. It was time I stopped letting others control my happiness.

I considered my words for a moment, taking several deep breaths. "Ever since the outage, things have been weird. Some dude has been following me. I was trying to get away from him when I ran into you."

Brannon's expression grew serious. "That's nuts. You should have told me. What does he want?"

I hesitated. "My phone."

Brannon burrowed his brows, creating a crease between his eyes. "Huh?"

"He thinks there's something hidden in my phone." I laughed at how ridiculous this must sound. "Crazy, right?"

"Kind of." A slight smile tugged at his lips. "Then again, what if your mom hid something before she disappeared? Like in a safe." When I frowned, he continued. "My parents keep a locked safe in our basement. What if your mom hid something important in your house, something she didn't want you to know about? If you could find the hiding place—"

"I don't know what to look for," I interrupted.

Brannon's lips twitched. "Yeah. Good point."

We reached the front of the Marble Park and Brannon took my empty cup, tossing both into a trash can. I didn't want to talk about the guy chasing me, or how the RD couldn't locate my mom. I wanted to enjoy myself with the best-looking guy in school. In case it was my only time.

"I should probably get home. My dad's super protective of me these days." If I stayed away too long, Dad would start calling. Plus, I had an algebra test tomorrow and a literature essay due.

"Yeah, I can imagine. My parents are worried too, after the shooting and all."

I pulled myself up into the truck while Brannon connected his phone to the speakers. He backed out of the parking lot, singing along to some country song. Well, singing was an overstatement. More like crooning off pitch. But it did the job. I laughed, and he smiled. Brannon leaned over the console, keeping one hand on the wheel while stroking my face with the other.

"There's a smile." Brannon winked, then returned his hand to the wheel.

He started to turn down Horse Farm Road, but I stopped him. "My brother and I are staying at my dad's place."

"Oh, sorry. Vic said you lived near him." Vic, Brannon's best friend, lived one street over from me in Paddock Springs.

"Yeah, I do. But my dad lives in the technology district. Hang a left at the next light."

Brannon turned down the music. "I was thinking about the guy who wants your phone, and I want to help. What if we stop by your house and have a look around? I know you don't know what to look for, but if it would keep you safe, I'd feel better."

His sentiment surprised me, and I placed my hand on his arm. He let go of the steering wheel and interlaced his fingers with mine. My body lit on fire as receptors shot through my nerves. Shock waves reached my brain at an alarming rate. Brannon asked me a question, but I forgot what it was. Something about my house? Tingling sensations flowed as he rubbed his thumb across my hand. Finley was wrong. Brannon was caring, sweet, and genuine. *And he thinks I'm pretty.* I grinned and bit my lower lip.

"Is that a yes?"

"What?" My face flushed.

Brannon laughed and let go of my hand. "Do you want to stop by your house?"

"Oh. No. We don't have a locked safe or anything like that. But thanks."

"Okay. Maybe next time. Which way?"

So, there will be a next time.

CHAPTER 24

Tuesday, September 26

Surviving two days of rumors at Peachtree Park High made me really want to print those t-shirts. I nodded to the Reinforcement Officer assigned to sit outside my father's townhome before unlocking the front door. I dropped my gym bag in Dad's laundry room, putting my sweaty jersey from today's practice into the washing machine before heading to the kitchen. Zac sat on a barstool eating his regular afternoon snack of chocolate ice cream, almost like old times. Almost.

Zac glanced up from his bowl. "How did today go?"

"Just like day one. Rumors and more rumors. A normal day at PPHS." I poured a large glass of water and gulped it down.

"Did you see Brannon?" He wiggled his eyebrows up and down.

I tousled his hair. "Too much information for someone your age. Want to play a simulation game?"

Zac jumped out of his seat. "Yeah. Come on. I downloaded a new one."

"You're not in the sim where you shoot at people anymore?"

He shot me a concerned expression. "Nope. That got too real."

I couldn't agree more. I followed him upstairs to the loft where Dad had created a makeshift room. It beat the couch, but the finality of it filled me with dread. Homesickness crept in and a wave of sadness washed over me. I longed for the predictability of my room, my space, and my things. "Did you and Dad ever hear from Aunt Kate?"

"Nope. She disappeared too." He slipped on his augmented reality headset. "Dad said they have a lead, but he doesn't share much with me. He treats me like a baby."

I leaned into him. "No, he doesn't. He wants to keep you safe. Like I do."

"I'm fine, Rami. Quit worrying about me."

But I couldn't, at least not until Mom came home. I promised Mom I'd protect Zac.

When the doorbell rang, I pulled off my headset. "It's for me." I darted downstairs to open the door for Theresa and Finley. I had asked Finley to come, too, in case things got awkward. Theresa and I weren't really friends, but between our shared interest in computer coding and her offering to help, I hated to turn her away.

Fin stopped to chat with Zac, so Theresa followed me to my room. She glanced around before choosing the chair by the desk. Other than my clothes, I had no personal belongings in the room. No pictures, no artwork, nothing to identify this space as mine.

"I haven't been able to get my stuff yet," I said, as if I expected the question.

"That must be hard." She gave a slight smile.

Surprised by her genuine sincerity, I nodded. "It is. My dad and I, well, it's complicated. But he's been good to me, so I shouldn't complain."

"My parents are divorced, too. I live with my mom and sister." She shuffled in the chair. "How long have your parents been divorced?"

"About a year, but my dad moved out long before that."

Theresa picked up the picture of my horse Cinnamon that I'd set on the desk when I first arrived. "I didn't realize you rode."

"I don't. Well, not anymore." When she stayed quiet, I added, "Do you ride?"

She shook her head. "No way. I'm so clumsy, I'd probably make the horse fall."

I laughed and plopped down on my bed. Finley strolled in, babbling about Zac's new game, but I barely listened. I thought about Theresa, how she knew everyone at school because of *The Grove*. Maybe she *could* help.

Finley sat on the floor across from Theresa. "So, you had some questions for Rami?"

"Oh, right," she said, as if forgetting why she came. "I'm sorry about your mom. I can't imagine..." Her voice trailed off.

"You'd think with all the cameras..." I bit my lower lip.

She did a quick intake of the room and lowered her voice to a mere whisper. "Where's your STaR health device?"

I jumped up and closed the bedroom door. "In the kitchen. Same with Zac's." I squirmed in my seat. "I'm not sure how you can help. The RD doesn't have any leads."

"That's just it. We have connections the ROs don't have. Not only do students have access to each other, but everyone has an Allicio account. If everyone's on the lookout for your mom, someone might remember an important detail."

I shifted in my seat, unsure how much of my personal life I wanted on *The Grove*, let alone Allicio. After my fiasco with the reporter, social media hadn't exactly been kind to me. Plus, with Dominic still at large, Zac wasn't safe. Even after I told Murray almost everything, they still hadn't arrested Dominic. Putting more information about the case online made me uneasy. "What do you think, Fin?"

He ran his fingers through his dark wavy hair, a habit he had whenever he wrestled through a problem. "It can't hurt. Why not try?"

Still uncomfortable, I paced the room. "What questions do you have?"

Theresa asked about when and where my mom's car was found, what she wore, and what leads the RD had chased so far. I shared a little about Kate and how I wanted to find her. Theresa took notes, stopping to ask more questions.

"I'll post this to *The Grove* tonight, and tomorrow I'll post a few more details to keep it going. It'll have my contact information, so hopefully, no one will bother you, Rami." Theresa closed her notebook and clutched it close to her chest. "One more thing. I'm still confused about how your Aunt Kate fits into all this?"

Theresa had just asked the million-dollar question, the one that kept me up at night. I tried to keep my voice indifferent, but my words came out clipped. "If the RD suspects her, they're not saying."

Theresa stood and paced toward the exit. "I think that's what you need to find out next. Something tells me she's involved." She paused in the doorway. "This may sound stupid, but I'm a big fan of *The Inheritance Games* series."

I stared in disbelief. Books weren't banned but every piece of written material had to pass the Threats Division inspection. Somehow, *The Inheritance Games*, *The Hawthorne Legacy*, and *The Final Gambit* made the cut. Probably because they didn't involve government takeover. "The novels by Jennifer Lynn Barnes? Those are some of my favorites, too."

Theresa's face lit up. "Seriously? I can't believe you've read them. I mean, I know they're old, but they were my mom's favorite when she was a teen. We used to read them together. When I could read them myself, I'd stay up late at night reading under my covers with a flashlight."

I glanced at Finley for the first time since Theresa and I started our nerdy book talk. He appeared either clueless or disinterested.

Theresa stepped into the doorway. "Anyway. Avery Grambs kept searching until she solved the mystery. She refused to give up. If there's anything I've learned, it's that you can't be afraid to seek the truth."

Finley and I followed her downstairs, and I grinned, surprised how much Theresa and I were alike. As she drove away, I turned to Finley, a glint in my eye.

"Oh no. I recognize that look," Fin said as I shut the front door. "And I have a feeling I'm not going to like what you're about to say."

I raised an eyebrow. "I'm that predictable?"

He swooshed the bangs off his forehead. "Yep. So, hit me."

"We're going after Kate."

Part II

"Technology is a useful servant but a dangerous master."

Christian Lous Lange

CHAPTER 25

Thursday, October 5

The weeks passed in slow motion as I tried being a *normal teenager*, as Officer Murray had phrased it. School, volleyball, homework, repeat. I stayed off chat sites and didn't go anywhere near decrypting anyone's online ID.

I'd promised Coach Sanchez that I'd get my head in the game, despite my circumstances, and I didn't let her down. Last week, I set the final score to beat our biggest competitor and earned my spot back in the starting lineup. Bald Eagle hadn't contacted me and Dominic hadn't surfaced. No pictures or texts mysteriously appeared on my phone. Maybe Murray did his job after all.

I lingered in the doorway of Dad's dining room that he'd transformed into a makeshift office since working from home. When he spotted me, he held up one finger. Zac stumbled down the stairs, hair a mess, and stopped at the kitchen counter. He poured cereal into a bowl.

"We don't have school today," I said, setting the milk jug next to him. I slipped off my cross-body purse containing my phone and the same tube of lip gloss I'd had days before and set it next to the milk. "Teacher workday. You could have slept in."

I told myself to sleep in, but I couldn't relax until I understood Kate's involvement in my mom's disappearance. Ever since the shooting, my dad had sentenced me to house arrest. Eleven days and counting. It was stifling. With no school today, I saw an opportunity to escape his watch and I couldn't blow it.

Zac stopped chewing and hit his forehead with his palm. I think he tried to say he forgot, but with milk and cereal swirling around, his words were indecipherable.

"You forgot, didn't you?"

He swallowed. "Yep. Well, that stinks."

"Kind of random having a teacher workday midweek, right? Anyway, you should go back to bed."

Zac smirked. "Or I could get in a full day of gaming."

I crinkled my nose. "How about the skate park?"

"Even better." He grinned.

I leaned across the counter, resting my chin in my hands. "Promise me you won't freak out when I tell you something."

Zac tilted his head to the side. "Depends on what you say."

"Fair enough." I braced myself for a lecture from a twelve-year-old. "Finley and I are trying to find Aunt Kate."

He dropped his spoon, splashing milk onto my sleeve. "Why?"

Zac deserved the truth. I stood up and took a deep breath. "Because I think she's involved in everything that's happened. Aunt Kate works for Centurion, the same company as Dominic Bell. The man that shot up Finley's house."

Zac's mouth twitched. "How long have you known this?"

A shiver slithered down my spine. "A while."

"And you didn't tell me?" Zac's voice tensed.

"I have my reasons," I said. Dad and I agreed not to tell Zac about the threat on his life.

Zac blinked rapidly, and I wondered if he was fighting back anger or tears. "Geez, Rames. She may have information about Mom."

"I know. That's why I have to find her."

"Have you asked Dad if you can go?"

I grunted. *How would I convince Dad to let me leave?* "No. Not yet."

"Good luck getting him to agree." Zac shifted on the barstool. "How long will you be gone?"

"I hope only an hour. I'll ask Fin to drive you to the skate park when we get back."

He considered this, then nodded. "Be careful."

"Rami?" Dad called from his so-called office.

I glanced at Zac before stepping around the corner. No point in beating around the bush. "Hey. Um, Finley's taking me to Aunt Kate's place today."

Dad kept his eyes averted. "Not today. I'm heading to the office in a bit. Stay home with Zac."

"I don't need a babysitter," Zac shouted from the other room. "And there's an RO outside keeping watch."

Dad sighed and raised his voice. "True, Zac. But Rami needs to stay here." He pulled the earbuds from his ears and lowered his voice to a mere whisper. "Rami. Let the RD handle Kate. You need to worry about yourself."

"I'm worried about Mom," I said with more force than intended.

"You agreed to cooperate with the investigation. That included no more vigilante activity."

I matched his hushed tone. "And I'm not breaking my agreement. I just want to ask her a few questions."

Dad shook his head. "Not a good idea for you or Finley. He's in enough trouble."

Getting nowhere, I shifted directions. I squeezed my eyes shut and forced fake tears. "Dad, please. Kate has always been there for me. I need to talk to someone who gets me." This wasn't a total lie. I had called Kate from time to time, but I rarely confided in her. Mom proved to be my best confidant, but she wasn't here.

Dad sat back and folded his arms across his chest. "What makes you think she'll miraculously appear when you show up?"

A valid question, one I'd asked myself all week, but I stuck with my story. "She trusts me, and I trust her. She'll talk to me."

Dad mulled this over. "Take your phone. I enabled Finder Seek. If you go anywhere else, it will alert me." I cringed at the privacy violation that allowed him to track my every move. But I kept my thoughts to myself because I needed Dad to believe me. "One hour, Rami. No exceptions. Then come straight back here."

I nodded in agreement, grabbed my purse off the kitchen counter, and waited for Finley in the driveway.

CHAPTER 26

Thursday, October 5

Finley traveled on backroads to downtown, where skyscraper-sized buildings boxed us in. The GPS led us to an upscale high-rise condo complex with a gated entrance. A keypad wedged into the brick column near the gate required a code, a code I didn't have. I'd only been here once. Kate always came to our house.

After waiting for twenty minutes with no cars entering or exiting, I had to come up with another plan. "Where is Centurion's office?"

Finley narrowed his gaze. "Why?"

"What if Kate's been hiding outside the city this whole time? I mean, she could hideout in Chastain or Tuxedo Park for months undetected." I swiveled in my seat as ideas came to life. "Or maybe Centurion's been hiding her."

Finley frowned, then let out a long stream of air. He typed the address into GPS. "Centurion is in midtown, six minutes away. You sure you want to do this?"

Finder Seek would trace me. I could shut the phone down so the app couldn't track me, but Dad would freak out and I'd be back on house arrest. "I don't see any other option."

He backed up the Jeep and headed north for several miles. We turned into what appeared to be the entrance of a private country club. Expansive trees lined a stacked stone wall leading to a six-foot wrought iron fence that stretched for several blocks.

"Is this the right place?" I asked, searching for anything that resembled an office building.

"It's where GPS said to turn."

We pulled up to an unmanned guard entrance. Finley slowed down but didn't stop. He drove down a long, curvy road until a massive building filled with windows came into view. White columns held a towering roof above the entrance, making it appear more like a five-star hotel than an office complex. We pulled into the attached multilayer parking garage, and Finley parked at level three. I placed my purse on the back seat, slipped on my coat, and put my phone in the outside pocket. Down one set of stairs, a covered glass walkway connected the garage to the building.

We stepped into a lobby with shiny white marble floors and a marble desk, but no one sat behind the counter. I glanced around, expecting noise or employees coming and going with all the cars I'd seen on the parking deck. But the building appeared vacant. Finley stood in the middle of the lobby, staring at something on the ceiling. He held up his phone and snapped a photo.

"What are you doing?" I said in hushed tones, waving him toward me.

He stuck his phone in the front pocket of his jeans and glanced over his shoulder. "Those are some serious high-tech security cameras. Why would they need military-style surveillance if no one's around?"

"Why are you taking pictures? Isn't that like announcing to whoever is viewing the footage, 'Here I am.' I thought we were staying under the radar?"

"Oh, right," Finley remarked, as if remembering why we'd come.

My shoes squeaked on the floor as I walked toward the elevator. The sign listed nine floors with various company names assigned to each floor, names I didn't recognize until I came to the third floor. Finley pressed the button, and we stepped inside. When the door opened, we entered an expansive room with a small desk at the front. Cubicles lined the wall of windows, displaying the downtown skyline. Finley took long strides, glancing from side to side at the desks stripped of equipment. Charging cords hung like limp noodles across the bare wood with no computers, phones, or files left in any of the cubicles. I opened drawers and cabinets, expecting to find pens and sticky notes, but they too were empty.

Finley stared across the desk. "A desk with no computer and no phone?"

"And no one to greet us. Again." My phone vibrated in the pocket of my coat. I pulled it out and cringed. Two missed calls and an unread text message. I didn't need to read it to know Dad's Finder Seek app had spotted me out of place. I placed the phone back in my pocket and followed Finley to a large metal cabinet pressed up against the wall.

"Someone has intentionally stripped this place," he said.

I shuddered. "It's as if it never existed."

"A ghost company."

I frowned. "What?"

"Centurion could be a front for something else entirely. A legit company doesn't pack up and move out without a trace."

Chill bumps rolled down my arms. "What *is* this place?"

A loud thud echoed in the empty room, and instinctively, I stepped behind Finley, pulling my jacket tighter around my body. "What was that?" Finley's hand jerked up to silence me. He stepped toward a long hallway with a closed door at the end. I pulled Finley back toward me. "This is a bad idea. Let's get out here."

"Stay here," he said, his voice controlled.

But I didn't listen. I followed him to a large room with dozens of servers stacked from floor to ceiling. Database towers filled with colored lights, buttons, and switches took up every inch of space.

"Tech companies have multiple data centers in different locations," Finley explained, even though I hadn't asked. "This must have been just one. I'm guessing they have servers on every floor of the building because there's no way this floor alone could house enough data to make much difference. But it's strange. Why purchase a fancy building in an upscale part of town rather than a simple warehouse? And why shut it down?"

"Because they're hiding something," I replied

A red light blinked in the darkness, and Finley strode deeper into the room. He flipped a switch, then slid a lever up and sideways. "These have been wiped," he whispered.

"How can you tell?"

He pointed to the red blinking light. "If it were an active database, a code would have appeared when I pressed this button. Instead, I got an error. Someone moved the data to the cloud."

I started to ask Finley about the relevance of moving data to the cloud when a shadowed silhouette flashed on the back wall. My skin tingled. “Hello?”

“Who’s there?” Finley had gone rigid, anxious, and alert within seconds.

A dark figure crept around the mainframe.

CHAPTER 27

Thursday, October 5

A woman approached dressed in solid black—jeans, combat boots, a turtleneck sweater, and a ball cap—so dark she could slip into the night unnoticed. I threw my hands to my face, covering my open mouth. Aunt Kate's shadowed silhouette stood before me. She rushed to my side. "Rami? Oh, thank God you're okay."

Kate's right hand, resting on my shoulder, was bound in a flesh-colored bandage. I gave her a slight push as anger spewed from my lips. "Where have you been? Mom's been missing for two weeks, and no one's heard from you. The minute I show up, you magically appear?"

Kate's shoulders drooped. "I'm after the same thing you are, Rami."

My jaw tightened. "Yeah? What's that?"

"Answers." Kate's gaze shifted from Finley back to me. "Who is this?"

"Finley. My computer genius friend who tracked you down," I said.

Kate raised an eyebrow. "You found the fail-safe switch on the target server. Impressive."

Finley grinned. "Thanks."

But I wasn't that easily impressed. "Start talking or I'm calling the RD."

Kate put her hands together in a praying position under her chin. *Just like my mom.* The resemblance overwhelmed me. "I know you're scared, Rami, but I'm doing everything I can to protect you."

My frustration boiled over. "It's funny how everyone says they're protecting me, yet no one is actually doing it. Someone shot at me, chased me, and threatened Zac. Sorry if I don't buy your sympathy."

Finley placed his hand on the small of my back. Whether to calm me or protect me from Kate, I couldn't be sure. "How did you know Rami would be here?"

"Ian," she said.

My eyes widened. "My dad? You and my dad—"

"It's not what you think," Kate insisted. "Look, we don't have much time."

"Why are you here?" Finley removed his hand from my waist and closed the small gap between himself and Kate. His voice tensed, and I wondered if he believed Kate's story.

Kate's dilated pupils darted left, then right. "I left something here in plain sight. For safe keeping. I had to wait until they cleared out to come back for it."

Finley narrowed his gaze. "Left what here? They stripped this place clean."

"Proof." Kate took a deep breath. "Rami. I need you to trust me."

My temper flared. “Trust you? How can I trust you when everything that’s happened to my family points back to you? Did you have something to do with Mom’s disappearance?”

Kate’s tone changed from commanding to panic. “No! I would never hurt Annie. She—”

“She what?” Emotion leaked from my lips.

“This is bigger than you, Rami. Larger than any of us,” she said.

By now, I was seething. “What are you talking about?”

“I can’t explain right now. There’s no time. But believe me when I tell you I’m trying to protect you,” Kate said.

“Protect me from what?”

Kate glanced at the ceiling and lowered her voice to a discreet whisper. “Following the pandemic, President Young purchased location data from a mobile research group. The data determined whether people complied with the health restrictions during the pandemic. A study of human behavior, if you will. It justified the need for the Department of Safety Threats and Reinforcement. The Safety Division used the data to create health protocols while the Threats Division used it to control information.”

I rolled my eyes. “Nice history lesson, but I’m not at school. And you still haven’t answered my question. Protect me from what?”

Kate let out a deep sigh. “Centurion Technologies recruited me to create a tracking program for Allicio. We call it Bifurcation Tracking Analysis. It separates users into distinct groups based on their attitude, personality, and preferences. From there, we design appropriate content.”

“So, Centurion is part of STaR?” I asked.

“We’re more like independent contractors,” she said. *Independent contractors. Where had I heard that term before?* “My team and I created digital profiles on every Allicio user. In the tech world, it's referred to as intelligent surveillance."

"That's legal?" Finley asked.

Kate raised her brows. "Intelligent surveillance is nothing new. Social media platforms did this long before you were born with little, if any, regulation. Several months ago, I expressed my concern about the level of data Centurion asked me to collect and what STaR planned to do with the information."

Finley narrowed his gaze. "And?"

Kate fiddled with the large server closest to the exit. She tapped a button, causing a light to blink on and off. With a pair of tweezers, she reached between two wire casings of computer hardware with sets of vertical blue flashing lights. "Government takeover didn't happen overnight, you know. Some people spent years preparing."

Removing the tweezers, she slipped something into her pocket and turned back to face Finley and me. "The pandemic only lasted two years. By then, scientists around the world had discovered a cure. They stopped the death rate from being worse than it was. But that didn't stop those who sought power from ushering in a new leader. President Young was sworn in under the guise that we *needed* her leadership to contain the virus. But all that was false."

My chest tightened. "Everything I learned in school—"

"Is censored, spun to make us all believe we're safe under President Young," Kate said.

"But she created STaR to keep us safe," Finley said.

Kate shook her head. "She created STaR to control us. It was never about the virus. It was always about control."

My mind swirled like water flowing down a drain. "Is *every* tech company controlled by STaR?"

Kate offered a sad smile, her voice full of condescension. "Did you really think the Threats Division would allow free thought and free speech? Monitoring Allicio is their way of keeping you and your friends under control. They control what you see, what you read. The goal is to control how you *think*."

"I don't understand. If STaR is bad, why do you work for them?" I said.

We followed her to the small conference room next door with a long wooden table and burgundy leather chairs. "I didn't know any better until Annie convinced me—"

"My mom?" I gasped.

"She opened my eyes to what was really happening, Rami. I discovered what Centurion intended to do with the data and how they planned to use it against us." Kate threw her arms out toward Finley and me. "Against *you*. When I tried to shut it down, everything spun out of control."

I placed my fingers on either side of my temples to stop my head from throbbing. "You tried to shut down Allicio?"

Kate shook her head. "Not Allicio. I don't have that kind of power. I tried to stop Allicio's tracking algorithm. The one I created." Keeping her body flat against the wall, she peered outside, scanning the parking garage below. "You were never supposed to be involved, Rami."

But nothing about her situation made me feel sorry for her. I was certain Aunt Kate had somehow been responsible for my mom's disappearance. I had almost died because of her so-called research. Unanswered questions continued to plague me. Why is *my* family involved? And what was Centurion Technologies planning?

"Two weeks ago, someone blew my cover," Kate continued, as if sensing my frustration. "I stored the codes and hid them. The next morning, the outage happened."

Finley's jaw dropped. "Wait. You caused the network outage? The one that took down millions of STaR's health monitors and mobile phones?"

Her lip twitched as she struggled to keep her voice low. "No, I didn't cause it. It was a distraction, a way for Centurion to release the program without me. By then, they knew I had defected."

Finley interlocked his fingers atop his head and paced the room. "This doesn't make sense. You still haven't told us what Centurion is doing with the information they collect from Allicio."

Kate didn't respond. Instead, she held up her palm and pressed her finger to her lips. "Rami? Does your phone have the update?"

Her question startled me. "Yeah, why?"

Without answering, Kate lunged forward and grasped my arm with extreme force. "They followed you."

I tilted my head to one side. "Who followed me?"

She cursed under her breath. "We have to go. Now." Her grip on me tightened as she pulled me toward a door at the opposite end of the room.

"Wait." I tugged my arm away. "I've been instructed to find you and bring you in."

Kate hesitated. "Who told you that?"

"A National Agent, for one. And some lunatic named Dominic Bell. Apparently, he's a friend of yours?" Sarcasm dripped from my lips.

Kate's face drained of all color. For the first time, she appeared afraid. "Dominic is not my friend. I copied the code to expose

Centurion. That's why I'm here. To retrieve the copy. Rami, please. We must go. Now."

Kate raced toward the staircase. Finley gave me a gentle shove, propelling me down two sets of stairs. Kate unlatched a locked door, where a red exit sign illuminated the dark hallway. Without a word, she pulled me into an awkward hug, but my arms hung limp at my sides. Kate reached for my hand and stuck a small silver piece of metal into my palm. With her other hand, she curled my fingers into a tight fist.

She stood so close, no one could possibly overhear her strained voice that had dropped to a mere whisper. "Take this and keep it safe, no matter what. Do you hear me?" When I nodded, she said, "This thing is bigger than you can imagine."

"I don't understand," I said, frantic for answers. "Where are you going? You haven't told me where to find my mom."

"The other half is hidden…" Kate's voice trailed off as she sprinted in the opposite direction.

I shoved the silver piece in my coat pocket and reached out for her, but it was too late. "Kate, wait!"

Finley clamped his hand on my mouth. "Rami, come on!"

He grabbed my hand and shoved me toward the exit. We raced through the covered parking garage. I followed Finley up the stairs and through a maze of vehicles to his Jeep. He hit reverse before my door even closed, tires squealing, as we raced away.

CHAPTER 28

Thursday, October 5

Finley sped north, zigzagging in and out of traffic. He entered the highway, clutching the steering wheel, until the whites of his knuckles appeared. The accelerator read twenty miles per hour over the speed limit, but I didn't dare tell him to slow down.

I buried my head in my hands as I tried to make sense of Kate's explanation for the recent events. Centurion had been tracking people based on their Allicio posts. Kate called it Bifurcation Tracking. But who were they watching and why? And what does Centurion plan to do with the information? More importantly, why is my mom involved?

Minutes later, when Finley approached the technology district, he exhaled like he'd held his breath the entire drive. He'd been silent since we left, and I wished I could read his mind. I slipped off my coat and reached for the tiny silver square I'd stuffed in the pocket. I held it up, as if exposing it to the sunlight would bear its contents. No bigger than my thumbnail, the square bore no markings, no logo, and no indication of what might be stored on it.

"Where did you get that?" Finley asked, darting his eyes from the road to me.

"Kate shoved it in my hand. She told me to keep it safe. Before she left, she mumbled something like 'other half hidden.' I have no idea what it means."

When Finley stopped at a red light, I handed him the tiny fragment. He fingered it in his palm, scrutinizing it, before handing it back to me. "It's a micro flash drive, most likely encrypted."

Finley was already in trouble for hacking, and I wasn't sure after the stunt I pulled today if I could protect him. While Finley droned on about how he built his computer, I slid the flash drive back into my coat pocket to keep it safe until Kate resurfaced. *If* she resurfaced.

Other half hidden. What did Kate mean?

Something Brannon said at Marble Park a few days ago nagged at me. His words tried to fall into place at the edge of my memory, but so much had happened, I couldn't put it into context. Suddenly, it hit me. When I told Brannon that Dominic had combed through my phone, he asked if my mom might have hidden something at my house.

"Finley, stop!" I shouted.

Finley slammed on the brakes, swerved to avoid hitting another car, then came to a stop on the side of the two-lane road. "What the—"

"Kate said she hid the proof in plain sight. Take me to my house."

Finley shook his head. "No. I need to take you to your dad's. You heard what he said about Finder Seek."

"I'll worry about that later. Listen, if my mom hid something and Centurion found out, that could be why she disappeared. What if it's still there?"

Finley threw up his hands. "What are you even looking for?"

"I'm not sure," I admitted.

He paused, then made a U-turn toward Paddock Springs. "I don't like this, Rami. I smell trouble. If nothing turns up in five minutes, we're out of there. Got it?"

Finley parked in the driveway, and I grabbed my purse from the back seat and slipped my coat back on. I hurried to the backyard to fetch the hideaway key, but when I reached behind the planter, I stopped short. Tiny fragments of broken glass covered the steps. My shaky fingers fumbled for the knob.

In the kitchen, drawers and cabinets sat opened and exposed with broken dishes scattered across the tile floor. Torn sofa cushions in the family room sat on the floor with piles of stuffing nearby. I clutched my chest and my mouth hung open in disbelief. As if on autopilot, I bolted for my room. My clothes, still on hangers, were thrown on the carpet and the mattress tossed aside.

I raced back downstairs to Mom's computer room near the kitchen. Like the rest of the house, someone had ransacked it. My mother was old-fashioned. She preferred writing things on paper rather than using electronic devices. She'd attach the papers together with small metal paper clips. But now, those papers littered the area.

My phone buzzed, and I jumped out of my skin. I glanced at the screen. *Dad*. I sent the call to voicemail, and a series of pings came next, which I also ignored.

"Rami, let's get out of here." Finley's voice held an edge of fear.

We stood side by side staring at the shattered frames facedown on the bookshelves. The only thing left standing was my enormous horse trophy turned backward, as if someone had lifted it, then shoved it aside. It stood oddly out of place.

Finley tapped my arm. "Rami?"

Ignoring his protests, I moved toward the shelf and examined the trophy for several seconds. Why was it the only thing unharmed in the entire house? It wasn't a flimsy, lightweight aluminum type like Zac had received for participating in baseball. My trophy contained lead glass and marble. I held it with both hands, examining every inch and crevice, and wondered if my intruder had done the same. A small crystal horse rested on top of the seamless glass. A label with my name, date, and show title sat on the stone base. I tried to peel it, but it didn't budge, so I turned the trophy upside down, searching underneath for holes. I was about to give up when something caught my eye. I took the stairs two at a time in search of tweezers in Mom's bathroom drawer. When my search came up empty, I zipped back to the family room.

Finley caught me by the arm, his eyes wide with concern. "What are you doing?"

"Remember the photo of me on my horse, Cinnamon? The one Theresa noticed in my room? I found it in my bag right after Mom disappeared. I think it's a clue."

"A clue for what?"

"Of all the pictures from my childhood, why that one? To get me to trust my dad?"

Finley rubbed his chin, as if pondering my hypothesis. "I'm not sure, Rames. Where are you going with this?"

I circled the room, landing my gaze again on the trophy and how it appeared out of place. "My connection to both Mom and Dad is my horse. The horse photograph, the horse trophy. My mom left me clues."

Without another word, I grabbed the trophy from the shelf and sprinted to the back door. With a glint in my eye, I smashed it against the brick of my home. The miniature horse broke off, splitting into multiple chunks of glass. But the marble base held on tight. Finley tried to stop me, but I pulled away. I lifted the trophy overhead and heaved it onto the concrete walkway. The base separated from the glass, shattering into hundreds of tiny pieces. I crouched onto the walkway, sorting through microscopic shards of glass, when a piece of gold reflected in the light. I picked up a miniature rectangular card and charged inside.

Finley closed the door behind me. "Are you crazy? What if someone's watching your house? We need to go."

"One more minute, Fin," I said, reaching for a paper clip in the drawer of Mom's computer desk.

I unfolded the metal paper clip and pressed it against the tiny hole in the side of my phone. The phone's SIM card popped out, and as expected, it was a perfect match for the one I now held in my grasp. Only the one from my phone bore Connect Mobile's iconic symbol—a red C encompassing a scarlet globe.

"It's a SIM card," I said, holding it up to show Finley. "That's why Dominic wants my phone. They suspected my mom hid this with me. And she did, but not in my phone. Maybe she knew they'd come after me, so she left me clues. My mom tried to protect me, Fin."

For the first time in days, my mind was clear. My mother had left me a trail of clues, placing the picture of my horse Cinnamon in my duffle bag, and arranging my trophy so it stood above every other item on the bookshelf. These two files held the key to her whereabouts and her captors. And although Finley could retrieve the information, he agreed to work with the RD in exchange for a lighter sentence. I'd have to decrypt them myself.

"You need to leave, Fin."

"Why? What are you doing?"

"I'm calling the RD and you can't be here when they show up."

For once, Finley didn't question me. When he was out the door, I took a pair of yellow rubber gloves from under the kitchen sink, grabbed a rag from the laundry room that Mom used to dust furniture, and meticulously wiped fingerprints from the broken trophy pieces the way I'd seen it done in spy movies. Scooping as many shards of glass as possible into my gloved hands, I placed the slivers on the family room rug, arranging them as if the trophy had been hurled from the bookshelf and shattered.

My phone vibrated inside my coat pocket. Again. I ignored the past five calls, but if I didn't answer, Dad would come for me. The Finder Seek app had tracked me since we left Kate's apartment. Once I was sure the trophy pieces were in place, I answered.

"Dad?" My voice cracked.

"Rami, you didn't listen!" He shouted into the receiver and I pulled it away from my ear. "Finder Seek shows you went to an office building downtown, then to your house."

I ignored the privacy violation of the app I'd grown to hate. My voice trembled as I pretended to be terrified. "Dad? You need to call the Reinforcement Division. Someone broke my horse trophy."

CHAPTER 29

Thursday, October 5

Even if Dominic were hiding in the shadows, I suspected he wouldn't chance getting caught by the RD after spending weeks undetected. While I waited for the RD to arrive, I replaced the yellow rubber gloves under the kitchen sink and grabbed a white trash bag. Thinking we'd only stay with Dad for a day or two until Mom came home, Zac and I hadn't packed much, and we both needed more clothes.

Although nearly all financial transactions took place using our STaR-issued phones, Dad had given me some cash bills since my phone didn't work. Cash was black market currency. I could swap it for almost anything. I pulled the bills out of an inner zipper pocket in my backpack, stuffed them into my coat pocket, and raced upstairs.

First, I stopped in Zac's room, stuffing sweats and t-shirts into the trash bag. Nollie's favorite toy she curled up with every night sat on Zac's bed. I grabbed the toy and a few skateboarding things I thought would make Zac smile, put them in the bag, then headed across the hall to my room.

On my floor where my clothes sat scattered, I yanked long-sleeved shirts and hoodies from their hangers, and snagged a few pairs of skinny jeans and a pair of warm boots before setting some lacy panties on top. From underneath my bathroom cabinet, I took out a pink box of feminine products, unwrapped one, and placed both the micro flash drive and SIM card inside the pink wrapper. Then I arranged it with the others inside the box.

Crouching in front of my dresser, I reached between the bottom dresser drawer and the back frame that held the dresser together and placed the wad of bills against the wooden frame. Satisfied, I strolled downstairs and waited.

When Officer Gaits arrived on the scene, I sat alone on the torn cushioned sofa drying fake tears. My purse hung across my chest over my coat and the plastic bag rested on my lap as I waited to share its contents with Gaits.

He took three steps inside, stopped, and spoke into his mic. "Officer Gaits, ID 67431."

The mic crackled. "Go ahead," replied the dispatcher.

"I'm going to need forensics here."

"Roger that." The dispatcher's voice repeated a series of numbers and codes with Gaits before he joined me in the war-torn room. He watched me, his face a mixture of confusion and concern. "Want to tell me what happened and what you're doing here?"

I couldn't have planned the timing better myself. It helped that I had seasonal allergies and suffered from post-nasal drip this time of year as I sniffled and wiped my nose with the back of my hand. After a few deep breaths, I opened the garbage bag. "I stopped by to get more clothes and a few personal items."

Gaits peered into the bag. Red spots formed on his freckled face, one resembling the big dipper. I hung my head and pretended to cry as a grin slowly crept up my cheeks. *Checkmate.*

Gaits shuffled his feet on the carpet, wiping sweat from his forehead. "Did you move anything? Touch anything before you called?"

"I put the cushions back, so I'd have somewhere to sit while I waited." I choked back tears. "When I saw the pictures of my mom thrown to the side as if she were dead, I had to pick them up. I stacked them on the bottom shelf."

Gaits nodded, as if believing my story, and asked me to start from the beginning. I explained how I had walked through each room in complete shock. I took my time, giving him details about the spare key and the broken glass on the back steps.

"How did you get here?" Gaits asked, interrupting me.

His question caught me off guard, but I quickly recovered. "Finley dropped me off."

This time, Gaits raised a brow. "He didn't come inside?"

I shook my head. "No. I planned to go to Lela's house after grabbing my clothes."

In my mind, the story made perfect sense, and by the time Officer Murray arrived with the forensic team, I was ready to leave. But Lela flew through the door before Murray could stop her. She fell onto the couch next to me, squeezing the life out of me.

"Oh...my...what...?" Lela's mouth hung open.

"Get her out of here," Murray hollered to the officer next to the front door. "She's contaminating my crime scene."

"Crime scene?" Lela screeched. A young male officer dusting for prints escorted Lela outside, but she cried over her shoulder, "I'll be right here, Rami. I'm not going anywhere."

"Set up a perimeter and keep everyone out," Murray barked once Lela was out of earshot. Then he turned his wrath on me. "Officer Gaits told me your version of the events, but I'd like to hear it from you. Start by telling me how you found yourself in the middle of trouble again."

Confident I had the perfect cover story, I began with the broken glass on the steps outside to gathering my clothes in a trash bag. For added effect, I showed him the lacy panties and pink box of feminine items. He glanced down without reaction. His response was disappointing, but I didn't let it falter me.

"You realize that by trampling up and down the stairs to get your so-called personal items, you tampered with the crime scene. It has me thinking you're inserting yourself into the case again." Murray glared at me, his eyes ablaze. "Why didn't you call me? Your phone works, right? Or did it mysteriously shut down again?"

His obvious distrust of me created problems. I regrouped, gasping for breath as if I could no longer hold back the tears, and dabbed at my eyes for added effect. "I was in shock. I mean, wouldn't you be if you found your house ransacked? What if your wife was missing, and you came home to this? How would that make you feel?"

He didn't play into my drama, and I suspected he knew I lied. When he pointed to my trophy and ordered the crime scene investigator to take pictures and dust for fingerprints, my palms began to sweat. Fearing he could see right through me, I cleared my throat. "I need to go to the bathroom."

Murray paused for an uncomfortable few seconds before motioning to the only female RO in the room to escort me. I reached for the white trash bag and raced for the bathroom. Once safely behind a locked door, I splashed cool water on my face, regained my composure, and reemerged with the plastic bag still in tow. With Murray and Gaits occupied in the kitchen, I slipped out unnoticed. A small crowd had gathered in the front yard. Off to one corner, Brannon and Lela stood side by side behind a wall of Reinforcement Officers with hands on their weapons. It seemed like overkill. Brannon gave a slight wave, and I headed his way.

He stood inches from my face, and I smelled his familiar spice-scented cologne. "I was on my way to Vic's place when I saw the RD. Are you okay? What's going on?"

My heart melted. *Brannon stopped to check on me.* "I'm fine. I came home to get my clothes and found my house trashed." I edged behind the officers and motioned to the white bag.

He pointed toward the swarm of Reinforcement Officers buzzing around the house. "Do they know who did this?"

"I'm not sure," I confessed, before turning my attention to my dad sprinting across the grass.

Dad pulled me close, then cradled his arm around my shoulder. "Go to the car, Rami."

I'm sorry, I mouthed to Brannon, no sound escaping from my lips, and followed Dad to his vehicle. He opened the passenger door, and I climbed in, keeping the garbage bag clutched against my chest. Throughout the short drive home, Dad's expression remained unreadable, and his silence unnerved me. When we reached the townhome, Zac followed me to my room, where I placed the trash bag, my purse, and my coat on the bed. He grilled me with questions.

"Who did that to our house? Why were you there?" Zac stood with his hands on his hips, reminding me of Mom when I came home late from a party last year.

"I'm not sure who did it. And I went there to get our clothes." Nollie sniffed at my bag, but I waited until the firing squad subdued before revealing my surprise.

"You should've listened to Dad and come here. Dad says you're getting in trouble on purpose. For attention." His expression bore sadness as he slumped to the bed. He waited for a response, but I remained quiet. "Did you at least find Aunt Kate?"

"Yeah. I found her," I admitted, unsure of how much of my conversation with Kate I should reveal. I opened the bag and pulled out his skateboard memorabilia. "I didn't think you'd want the RD to have those." Zac's grin reached his eyes. Then I reached to the bottom of the sack for Nollie's favorite stuffed bear. Nollie grasped it in her jaw and leaped into Zac's lap.

"Nollie! Your bear-bear." He stroked her soft fur before cutting his eyes to me. "Thanks, Rames."

I cupped his chin between my palms. "I'm going to find Mom. I promise."

CHAPTER 30

Friday, October 6

For the past two weeks, I struggled to comply with Officer Murray's demands—stay away from the investigation and no vigilante activity. The latter was no problem. I didn't want to be anywhere near Dominic and his cronies. But I desperately wanted to understand the significance of the SIM card I'd found yesterday stashed in my horse trophy. All clues pointed to the fact that Mom knew someone was after her. Centurion? The Threats Division?

It had been fifteen days since she'd disappeared, and with every passing day, I'd lost hope of finding her alive. Mom's story had made national news. UNN referred to her as "Ghost Mom"—the lady who had disappeared without a trace, just like the television program about missing persons. Her favorite TV show had become my reality.

Although Dominic was on the RD's most wanted list for upending STaR's safety protocols, it didn't mean I was safe. Dominic could still snatch Zac the instant he was out of my sight because I had what he wanted—the second file. The one he suspected was inside my phone. Despite my best efforts, I was no tech genius. I couldn't decrypt the flash drive.

Ever since the shooting at Finley's house, I'd gone straight home after volleyball practice to keep an eye on Zac. Just in case. But today, I told Zac I'd be late getting home. I made sure the RO that sat outside in his car also knew I'd be late.

Finley called last night and asked me to meet him after school, but wouldn't say why. In fact, he refused to talk on the phone, insisting we meet in person. I got the distinct impression that Finley decided we should no longer be friends and wanted to tell me in person rather than over the phone. I had turned his ordinary life upside down. In some ways, I felt relieved knowing he was safer without me. But a deep sadness washed over me, as if someone I'd grown to care for was moving far away.

I spent the day in a haze, distracted over Finley's odd behavior on the phone. My chemistry teacher assigned us to groups to complete the study guide, and once again, I'd failed to hold up my end of the bargain. I had nothing to offer this group except conspiracy theories, which would not have helped us pass our test, so I silently stared at my blank piece of paper for the duration of class.

By the time the bell rang, I tried to escape unnoticed, but Theresa called after me. "Hey, wait up." Theresa dodged a boy racing out the door before catching up to me. "Are you okay? You were so quiet in class."

My shoulders slumped. "I'm sorry I didn't help the group."

Theresa shook her head. "Don't worry about it. You have a lot going on." She followed me into the hall, and I wondered if she was drumming up a new story. "I thought you'd want to know a kid responded to the story in *The Grove*. Said he takes a work-study class first period at an office complex on Technology Park Drive.

He claims your mom was in a big hurry and cut him off. He had to swerve to avoid hitting her. That got my attention because her law firm is in the opposite direction of the technology district."

The wheels spun in my mind. "You think he's credible?"

"Yep. His story checked out."

I glanced over my shoulder, a nervous habit I'd picked up the past two weeks. "Did you report this to the RD?" When she nodded, I stepped closer and whispered, "I found Kate." Theresa's eyes widened in recognition. Kate was the missing link to everything that had happened. The outage, the shooting, and the destruction at my home. "Keep the story running for now. Maybe this tip will inspire others to come forward. Oh, and Theresa? Thank you."

She smiled, and we separated into the sea of students heading out the door. When I spotted Brannon, my mood shifted. His smiling face was a warm welcome to this awful day. He leaned into me, and I breathed in his warmth.

"Have you been avoiding me?" Brannon smiled, flashing his pearly white teeth.

"No...no," I stammered. "I've been busy with volleyball and school." I left out the part about staying close to Zac.

"Good. Because I miss talking to you."

I beamed. "You do? I mean, I enjoy talking to you, too."

"Want to grab a coffee? Hang out at Marble Park again?"

I crinkled my brows. "Another day?"

He frowned, mimicking my expression, then smiled. "Fine. What about tomorrow night? We can see a movie or something. I'd pick you up."

I squeezed my lips together to keep from answering, but I might as well have announced my feelings. "Yes!" I said, before I could stop myself.

Brannon bobbed his chin and snickered. "Cool. Seven o'clock?" He started to step away, then stopped himself. "Hey? What happened to the thing with your phone? Did you ever find what the crazy stalker guy wanted?"

Brannon had done nothing but try to help me, but something held me back from admitting the truth. I couldn't lie to his face, so I dodged the subject. "I really don't know what that was all about. I just think he was crazy."

"But you went to your house to look for it, right? And found someone had broken in?"

"Yeah."

"So, you must have found something, right?"

The hair on the back of my neck bristled. "I'm not sure what you mean."

Brannon's expression changed from indifferent to fearful. "Something out of the ordinary? Like what a crazy stalker would think is important."

My skin tightened, uncomfortable with his line of questioning. What was it he wanted me to admit? There was something strange about his tone. Brannon, who had always appeared in control, seemed shaken. This exchange felt even more weird than my phone conversation with Finley last night. "Um, I need to get going, Brannon. See you tomorrow?" I offered a slight smile.

The look on his face made my stomach tighten. *Frustration or anger?* I couldn't be sure, but it faded as quickly as it arrived, replaced with his usual heart-stopping grin. "Right. Seven o'clock."

Still reeling from my exchange with Brannon, I entered the empty gym to meet Finley. My phone buzzed and when I looked down, a video appeared on my screen. Dominic held a knife up to the camera and laughed.

After devoting hours to augmented reality games, Zac had developed a fascination with military weaponry. Especially knives. Mom didn't allow any weapons except for the old Swiss Army pocketknife Dad passed down to him, which I now knew Zac had sharpened to military grade. Zac kept a journal with pictures of the blades he wanted to collect.

And in the video, Dominic slid one of those knives across his throat. Dominic's video vanished as quickly as it appeared, and in its wake, a text message appeared.

I'm coming for you.

He knows I found the SIM card. My fingers fumbled with the buttons as I tried to respond, but it was no use. It disappeared from the messages app before I could answer, exactly as the others had done. My phone had the update. How could this still be happening?

My breath zapped from my lungs. I bent over. Dominic knew if the messages vanished, no one would believe me. I had no proof. The Reinforcement Division had found no hard evidence of any text message from an unknown number or any of the pictures I claimed Dominic sent to me.

I had gotten too comfortable. Too proud of myself for finding Kate and her hidden code. Kate instructed me to keep the files safe, but I shouldn't have listened to her. It was her fault I was in the mess in the first place. I should have gotten rid of them. How could I have been so stupid?

Someone was still after me. And Zac. Had Theresa running a story in *The Grove* triggered a response from Dominic? Or was Kate pretending to protect me but still working with Centurion?

All the air leaked from my lungs. With both hands, I clutched my chest, then my phone crashed on the wooden floor, its case protecting it from shattering. The noise echoed in the empty gymnasium like thunderous applause. I wanted to stomp on my mobile and crush it, but I didn't because Zac might need to get ahold of me. Everything I'd done was to protect him.

Lela called my name, but my feet stuck in place as if cemented in concrete. Unable to respond, Lela dragged me deeper into the gym where Finley stood hidden in the shadows of the dim fluorescent lights. He touched his finger to his lips and motioned to the exit.

Outside, Finley leaned against the brick building, glancing around before lowering his voice to a mere whisper. "Walk to Lela's car, then drive to my house. Park at the end of the cul-de-sac. Walk through the neighbor's backyard. Hop my fence and meet me in the basement."

"What? Why?" Lela gave Finley a once-over. "You could have just texted us to come over."

Finley clenched his jaw. "There's a story being leaked to the press. You won't want to be here when it happens."

"What are you talking about, Finley?" Lela snapped. "You sound like a nutcase."

"This is serious, Lela. If you don't believe me, then don't come," Finley barked.

Lela was right. Finley had been acting strange since his phone call with me yesterday, and Brannon's odd behavior had me second-guessing our relationship. But Dominic had sent me a warning, and if Finley had information that could help explain everything, I wanted to hear it.

I clutched Lela by the elbow. "Come on, Lela. Let's go."

CHAPTER 31

Friday, October 6

In the parking lot, Quince leaned against Lela's car, narrowing his eyes as I approached. We hadn't spoken since the shooting at Finley's house, and I got the sense Quince was debating whether to trust me again. He glanced my way, then turned his attention to Lela. "What took you so long?"

Lela gave me a sidelong glance. "Nothing. We're good. Everything's fine." Lela spoke in staccato whenever she was nervous.

"Hi, Quince," I said. No response. "Um, we're going to Finley's. You should come with us."

Quince hesitated, then climbed in the car, grumbling about Lela's driving. His familiar banter brought a smile to my cheeks. I missed these times with my friends, back before my world turned upside down. I could only hope that whatever knowledge Finley possessed would keep Lela and Quince out of danger.

We reached Finley's neighborhood and followed his bizarre instructions to park in the cul-de-sac and trudge through two backyards, one with a large wooden playset, the other with a lacrosse net and bounce-back, before climbing the fence and landing in his yard. I expected Ranger to bark, but the yard was silent, and the basement door stood wide open. Before stepping inside, I paused in the doorway, the memory of the gun firing through the window still fresh. The room held a faint scent of cleaner mixed with paint fumes, and the contractors had repaired the broken window and wall with no trace of what happened mere days ago. Almost as if it had never happened.

A slight chill trickled down my spine, although I couldn't decipher whether it was from the cold or the recollection of the shooting. Finley turned the lock on the door behind me and gestured to the news on TV.

"Breaking news this hour out of Atlanta, where local authorities received an anonymous tip about a bomb threat at Peachtree Park High School, in the Southeastern region, where days ago a power outage took down millions of mobile phones. The few remaining students and faculty in the building have been evacuated. Sources tell us that traces of bomb paraphernalia and detonators were located on school grounds. The local Reinforcement Division is not releasing the suspect's names at this time. However, UNN received a tip that a group of students from the school may be involved. We take you live to our reporter covering this developing story. What can you tell us about the situation?"

The camera panned across the school's parking lot full of ROs and Agents wearing the striped, red uniform. Although the reporter didn't specify, I got the district impression that the students he referred to were standing next to me. The thought made my blood run cold.

Quince squared his shoulders and approached Finley. "What's going on, man?"

Finley switched the set off. "I was told to get you somewhere safe before this aired. That's all I knew."

"Who told you this was going to happen?" Quince demanded.

"We're safe here?" Lela said.

Finley shook his head, glancing from Quince to Lela. "No. We need to leave."

He stuffed his brown leather bag with papers from his desk, slung it across his chest, and opened the bottom drawer of a metal file cabinet before filling the room with loud music that I didn't recognize. The music choice seemed so out of character for Finley, I had to take a step back. Fin was more of an old-school rocker type who liked to play air guitar while driving. Something felt off, but the music drowned out the questions I shouted his way.

Without warning, Finley wrapped his arm around my waist, pressing his body against mine. I'd never been this close to him before, and something inside me stirred. His chest felt strong and tight, and I wondered why I'd never noticed. He brushed his lips against my ear. My body shuddered. He had caught me unprepared, and my reaction troubled me. I tried to pull away, but Finley maintained his grip.

"Shut down your phone and put it inside the open file cabinet. Don't take it with you," he said, his gravelly voice a mix of confidence and fear. "Please, Rames. Trust me."

When Fin let go, I stood speechless, more from the sensation of our bodies touching than his words. Unable to meet his gaze, I fiddled with my phone, then placed it in the drawer. Finley whispered to Lela to do the same, and she and Quince dropped their phones next to mine as Finley locked the cabinet with a key.

I followed Finley out a side door I didn't even know he had while the music blared through the speakers. Once outside, he sprinted across the mulch toward a strip of tall cypress trees. We edged along the thick carpet of fallen branches, crossed a small creek, and ran uphill after Finley. As we approached the crest of the hill, Finley slowed near some pines that had dropped their cones and needles below.

"Finley! Stop, please," I begged. "What are we doing out here? And who is trying to bomb our school?"

He stopped, his eyes darting about, searching. Then he closed the gap between us and dropped his voice to a restrained whisper. "We are."

"That's ridiculous." Lela rolled her eyes. "Why would we bomb our school? If I had my phone, I would clear this up in two seconds with a post to Allicio."

"Allicio is exactly what we're avoiding," Finley said, walking between the pines.

Lela exhaled and jutted out her chin. "Why?"

"Okay, look. What do the four of us have in common?" Finley ducked under a large branch and held it back to keep it from popping me in the face.

I played along. "We all have phones."

"So does more than half of the world's population," said Quince, his voice rising in pitch. "So what?"

"Quince is right," I said. "Where are you going with this, Fin?"

Finley swallowed hard, making his Adam's apple bob up and down. "But half of the world's population doesn't have a STaR-issued phone. At least not yet. Dominic insisted Rami get the update on her phone. He *needed* you to have it."

My thoughts jumbled. "Oh-kay."

Finley took a slow, yet deliberate step closer to me. "The update contains a GPS tracker."

Chills ran down my spine. "Our phones have been tracking us ever since the software update?"

Finley nodded and adjusted the bag across his chest. "Yeah. A few months ago, Connect Mobile and Centurion bought a company called Topothesia. Sound familiar?"

Knots filled my stomach. "The company my dad works for. How—"

"Your dad developed Finder Seek, the perfect tracking app, and Centurion needed a tracker. Right before the merger finalized, they caused a mobile outage that required a software update. Everyone who got the update now has the tracker installed on their phone."

The day I tried to get the update at Connect Mobile, Little Miss Sunshine alluded to a merger, and Aunt Kate confirmed my suspicion. All the tech companies in Atlanta were actually controlled by STaR.

"That's how your aunt knew you were at Centurion's office that day," Finley continued. "She tracked you using the app your dad created. It's genius if you think about it."

Quince's face turned a shade of pink. "Genius? It's sick, man."

Finley's jaw tightened. "I didn't mean it that way. I meant...never mind. The point is that everywhere we've gone, Centurion finds us first. They've been one step ahead of us the entire time."

CHAPTER 32

Friday, October 6

We reached a building entangled by a thick band of vines. Cobwebs surrounded the place, and I brushed a spider from my shirt. Finley dug through the vines and a large metal door came into view, revealing an abandoned service station. Within months of taking office, President Young decreased oil production which forced car manufacturers to increase electric vehicle production. The need for gas stations decreased and most eventually closed their doors.

Finley yanked at the stuck door, lifted it overhead, and motioned us inside. A rusted truck sat above a workstation in the center of the room, its parts stripped clean, and spare parts lay strewn across the cement floor.

"What is this place?" Lela asked, wiping away a spider web.

"I used to come here as a kid with my friends. Our hideout. Virtually invisible on satellite." Finley set his satchel on the dusty floor and pointed to the car batteries piled in a corner. "We got those working once. A little wire and one battery later, we attached it to my go-kart. Ran it until we crashed it into the gas pump."

I tried to visualize young Finley racing go-karts, back before his computer and phone were the most important things in his life. I removed a wrench from a rickety wooden crate. "Is this yours?"

Finley grinned. "I remember this old thing. My dad gave it to me when I was twelve. I lost it and he grounded me for a week." He rubbed his thumbs over the handle.

I'd never met Finley's dad. His parents divorced when he was five, and his mom never remarried.

Lela gestured to a stack of oil cans filled with bullet holes. "What happened there?"

"Target practice," said Finley. "We lined them up outside and shot them with a BB gun."

I did a double-take. "*You* shot a gun?"

"There's more to me than you realize." Finley lifted one eyebrow and one side of his mouth curled upward.

My face flushed with heat, caught off-guard. *Again*. Never in my wildest dreams would I have imagined my friend—turned hacker—shooting a gun. The realization both excited and terrified me. I wanted to ask him a million questions, to clarify what happened between us earlier. But my feelings for him, if that's what they were, would have to wait. There had to be a reason he led us to the middle of nowhere and away from cameras.

I collapsed onto the crate and leaned forward, resting my elbows on my knees. "Fin? What does the tracker on our phones have to do with the bomb threat at school?"

"Remember when Dominic shot at us? While the ROs were busy investigating the shooting, someone ransacked Rami's house looking for the stolen computer codes. The shooting was a distraction, just like this bomb threat. Right now, National Agents are swarming Peachtree Park High, looking for a bomb that's not there."

Quince narrowed his gaze. "How do you know all this?"

Finley interlocked his fingers atop his head. "Look, man, all I can tell you is I've been in touch with someone who warned me."

Now it was my turn to question him. "Who warned you?"

"I did," a voice replied, emerging from behind me.

My heart stopped. I turned around. "Aunt Kate?"

Quince lunged at Kate. "Who are you and what the—"

"If you'll let me, I'll explain everything." Kate threw her arms up in surrender.

Finley stepped between Kate and Quince. "Kate Evans works for Centurion, the ones responsible for the outage, the shooting, and the disappearance of Mrs. Carlton. I hid her here until I could be sure they didn't trail us."

"They?" Quince's face reddened.

Ignoring Quince, Kate crouched on the floor in front of me. "Everything Finley told you is true. The software update is a GPS tracker."

Kate placed her fingers on either side of my face. On her right hand, a tiny laceration had been badly stitched. Dried blood crusted around the wound. Although I wanted to ask her about it, my anger surged. I peeled Kate's fingers from my face and gritted my teeth. "Why did Centurion install a tracker on our phones?"

Kate shrugged. "It was easier. Less painful and less intrusive than a microchip. No one would know the difference." She picked up Finley's rusty wrench and studied it. "A long time ago, this wrench tightened and loosened bolts. It served its intended purpose. But after some time, and perhaps being left out in the rain a few too many times, it rusted and was no longer useful."

"Thanks for the science lesson on corrosion. Your point?" Quince interrupted, vocalizing my exact thought.

Kate set the wrench on the ground, wiped her dirty hands on her jeans, and gazed at the back wall of the old garage. "Social networks understand everyone has a belief system. If they divide us based on our beliefs, we can be controlled, manipulated if you will. Social media's original intent was to connect people, to share ideas and common thoughts, to agree peacefully with civility. But over time, its intended purpose changed."

Anger surged with each rise and fall of my chest. "You haven't answered my question, Kate. A tracker for what?"

"Three years ago, Connect Mobile hired Centurion to create a social media app called Allicio. Heard of it?" A smirk filled her face.

"Of course we've heard of it," Lela said. "So have two billion other people."

Kate nodded. "Download the app on your STaR-issued device and the Threats Division has every piece of information on you at their disposal. And not just in America. Every user worldwide who downloads Allicio has a digital profile that the TD can access. STaR can use the data to exploit anyone anytime they want. While kids your age love Allicio, some people who remember life before STaR, before President Young, think the app as dangerous.

"Rumblings of a resistance began circulating online, using STaR's own social media app. The Threats Division tried to shut down anyone spreading disinformation and suppress what they perceived as propaganda, but TD workers assigned to Allicio are overworked and understaffed. That left space for resisters to communicate and organize."

"Organize what?" I asked.

"Revolution. STaR needed a way to keep the next generation—" Kate swung her arms around the room. "—your generation from *wanting* to overthrow the government."

Quince's nostrils flared. "How are they going to do that?"

"By convincing everyone that they're safer under STaR's control. Bifurcation Tracking, the program my team and I developed, divides individuals into groups based on what they believe. Centurion assumed if we could understand a group's belief system, we could use that data to either encourage certain content or suppress the posts." Kate spoke rapidly, her words clipped.

I placed my fingertips on my temples. "Let me get this straight. You installed a tracker in our phones so you could control our social media?"

She placed her hands below her chin and let out a long sigh. "So we can control *you*. Manipulate what you see on Allicio to encourage you to think a certain way. Gradually change your perspective, leaving you with the impression that STaR wants what's best for you. Governments of the past often used propaganda to control their citizens." She paused, though whether for our sake or hers I couldn't determine. "I swear to you I tried to stop the program, but I was too late. The only option was to copy the data."

"Why didn't you destroy the data?" Quince shouted.

"It's not that easy. The Threats Division controls Connect Mobile and Centurion. We're constantly monitored." She held out her right hand and rubbed the wound with her other thumb. "Every Connect Mobile employee and contractor is microchipped, including me. At least I was until I cut it out. My best chance of stopping this thing was to copy the data onto a micro flash drive and let someone outside the organization disable the program."

"The other half hidden," I muttered, recalling Kate's words.

Kate nodded. "I saved the other half on a SIM card, similar to the one on your phone. It contains an extensive database of everyone Centurion is watching."

I let out a loud sigh. "Why two different files?"

"The code fit on an encrypted flash drive, but the contacts were another issue. They had to be stored as a mobile file because that's where most people access Allicio."

I scooted in my seat, the crate suddenly hard and unforgiving. Exactly the way I felt toward Kate. "My mom doesn't know the first thing about coding. Why involve her?"

"Annie convinced me what STaR is doing is wrong. If I had listened sooner, none of this would have happened." A tear trickled down Kate's cheek. "Centurion was on to me. They knew I'd defected. I needed to give the codes to someone I trusted. Someone who could deliver them into the right hands. Annie and I planned to meet at Topothesia the day she disappeared, thinking a public place would rouse less suspicion. She was going to hand the files to the group."

I blinked over and over to clear my head. "What group?"

Kate wiped her cheek and swallowed hard. "The Threats Division is holding Annie hostage because your mom is part of The Resistance."

CHAPTER 33

Friday, October 6

My mind swirled like the fall leaves that gathered in our yard. *This is bigger than you, Rami. Larger than any of us*, Kate had said. But my mom involved in a resistance? No way. Anger surged through my veins and I jumped up, ready to bolt. "You're lying. My mom would never be involved in something so reckless."

Kate sighed. "Late night meetings at church? Secret outdoor gatherings?"

I shook my head. "She led a support group for those suffering from chronic illness."

"She led meetings for The Resistance," Kate insisted.

"No, no, no," I shouted through a clenched jaw. I sank to the ground, burying my head in my hands. Why hadn't Kate told me this before? How could she keep this from me? For fifteen days, my mother had been missing, and all this time Kate knew who took her? Deep sorrow replaced my anger as I pictured my mom tortured, or possibly dead. Kate's involvement with Centurion had cost me everything.

Kate sat down on the dirty floor next to me. "God, if I could go back and do it all over again."

"But you can't. You made your choice, Aunt Kate, and my mom suffered the consequences." Tears burned my eyes as they spilled onto my cheeks. "How could you, Kate? How could you leave her and not turn yourself in instead?" But even as the words escaped from my lips, I knew the answer.

Kate reached for my shoulders. "Think about it, Rami. What do you know about your mom?"

Mom refused to speak out against STaR. Ever. She chastised me for doing so the day she vanished. Love, loyalty, family devotion. Words Mom preached to Zac and me. Even after Dad left, my mother refused to speak ill of him, refused to turn against him. While hate harbored in my heart, Mom forgave and continued to love those who hurt her. "You need to forgive your father," she'd said. "Bitterness is like a cancer, Rami. It creeps inside our bone marrow, eating us from the inside out. We grow cold and angry, and become incapable of loving others." The realization hit like a tidal wave.

"Mom wouldn't give you up," I said, my words barely audible.

Kate lowered her head. "Annie made me swear to finish this, no matter what happened. She kept saying, 'You have to stop this, Kate.'"

A few weeks ago, my mother cut her hair to look exactly like Kate, styling it the way Kate does. She placed my horse trophy front and center on the family room bookshelves and slipped a picture of my horse Cinnamon into my duffle bag. Had she known the TD was after her?

As if reading my thoughts, Kate continued. "The TD planned to raid the church and arrest the resisters, like they've done in other regions. I think your mom intentionally took my place so I could destroy Centurion." Kate edged closer, cradling my chin in her hands the way my mother did whenever I was upset. "Rami, you and Zac are the most important people in Annie's life. She loves you more than anything in the world. We made sure Officer Murray was—"

"Officer Murray?" I interrupted.

"Is with The Resistance. He was supposed to protect you," she said.

Finley whistled. "That explains why a Reinforcement Officer raced to Rami's house the night Mrs. Carlton disappeared. We wondered how the case got classified as a missing person so fast."

Kate offered a half-smile. "You made it hard for Murray. Lying, running, keeping secrets."

I stood and spun in circles, my mind reeling. "That doesn't make sense. Officer Murray had all of us believing Dad was involved. The RD implied Mom was a victim of foul play. They interviewed my dad repeatedly."

"Murray had his suspicions about your dad, despite what I told him," Kate said. "Plus, he had to maintain his cover. Listen, there's so much more I need to tell you, but we're running out of time."

Quince set his jaw. "Hold on. You had an officer from the local RD precinct protecting Rami, yet Dominic still got to her? No wonder Rami's been so paranoid. She thought the ROs couldn't be trusted. But all along, the person she couldn't trust was you."

Kate hung her head at Quince's accusation. "I'm so sorry, Rami. You were never supposed to be involved. I had so many layers of protection set up in case anything went wrong." Kate stood and stared out the window, then turned to me, her expression pained with regret. "It seems Annie refused to reveal where she hid the

SIM card, so Dominic turned to Rami. He was probably told to scare you, but not to harm you. Otherwise, you'd be...well...you can figure that out. When he couldn't find the card on your phone, he ensured your cooperation by threatening the one person he knew you'd save."

"Zac," Finley and Lela said together.

"Zac," Kate repeated. "Now he had you. You'd do whatever it took to save Zac."

Dominic thought Mom had hidden the SIM card in my phone. That's why he wanted my phone. He needed me to have the update so he could track me. My body collapsed forward until my elbows rested on my knees. I buried my hands in my head, allowing my long hair to cover my shattered face.

"My mom left me clues along the way. The horse picture, the trophy standing feet above everything else on the bookshelf. She knew Dominic would go for my phone, so she hid it where only I would figure it out."

"I'm not surprised," Kate said. "She never told me where she hid it. But your mom would have done anything to keep you and Zac safe."

Lela wrapped her arm instinctively around my shoulder. "I'm still not getting something. If Dominic knew Rami found the hidden chip, why not grab her yesterday?"

Kate gave her an intense gaze. "Dominic counted on Rami to bring them to me."

Lela exhaled. "And she did."

Kate nodded her head. "It's me they want. To stop me from destroying the program I created. Starting over would take years and cost millions of dollars. The TD will do anything to retrieve that data. It needs to get into the hands of The Resistance. Their techies will insert a virus to destroy the program. In exchange for the files, I made Officer Murray promise to protect you kids. He'll take you to a safe house. You'll be back in a day, two days max, and Officer Murray will clear your names from the school bombing."

"Whoa." Quince ran his fingers through his curly afro, making it stand up tall. "Safe house? Nope, not me. I'm not going anywhere with you."

"What about our parents? Do they know we're not coming home?" Lela asked.

"They know you're safe. That's all I could share with them. The less they know, the better," Kate insisted.

I formed my lips into a small O shape as I inhaled and exhaled, practicing the breathing technique Mom had taught me to use whenever I woke from a terrible nightmare. I stood defiantly in front of Kate. "I'm not leaving Zac."

"Zac will be safe. Zac, Ian, and Olivia will have twenty-four-seven protection," Kate said.

I planted my feet firmly in place. "It's non-negotiable."

Kate groaned. "I told Murray you'd say that. Like mother, like daughter."

"Look, lady," Quince said. "You have some wild theories and crazy stories. I don't want any part of this."

"Like it or not, you are a part of this," Kate replied. "Guilty by association, so to speak."

Lela's sad eyes roamed from Quince to me. "We're Rami's pawn chain, Quince. Remember?" She spun around to face me. "Wait! Quince doesn't have the update. He hates social media, never uses it. If no one is tracking him, he could stay here and be our eyes and ears. Break up with me, Quince."

"What?" Quince drew up his lips.

"I'm crazy, delusional, and hang out with conspiracy theorists. It will be our cover story," Lela continued, manic with ideas. "I disappear and you become our spy."

"Our informant," I said, mulling it over in my mind. "It just might work."

Finley rubbed his chin. "Prophylaxis."

"What?" I asked.

Finley surveyed the room, his self-assured gaze landing on me. "Another chess term. To prevent beforehand." When I frowned, Finley explained. "Prophylactic thinking means looking for a threat, or what move you think your opponent wants to make, then stopping the threat before it happens."

Kate groaned. "This isn't a game, Finley. The Threats Division will stop at nothing to get this information. Our lives are all in danger."

"Then we keep Quince out of danger." Finley gathered his things and shoved Quince toward the door. "Get out of here, man. Get as far away from this place as you can. Leave your phone where it is. I'll buy you a new one when I get back."

Quince bristled, but gave a slight nod. "Lela? Please don't do this. Let me take you home."

Lela threw her arms around Quince and tears spilled onto his shirt. "I'm sorry. I have to stay with Rami. But I'll be back soon. I promise." They kissed until Finley cleared his throat.

"Go, Quince. Please," Finley pleaded. He opened the door and Quince disappeared through a tangle of vines.

Within minutes, the crunch of gravel beneath car tires filled the quietness of our space. Kate stepped outside and crept toward a parked car hidden in a patch of thick brush. I wondered why I hadn't noticed it before. Finley raced to the window, and Lela and I ducked below, watching a dark sedan emerge from the nearby woods and park near Kate's car. Kate opened her car door and retrieved a small white envelope, leaving her door ajar. She handed the envelope to Officer Murray who tucked it inside his jacket. Then he leaned into Kate, as if to kiss her, but she turned, and the embrace landed on her cheek. He took her hands in his and Kate nodded at something he'd said. They parted and together ambled our way.

The two stepped inside and searched the dark room until she spotted us crouched below the front window. "Rami? Officer Murray is here. He'll take you to the safe house. I'll gather your belongings and bring them as soon as I can."

No one moved. Perhaps the others felt as skeptical of this plan as me. *Could we trust Kate?* And how did we know Murray was trustworthy? Although I'd asked to speak with him at the RD precinct, I still had my doubts about his loyalty.

Emotions tumbled inside like sheets in a clothes dryer. "Where will you go?"

Kate gave Murray a sidelong glance. "I need to fix this. I'll bring your mom home, Rami. I promise." She held out her arms in a wide embrace, and I went to her, allowing the warmth of her body to envelop me. It was a small but powerful gesture.

Finley, Lela, and I moved toward the exit when Murray's handheld sounded.

"Murray? We've got company."

CHAPTER 34

Friday, October 6

The humming of incoming drones filled the silent space. Officer Murray let out a string of four-letter words before shoving me to the ground. "Get down." Gunfire ricocheted off the aluminum garage door.

Lela covered her mouth to suppress what I assumed were screams. We climbed under the rusty truck, Finley trailing close behind. Then silence. Warning shots, perhaps, letting us know Dominic had found us? Every nerve in my body stood on end. Murray shuffled around the station, speaking in hushed tones into his handheld. Others answered in clipped conversation. A hand touched me, and I jumped, hitting my head on what was left of the truck's engine.

"Rami? Hand me the flash drive and SIM," Kate whispered.

"They're in my backpack." I pointed to the window where I had crouched with Lela when we heard Murray's car approach. I slid on my stomach to get out of the truck's cover and Lela grabbed me.

"Don't leave me, Rames." Her voice shook.

"I'll be right back. I promise."

I scrunched down and waddled across the room like a duck, scared out of my mind to stand up. When I found the backpack, I unzipped it and reached for the pink wrapper where I'd safely tucked the files yesterday. I had sealed the wrapper with strips of clear two-sided tape given to me by Olivia. She kept the tape in a small pink tin. If anyone had searched my backpack, they would have found the pink tin along with a box of feminine products and tossed them both aside.

Suddenly, I stopped and tucked the wrapper back into the tampon box buried deep in the backpack. Aware that Kate held out her hand expectantly, my doubts resurfaced.

When Kate emerged yesterday, she could have told me someone had kidnapped my mom. Why didn't she tell me? And why hadn't Mom told Kate where she'd hidden the SIM card? Did my mom doubt Kate's loyalty? Kate needed the SIM to destroy the program. Without it, Centurion would continue to hunt for her. But once she had both files in her possession, she no longer needed me.

"Once Zac and I are safe, I'll give them to you," I said, my tone more authoritative than I felt.

"Don't be ridiculous, Rami. Hand them to me! We don't have much time!"

"No. Not until Zac is safe." I zipped my backpack and clutched it close to my chest.

Kate's eyes bore into mine, and she held her palm in place. "I'll pick up Zac, bring him there soon. You can trust me."

I wanted to be wrong about Kate. I wanted to believe her. But trust didn't come easy for me and she had made it hard. Kate worked for the Threats Division. She created a program to spy on social media accounts with no thought as to the repercussions of her actions. When things got bad, she let her twin sister take the fall. What kind of person does that?

I wedged myself between the wall and a large metal barrel, my voice almost inaudible. "Get Zac to safety, then I'll hand the files over to you. You have my word."

Kate's face reddened to a deep crimson, and I thought for a second she'd pounce on me and grab the backpack. Instead, she glanced over her shoulder and lowered her voice so no one couldn't possibly overhear. "How did Dominic know we were here?" She shook her like her thoughts had become jumbled, and she wanted to reorder them. "Rami? Hold on to the files until *I* get to the safe house. Do *not* give them to anyone else. Do you understand?"

I frowned, unsure whether I'd heard her correctly. But before I could clarify, Murray interrupted.

"Kate. Go. Now. The men outside will cover you," he said.

Kate locked me in her gaze, then backed away. "I'm not the enemy, Rami."

"Follow me," Murray commanded.

Finley threw his arm over Lela and whisked her down a set of stairs. But I lingered behind, watching Kate. Had I done the right thing by keeping the files?

"Rami! Let's go!" Finley sprinted toward me, waving his arms like an airport runway worker guiding an aircraft.

I glanced outside one last time as Kate reached her car. The driver's door remained open, just as she had left it. She climbed inside and turned on the ignition.

Boom!

The ground beneath me erupted, tossing me into the air like a doll. My body hit the concrete bay, causing extreme pain.

Muffled noise. A high-pitched tone in my ear. Shattered glass from blown-out windows lay all around. Smoke filled the room, each breath becoming more painful than the next. The pain in my ribs made it difficult to breathe. *Fire outside. Fire next to me. It was everywhere.* Finley lay motionless next to me. I reached for him. *Too far away.*

Dark spots filled my eyelids as I struggled to stay awake. I rolled to one side, attempting to climb to my knees. Bits of glass sank deeper into my skin. I screamed, only no sound escaped. The smoke had stripped my voice away. Heat scorched my skin and the smell of burning fuel filled my nostrils. Someone grabbed Fin and dragged him away. My eyes opened and closed. A man stood over me, helping me to my feet. My legs collapsed under me as he pulled me away from the flames that threatened to engulf me.

Fire. Explosion. Kate.

The memories came flooding back in rapid succession. I tried again to scream, but only a puppy-like whimper escaped my lips. "I can't leave her. I can't leave her."

Someone shoved me into a car. Muffled voices. The stench of burned flesh. Finley bent over, gasping for air. Lela shaking me. I was hysterical. Kate's car burned out of control. Debris filled the driveway.

"Stop! Help her!" I tugged at the locked door handle, slamming my hands against the window until they stung, my wails falling on deaf ears. "I'm sorry, Kate. I'm so sorry."

As Kate's lifeless body faded in the distance, so did my hope of ever finding Mom alive.

CHAPTER 35

Friday, October 6

I awoke with a start, unsure whether I had passed out from exhaustion, smoke inhalation, or both. A soft blue light shone from a panel near the windshield. Outside, the dark sky matched the ache in my heart. I tried to swallow, but my throat burned. Someone pressed a water bottle into my hand.

"Here. Drink this," the man ordered. I opened the bottle and drank its cool contents, glancing sideways at my captor. His light blue eyes were red and puffy. My eyes squeezed shut at the memory of Kate holding hands with the man next to me. The man she'd trusted to keep me safe.

My mind wandered back to the morning when everything changed. The faint smell of a burned bagel creeping upstairs, my mom glued to the news about a power outage. What if I had never left the house that day? What if I had pressed Mom for answers? What if I hadn't lied to Zac, Dad, and the RD? We'd be at home with Mom in boring Atlanta, where nothing bad ever happened. And Kate would be... I stopped myself as tears filled the corners of my eyes.

"How long was I out?" I asked, my scratchy voice barely above a whisper.

Officer Murray didn't look at me. "One hour, give or take."

"Kate? Is she...?" I couldn't bring myself to ask what deep down I already knew. Murray offered a slight nod. "And my mom?"

"I don't know," he said, his eyes never leaving the road.

Fear rushed to the surface. They tried to kill me. They murdered Kate. Zac would be next. This wasn't supposed to happen. Kate said we'd be safe. She said she'd bring my mom home.

I lowered my head and sobbed. It started as muffled tears but grew into loud, painful cries that made my ribs ache. It hurt to breathe. It hurt to be alive knowing other Kate was dead and my mother's life hung in the balance. Lela sat up and wrapped her arms around my neck. I held onto her like a floatation device to keep me from drowning in sorrow.

When my tears dried, I wiped my cheeks and turned to face Finley. His shallow breaths fogged the window. A gash on the side of his forehead, red and swollen, gave way to a trail of dried blood.

"Fin? You shouldn't have come back for me. You could have been killed." Finley glanced in my direction, his expression hard to read. "Are you okay?"

He held a bottle to his lips, drank the remaining water, and turned back to the window without answering. Maybe he hadn't heard me. My ears rang, and I wasn't sure if my voice was even audible.

When will this nightmare end? Once again, I had put my friends in danger. I finished my water and turned to Murray, picturing him standing close to Kate minutes before she died. I imagined the words they must have exchanged and suddenly I understood. "You were in love with Kate, weren't you?"

Murray bobbed his head ever so slightly and brushed at a tear that leaked down his cheek. It was the first sign of emotion I'd seen in him. "We're almost at the safe house. You should rest while you can." He moved away from me and leaned against the outside door.

I didn't press the issue with him. I didn't need to. Murray told me all I needed to know, and my heart broke for both of us. We continued driving in silence, lost in our shared grief, winding around narrow two-lane roads that seemed to go on forever. We hadn't passed another house or even a car for miles.

As Murray drove in silence, I studied the car. ROs all drove the same car—black electric vehicles with four doors. They were easy to spot, and most kids knew how to avoid detection. But this one was different. An older model with no electronic monitor on the dash. The windows contained a tint so dark, no one could possibly see inside. With few streetlamps to illuminate the inside, I hadn't noticed the contents of my backpack sprawled across the floorboard at my feet until now. Officer Murray must have grabbed it during the explosion. Although I don't remember unzipping it, the explosion had knocked me unconscious, so my memory of the day's events might not be reliable.

I reached down to pick up everything, including the pink box of tampons, but it was empty. I tossed a stack of papers aside in search of the one wrapper I'd resealed with glue. At the very bottom of the backpack, tangled with my hair clip, I found the wrapper containing the flash drive and the SIM card.

I stared at Officer Murray leaning against the driver's side window. Had he rifled through my backpack when I was asleep? Did he dump the tampons out, or had they fallen out during the craziness of the explosion when he'd tossed the unzipped backpack into the car?

Murray turned onto a one-lane, semi-paved road, and we hit a rut. The car bounced, and Finley cried out in pain.

I whipped my head around. "Fin? You okay?"

Finley gave a slight nod and closed his eyes without answering. I faced the front and assembled everything inside my backpack the way I'd remembered it before the explosion.

On one side of the road, a meadow ran along a narrow creek. On the opposite side was a steep rock wall that extended up as far as the eye could see. Murray rounded a curve to a gravel driveway, then traveled straight up a mountain with tall pine trees on both sides. The car leveled out in front of a tiny cedar cabin with an evergreen-colored tin roof. On the front porch stood two men in bulletproof vests with high-powered weapons strapped across their shoulders. My muscles tensed. If we were safe, why did we need guards with weapons? The men approached the vehicle, and I got the distinct impression that they'd rather be anywhere in the world other than babysitting a bunch of kids.

Murray ushered us inside a small living space with a stacked stone fireplace against one wall with an empty cedar mantel above. Wood paneling that led up to cedar beams on the ceiling lined the remaining walls, forming the A-frame shaped roof. Although the open floor plan afforded a view of every room, the cabin felt dark and cramped. A beige sofa and two beige chairs sat in the main room, divided by a coffee table made from logs. One bedroom rested beyond the fireplace and another behind the staircase that led to an upstairs loft. A narrow hallway opened to a small kitchenette. Chills trailed up and down my spine.

"There's two bedrooms, two bathrooms, and a loft with couches. It's not fancy, but it's safe," he explained. "They've stocked the kitchen with food, so you should have everything you need. Keep the curtains drawn and stay inside. Don't venture out for any reason." Murray pointed to the men, who looked more bored with each passing minute. "They'll take off in the morning and two others will take their place, so if you see a car or two, don't be alarmed. Sorry to drop you off like this, but I can't stay." His voice cracked. "I don't want to rouse suspicion. I've assigned myself to the team working on your school's bomb threat. It's going to be a long night."

I turned to go, but Murray grabbed my shoulders, clutching them with such extreme force, I winced in pain. He lowered his voice to a mere whisper. "Give me the flash drive and SIM. That's our best chance of stopping Centurion." The sudden personality change gave me pause, and I didn't move. Murray's clenched his teeth. "Now."

"Did you go through my backpack after the explosion?" I asked, wondering if he could hear the anxiety in my words.

His face contorted. "What? No. Look, if you have the files—"

"I gave them to Kate," I lied, cutting him off. "At the gas station, before the explosion."

Murray tightened his grip. "I need those files, Rami. That's the only way."

I swallowed my fear as the lies flowed effortlessly. "Kate told me to keep them safe, no matter what."

"You were supposed to turn them into me! I got you here. You're safe. That was our agreement." When I stayed silent, Officer Murray cursed under his breath and dropped his grip. "Well, I guess it's over then."

He held my gaze, and his expression shifted. Relief? Resolve? I couldn't be sure. With that, he turned to go and locked the door behind him. Thin curtains covered every window, and a modest lamp resting on a wooden table in the corner provided the only light source. The darkness matched what I felt inside. I stood motionless in the dimly lit room, absorbing the shock of being abandoned.

Murray was in love with Kate. But when I'd told Kate I would give the files to him as soon as Zac reached safety, she changed course, instructing me to only give them to her. *I'm not the enemy*, she'd said. None of this made sense.

Lela looped her arm through mine. "What was that all about?"

I watched Murray drive away. "Nothing. Come on. Let's check this place out."

Finley sighed. "I'll take this room and you guys take the front bedroom."

Fin strolled to the room behind the stairs while Lela led the way to twin beds with matching quilts in patterns of evergreen trees, black bears, and deer. A cedar dresser sat opposite the beds with five drawers and an old-fashioned alarm clock. We didn't need the drawers. We wouldn't be here long enough to bother unpacking. Plus, we didn't even have any belongings.

Lela took one look around and collapsed on the bed, facedown. I searched the bathroom for first aid supplies but came up empty. I drifted to a tiny kitchenette with a mustard yellow refrigerator no taller than Zac and a matching yellow stovetop and oven. A round plastic-topped table with four chairs covered in yellow-daisy plastic fabric sat near a bay window. *How old is this place?*

I opened and closed cabinet doors until I found a red first aid box in an upper cabinet and a pair of scissors in the drawer beneath. From the box, I selected an antiseptic wipe packet, a tube of antibiotic ointment, a large gauze pad, and a roll of cloth tape. Finley wandered in and collapsed into one of the yellow chairs.

I brought the supplies to the table and sat down, leaning in close. "I need to get that cleaned up." He didn't answer, just gave a slight nod as I tore open the antiseptic wipe and massaged away the dried blood. Finley winced, and I pulled back. "Sorry. It's kind of deep. You really should have stitches." I continued taping the gash with the wipe until it appeared somewhat clean, then applied the antibiotic ointment to a large gauze pad and held it up. "Here, hold this while I cut the tape." I cut several strips of tape and stuck them to the gauze. "That will hold for now, but you should change the bandage every few hours."

After washing my hands, I pulled a long flesh-colored bandage from the red box. I sat in the chair next to Finley, pulled up my shirt, and wrapped it around my ribs. Its compression brought a welcome relief to my aching ribcage.

Finley nodded again, then seemed to gather his words. "Did you really give the files to Kate?" I shook my head, ashamed of my lies. "Why didn't you hand them to Officer Murray?"

I explained Kate's response just before she died, how she didn't want me to give them to anyone except her. Finley listened without comment, as if the reality of our situation had just sunk in. I needed him to make sense of everything for me, but he stood without a word and riffled through the cabinets until he located a jar of peanut butter. He spread the peanut butter onto two pieces of bread and smashed them together. He had hardly spoken since we left the station, and I had no idea where to begin.

"I reached for you, you know. In the explosion..." My voice trailed off as a sudden surge of emotion swept over me.

He fumbled with the twist tie on the bread, then lowered his head. "It's not your fault."

I sprang out of the chair and closed the distance between us. "Yes, it is. All of this is my fault."

This time, he turned to face me. "You would have done the same for me. Right?" For reasons I couldn't explain even to myself, I hesitated before answering. In that split second, Finley turned back to his sandwich. "Guess that says it all."

I touched his arm. "Fin?"

"Forget it, Rames. The moment is over."

I stood there, unable to formulate a response. *Why am I so emotionally disabled?*

Lela eased into the room and looped her arm through mine. "Rami would have done the same for any of us, Finley. She tried to save me the day of the shooting. What she's been through, well, there are no words."

Finley dropped the peanut butter knife in the sink. "We're safe. That's what counts." He turned back to the countertop. "More importantly. Does anyone want a sandwich?"

I stared at him in disbelief. "How can you possibly think about food right now?"

Finley shrugged. "I'm a guy. We're always hungry."

He sat at the table devouring his sandwich, but I couldn't stomach food at a time like this. Lela sat motionless. I scooted my chair closer to Lela. "Hey. Let's eat at The Orient tomorrow night after the game, okay? We're going to win tomorrow's game, you know."

"Yeah. Sure." Lela pretended to smile.

"The powerhouse starting lineup." I smiled. "You'll see."

When Lela didn't respond, I stared into the dark night sky. A sense of foreboding washed over me. What had I gotten us into?

CHAPTER 36

Tuesday, October 10

It had been four days since Officer Murray dropped us off in the middle of nowhere, with no word from him. Four days, eleven hours, and twenty minutes, to be exact. It wasn't that bad, if you liked beans from a can soaking in sticky syrup and macaroni from a box with some sort of powdered cheese. I was pretty sure these foods were not STaR approved.

Kate had promised we'd be back in one to two days, but that was before she died in a car bombing. Only one of Kate's promises came true. In the wee hours of the morning, someone brought Zac to the safe house. Zac woke me from a fitful sleep, and I held onto him longer than necessary. When he complained that hugging me was too much, I dropped my arms and followed him around the cabin for the next three days like a whimpering puppy who misses its mama, refusing to let him out of my sight.

Each day, I adjusted the compression bandage around my ribs as my breathing improved. The body aches and headaches had subsided, but the ringing in my ear lingered and my voice remained scratchy.

If the guards around our so-called safe house had any details about my mom or how The Resistance planned to expose Centurion, they hadn't said. I would have snuck out and taken Zac home by now if not for the constant watch. Four guards rotated morning and night, scanning the perimeter for intruders. They reminded me of Doberman pinschers, growling the second my toe hit the deck. Each day, I asked who they worked for, but all four refused to answer. They couldn't be RD employees, so how did Murray know them?

By mid-week, I nicknamed each guard, more out of boredom than anything else. Every afternoon, Donut and Muscolo showed up before the sun set. The two could not be any more different. Donut's belly made the buttons on his shirt pop open when he adjusted the belt around his thick waist. His short stature and oversized middle gave him the appearance of a pastry I once ordered from a bakery downtown. I wondered what Donut would do if he actually had to chase someone. Seems to me he'd fall flat on his face, or in this case, his belly.

His partner, Muscolo, the Italian word for muscle, must have spent every waking moment at the gym when he wasn't babysitting us. Regardless of temperature, he wore tight short-sleeved t-shirts that looked painfully constricting on his thick arms. In our limited conversations, Muscolo revealed through his accent that he had grown up in the Bronx. Standing well over six feet, he towered above Donut, giving him an edge for spotting oncoming interference. Muscolo reminded me of a drug lord. The resemblance should have made me feel safe, considering a gang was after me. But something about the guy scared me half to death. I stayed out of sight when he was on duty.

In the mornings, Freckles and Blue showed up as the sun rose above the mountains. I had learned in my brief exchanges with Blue that he had served in the Navy before STaR took over the organization. I supposed he had gotten used to wearing the same color because I'd never seen him in anything except blue. Not a boring blue like ROs wore, but a vibrant blue like my favorite butterfly. Today, Blue wore an azure-colored sock hat that covered his bald head and an azure turtleneck sweater.

Freckles was by far the more friendly of the two, although when Blue was around, she pretended not to notice me. Her caramel-colored complexion offered a stunning contrast to her almond-shaped eyes that scanned the yard effortlessly. A stunning shade of amber, her eyes held a slight twinkle whenever she ordered me inside, as if she and I would be friends under different circumstances. Her black hair held a tight curl, which each day she pulled into a bun at the nape of her neck. But it was her freckles, which stretched from forehead to chin, that gave her near-perfect skin tone its unique quality.

Each morning, I handed Freckles and Blue mugs of steaming hot coffee on the front porch. I learned that Blue took his coffee black while Freckles preferred sugar and only a splash of cream. I attempted to get information about Murray, but with each passing day, Freckles and Blue became more aloof in their responses, giving me the impression that things weren't going well back home.

The temperature had dropped to the low thirties, and I shivered as I handed the mugs to Blue and Freckles. Freckles cupped it between her hands, letting the steam vaporize on her face. Blue accepted the coffee, muttered a quick thanks, and set out to secure the perimeter. Once Blue began his rounds, I asked Freckles the same thing I'd asked since we arrived. Each day, she sipped her coffee without moving, as if expecting my question, and I got the feeling she would talk to me if it weren't for Blue.

"Have you heard anything about my mom?" I whispered. I could see my breath in the crisp air.

It seemed futile to ask, since Mom's chances of survival after all this time felt like less than one percent. With Kate out of the way, Centurion had no reason to keep my mother alive. But I refused to give up hope. Plus, every morning Zac asked what Freckles had said, and each day I continued to lie to Zac, explaining that Mom was safe. Lela said Zac needed the truth, but this was the only time Zac ever smiled. So, I kept up the pretense.

Freckles finished her coffee, handed the mug back to me, and stepped off the porch. "No, I haven't. I'm sorry."

Her answer was the same every time I asked, only today she added *I'm sorry*. It made me think I might break through her exterior wall. I followed her off the porch, not wanting to let her out of my sight yet. She gave me a slight shake of her head, a sign that I needed to go back to the house. But I had one more request. Tucked safely inside my sweater sat a letter I had written to Brannon. We never got to go out on our date, and I wanted to explain myself. Not that he would ever want to date me after the UNN implied I had planted a bomb at our school. But I thought he should hear it from me.

Quince was supposed to be our informant, but we had no contact with him or anyone else at home, so Lela wrote a detailed account of our situation, asking him to pass it on to Theresa May. We hoped Theresa would find Murray and get us out of here.

I handed Freckles one envelope containing Lela's letter to Quince and my letter to Brannon. "Freckles, wait." My face erupted in heat, traveling from my neck to my ears. "I... I mean, sorry, I don't know your real name."

She offered a half-smile, but a twinkle filled her amber eyes. "It's okay. What's this about?"

"Could you get this to Quince Harris? Please? It's important." I shuffled my feet on the frozen gravel walkway, desperately trying to come up with an excuse. "Halloween is coming up. The four of us always spend Halloween together at Lela's place." In truth, Lela and I spend Halloween together every year. Last year, when we met Finley and Quince, they became part of our tradition. But Freckles didn't need to know any of this.

She eyed me, then snatched the letter from my hand, tucking it into the pocket of her windbreaker. "Get back inside. It's freezing out here." Her concern for my warmth touched me, and as much as I wanted to keep her talking, I knew she had to follow orders. When I reached the bottom stair, Freckles tapped me on the shoulder. "I'll see what I can do."

Then she ambled toward the back of the house as Blue emerged around the corner.

CHAPTER 37

Wednesday, October 11

The loft came supplied with jigsaw puzzles and old board games I'd never heard of. It was like being transported to another dimension. After six days stuffed in a cabin, I played Monopoly six times, Battleship eight, and Scrabble twelve. I'd become quite literate at quirky words like *pyxidium*, *aryl*, and *zoarium*.

For days, Finley and Zac worked on a thousand-piece puzzle of the Amazon jungle, filled with waterfalls, rivers, monkeys, and tropical plants. Its bright colors were a warm welcome to the beige interior of the cabin.

Today, Zac selected Battleship, for which I was grateful after losing a million dollars' worth of property in Monopoly yesterday. At one point, I owned from Pacific Avenue to Boardwalk, but somehow Zac came out of nowhere to buy me out and force me into bankruptcy.

Zac placed the beat-up vintage box on the small coffee table between us, sliding one of the blue grid boxes to me. I set up my fleet, placing my ships on the bottom grid along the vertical and horizontal axes. We took turns firing shots by calling out grid coordinates and marking the hits.

"A7," said Zac.

"Miss," I said. "B12."

Zac grinned. "Miss."

Somewhere between E6 and E7, I narrowed the location of one of Zac's ships. "E7."

"Hit," Zac said. I continued along the E axis until Zac spoke the magic words. "You sank my battleship."

"Yes! After Monopoly, I deserve a win." I smiled at our friendly banter. But after Zac sunk my carrier occupying five spaces, my hopes of winning sank to the bottom of the sea.

"Guys," Finley shouted from the room below us, interrupting my plan to sink Zac's submarine. "Come check this out. Why didn't I think of this before?"

Zac gave me a sidelong glance, and I shrugged. We ambled downstairs, where Finley sat on the edge of the sofa holding a laptop—a laptop he wasn't supposed to bring to the cabin. He rubbed the gash on the side of his head, adjusting the medical tape away from the hairline. Lela stood in the open doorway to the bedroom, her expression hard to read.

"I thought we weren't supposed to have electronics because they're traceable," Zac remarked.

Finley pointed to a tiny black chip plugged into his USB drive. "Stealth IP. It keeps the network secure and is virtually untraceable. But that's not what this is about. I've been staring at the set of numbers and letters on Kate's flash drive for weeks—"

"Wait," Lela interrupted, facing me. "I thought you gave those to Kate?"

"Not exactly," I said.

Lela's eyes widened. "Rami? What's—"

"I made a copy, okay?" Finley interrupted, shooting me a quick glance. He turned up one side of his lip. "I assumed the patterns had something to do with the Bifurcation Tracking Analysis, but I couldn't figure it out. Battleship gave me the answer. See that? There it is."

"There what is?" Lela asked, leaning closer to the computer screen.

Finley stared wild-eyed. "The letters and numbers, they're coordinates. Longitude and latitude. But not just any coordinates." He gestured again to the map. "This, my friends, gives us the exact location of Centurion's headquarters. The mother ship data center."

"Whoa," Zac exhaled. "How do you know that?"

"Every computer that logs into a network has an identifiable code. I messed around with a few codes Kate had and traced two computers to a particular network. It's private, so I couldn't get an exact location. Until I put the two files together. By shifting the coordinates, this popped up." He moved his fingers across the touchscreen, enlarging the gray blob in the center of the map. "It's a building."

Lela stepped closer to the screen. "You're sure it's Centurion?"

"Positive. Once I entered the longitude and latitude coordinates, the activity blew up." Finley paused. "Sorry. Bad choice of words. The coordinates gave me the network location. Hit. Game over."

I tilted my head to the side. "So where is it?"

Finley shrunk the image and opened a new tab. "North of downtown, in the Southeastern region." He enlarged the image until patches of white became clear. "The topography is rocky.

And notice the patches of white on either side. What is the Southeastern region best known for?"

"Marble," Zac said without hesitation.

My mouth twitched, amazed at my little brother, who wasn't so little anymore. "Okay, but wouldn't The Resistance know about this location?"

"Only if Kate told them where to find it," said Finley.

"So, let's assume Kate told Officer Murray about the location. Why haven't they blown it up and come to get us?" Lela asked.

Fin's excitement waned. "That's what I want to ask Murray when he shows up. *If* he shows up."

CHAPTER 38

Wednesday, October 11

By late afternoon, exhaustion swept over me as I hashed out a plan to raid Centurion. Finley sat at the rickety kitchen table with his laptop. I stopped in the doorway and studied him, the way he ran his hands through his hair when he contemplated a tough decision, and how his head cocked to the right side when he read information on the internet. It felt so...comfortable. He threw a glance my way, and heat rose to my cheeks. I shuffled to the coffeepot with my head down.

"We're getting snow flurries," Finley said, bobbing his chin toward the window behind the small Formica table. "Can you believe it? It's not even November."

Outside, snow fell in tiny droplets, melting the instant it hit the ground. Snow dust swirled on the gravel drive and the tops of the trees swayed in the breeze. I wanted to race outside and capture the snowflakes on my tongue before they disappeared. But I couldn't. This cabin had become my captor.

Leaves crunched outside. The hum of a car. A chill shot through my veins. "Fin? Isn't it too early for shift change?" I peered out the tiny window above the sink, expecting Muscolo's black SUV.

Instead, Freckles raced past the window with her gun raised, and Blue pointed his weapon at the approaching sedan.

"Someone's here." My terse words filled the silent cabin.

I sprang into action, placing one finger against my lip and motioning for Zac to follow me to the bedroom I shared with Lela. She sat wide-eyed below the twin bed with the patched quilt wrapped around her. We huddled beneath the window as Finley peered behind the thin curtains.

Blue stood on high alert, his eyes searching. He approached the sedan, pointing his firearm at the window. Behind the sedan, Muscolo's black SUV roared up the hill. Donut and Muscolo jumped from the SUV, weapons raised, and sprinted in opposite directions around the tiny cedar cabin. When they returned, weapons lowered, Muscolo gestured to Freckles.

She opened the passenger door, and Quince bolted from the car.

Lela shrieked, sprinted across the cabin, and threw open the front door without a single ounce of hesitation, abandoning all protocol. I tried to stop her, to warn her it wasn't safe, but she ignored me and ran outside. Lela fell into Quince's arms, causing him to stumble backward. She buried her face in his winter coat. When he planted a kiss on Lela's lips, Zac turned away.

"Gross," he whispered.

But I smiled. My best friend had given up so much for me. Her happiness brought a sense of peace that everything would work out. I crept onto the porch, pulling my sweater tight around my waist as the bitter wind blew snow flurries all around me, and Zac and Finley stood close by.

Officer Murray climbed out next, releasing the back door for a tall figure with jet-black hair. My hands sprang to my mouth, covering a gasp, as Brannon Martinelli stepped toward the cabin.

"What's he doing here?" Finley said, his words tight and clipped.

"I... I'm not sure," I stammered.

"He shouldn't be here." Finley stormed past me and placed his finger in Murray's face. "Where have you been? And why is he here?"

Murray brushed past Finley. "Everyone inside. Now."

But I inched closer to Brannon, one cautious step at a time.

Brannon pulled me into an unapologetic hug. "Rami. Thank God you're okay."

My heart raced as his warm body pressed to mine. I ran my fingers along a large purple bruise on his right cheek, just below the eye. "What happened? Are you all right?"

Freckles tugged at my arm and shoved me to the porch. "You heard Officer Murray. Inside."

Brannon reached for my hand and together we entered the cabin behind the others. Finley stood near the stone fireplace, greeting Brannon with an icy stare. I dropped Brannon's hand and fiddled with my sweater to ward off the chill bumps that trailed down my arms. I wasn't sure which was colder—the temperature outside or the space between Finley and Brannon.

Lela and Quince snuggled together on the couch, Lela pummeling him with questions as Murray shut the door, leaving Blue and Freckles on the porch and Donut and Muscolo pacing the building's perimeter.

"What's going on, Quince? Did you get your phone back from Fin's basement? Can we leave now?" Lela's firing squad had begun.

"I imagine you all have a lot of questions," Murray interrupted.

"You think?" Finley's sarcastic tone surprised me, but I didn't blame him.

"Where is my mom? Did you rescue her?" Zac asked.

"Not yet, son," Murray said.

"Why not? You said we'd only be here for a day or two and that my mom would be safe." Zac swallowed hard.

I edged closer to Zac, keeping an eye on Officer Murray. Kate said I could trust him, but I was beginning to doubt her judgment. "You left us here for days with no word of what happened."

"Unfortunately, it couldn't be helped. Things got a bit more...complicated than I expected." Murray jutted his chin at Finley. "Can I talk to you for a second, Finley?"

Finley hesitated before following Murray into my bedroom. While we waited for his return, Lela and Quince whispered together, side by side on the sofa, and Zac fled to his room, leaving me alone with Brannon.

My throat went dry as I tried to form the words I'd rehearsed in my mind. "I didn't plant that bomb at our school, Brannon."

Brannon rubbed the gash on his face. "I believe you."

"You do?"

"Your letter. Quince gave it to me. Well, that plus *The Grove*."

I frowned, wondering what our school's news app had to do with my innocence. "*The Grove*?"

"Yeah. Theresa kept the story of you and your mom running every day. She said there was no way you could have planted a bomb when you were at her house that day after school." Brannon lowered himself onto a nearby chair, sinking into its soft cushion. "I never believed it was you anyway, for the record."

A smile formed, small at first, then encompassing my entire face. Theresa claimed to be my alibi the day of the bombing. The day I disappeared with Finley and Lela. *Why would she lie for me?*

"I'm just glad you're safe," Brannon said, interrupting my musing.

I crouched beneath him, sitting on my knees with my feet tucked underneath, tracing the sharp edge of his jaw to the bruise, which shifted between black and purple depending on the light. "Who did this to you, Brannon?"

His eyes held mine for a moment, then flickered upward. "Dominic Bell."

Dominic turned his rage on Brannon while I hid in this stuffy cabin, feeling sorry for myself. "How? Why?"

"Last night, after work, this guy jumped me in the parking lot of Little Cone. He wanted information about you, like why you weren't at school and stuff. He made it sound like you were in danger, and he was trying to protect you. Then he flipped out, like out of nowhere. The guy pulled me into a headlock, said I lied to him, and punched me in the face." Brannon clutched his cheek and winced. "I told him the truth, that I didn't have a clue where you were, but he didn't believe me."

I covered his hand with mine, stroking his bruised face. "I'm so sorry. I didn't mean to involve you in my problems."

Brannon leaned forward, resting his chin on the top of my head. "It's not your fault, Rami. I offered to help, and I let you down. I should have protected you." Brannon's sentiment filled me with warmth. He sat back in the chair. "The guy's a nutcase. My parents freaked out and demanded protection from the Reinforcement

Division. So, I came here for the night until they figure out what to do with me."

It was a lot to take in, and I needed a minute to process it. Dominic must have found out Quince was spying for us or saw Quince give the letter to Brannon. Maybe he thought I would reveal my location in the letter, only I'm not that stupid. So, he unleashed on Brannon. Brannon deserved answers, but I wasn't sure how much I should say.

I stood but didn't walk away. "I... I wasn't completely truthful with you when you asked me if I found something hidden at my house the day it got ransacked." I paused, searching his face for recognition. "The truth is, I found something. Something my mom had hid in case anything happened to her." I bit my lower lip and shuddered at the thought that Mom may have given herself up on purpose. "It's some sort of computer code. But I should probably talk to Officer Murray about it."

Brannon stood and lowered his voice to a mere whisper. "Do you still have it with you? Here?"

"What are you love birds whispering about?" Quince said.

Flustered, I hesitated. "Nothing, Quince."

Brannon edged closer, placing his lips against my ear. My skin tingled. "You hid it somewhere safe, right? Somewhere in the cabin, or maybe you gave it to Finley?"

I took a step back. "Look, I'll explain everything, but first I need to speak to Officer Murray." Brannon's lip twitched, but he simply nodded. I tiptoed to my bedroom, where I found Murray rifling through my things. I snatched my backpack and clutched it to my chest. "What do you think you're doing?"

Murray turned when I approached. “Grab a warm coat. Finley too. We’re going outside.” He charged out of the room, breezing past the others.

CHAPTER 39

Wednesday, October 11

Finley and I exchanged puzzled looks, but followed his instructions. We moved beyond the back deck to an old tool shed covered by tall birch trees. In the days since I arrived, the farthest I'd explored was the front walkway, and even that was breaking the rules. The shed smelled musty, and dirty garden tools hung against the wooden walls.

"I thought it best to speak in private." Murray's eyes searched the small space, landing on me. "So where are they?"

I glanced between him and Finley. "Where are what?"

"Don't play games with me, Rami," Murray said. "The Threats Division knows Finley accessed the data. Either you still have the original files and lied to me or Finley made a copy. Either way, we're all in danger."

I swallowed the fear that threatened to choke me. I shot Finley a look, but his face remained stoic. Years of chess had taught him how to keep his expression tight. "Really, Officer Murray. I don't know what you're talking about."

"Finley already admitted to locating Centurion's headquarters, so you can drop the innocent act, Rami. Lucky for you, Finley hid his location well. But it's only a matter of time before someone from the TD finds you. They want those files back and they won't stop until they have them."

Finley explained our plan to enter Centurion's data center, but Murray cut him off. "You can't walk into their headquarters. It doesn't work like that except maybe in an augmented reality simulation. As far as STaR is concerned, you're wanted terrorists." Murray's voice held an edge of condescension.

I bristled at his cocky disapproval. "Why didn't you shut them down and rescue my mom?" I held his gaze, mimicking his mocking tone.

"It's complicated," Murray said.

"Try me," I said.

He let out a long sigh, as if he'd been expecting this. "For twenty years, I served in the military, special ops unit, trained in international terrorism. STaR recruited me to an elite task force that works hand-in-hand with the Threats Division. I gather intel on internal threats, all while playing a local officer within the Reinforcement Division."

"And the guards? They're ex-military too?" I asked.

Murray nodded. "We served together. I called in a favor and they were happy to comply." I scoffed at the idea of anyone besides Freckles being happy to be here, but I kept the thought to myself. "They work in various positions in the government, but all believe in the cause."

I frowned. "Cause?"

"The RD has known about The Resistance for some time. Each region has their own unit and somehow they communicate with each other on Allicio, which is how I found Centurion. That's how I met Kate. I started investigating her and learned, like me, she'd defected."

"So you're an officer by day, spy by night?" I said.

Murray shrugged. "Something like that. Here's the point. I pass information back and forth to The Resistance while maintaining my position as the mole inside the RD, which means I have to operate under the guidelines of the RD. The Resistance needed Kate's files to take down Centurion. Without them, it will take months to duplicate Kate's work. You should have given them to me, Rami. Your lies cost us valuable time."

He let the words sink in as guilt plagued me. I lowered my head in shame as Murray continued. "The RD director asked me to find out who accessed the files. I had to lie to protect you. I told him it was someone inside the Threats Division." He turned up his lip. "I hate those guys. So, I blame it on Dominic Bell and tell the director he's a traitor. I assemble a team to bring him in when the director orders me to stand down."

Finley edged closer. "Who would have done that?"

"STaR's protector. Known only by code name The Guard. No one knows who runs The Guard or who's a member. They operate under the radar, with full government approval and few regulations. Their members exist inside every STaR division."

My shoulders stiffened. "You're telling me a covert government agency of spies told the spies within the Reinforcement Division to stand down?"

"Yes."

"So that's it? There's nothing else you can do?" When Murray didn't answer, fury quivered through my veins. "My mother has been missing for twenty days, Officer Murray. You've done nothing to recover her and now you're telling me this so-called secret government agency won't allow you to arrest Dominic Bell?" I clenched my jaw and shifted closer. "These people turned my life upside down. If you think for one minute I'm going to roll over and play possum, you're wrong."

Finley threaded his fingers through his wavy hair, the way I'd witnessed countless times. "Rames?" That one word in Finley's soft tone forced me to quiet down. Only Fin could speak my name in such a way that it felt calming, reassuring. He stepped between Murray and me. "Murray detected a lot of movement inside the building. There's a woman inside, Rami. She matches your mom's build."

My heart fluttered. "My mother is alive?"

Murray stiffened and shot Finley a sideways glance. "We don't know for sure. But if it is Annie, it means Centurion needs her alive."

I peered between Fin and Murray, narrowing my eyes. "What are you not telling me?"

Murray's self-assured demeanor vanished. "*If* she's alive, your mother is being held hostage."

The look on his face made me freeze. "Hostage? But why?"

"Because it's *you* they want."

My breath caught as dozens of thoughts emerged simultaneously. I placed a finger against each temple to ease the pounding inside my head. Cold chills trickled across my spine as if someone had poured ice in my shirt. *Bald Eagle wants me to find him.*

"He's going to kill me," I said. The weight of my words struck a chord, and Finley and Murray remained silent. I reached into the pocket of my sweatpants and pulled out the flash drive and SIM card, hoping and praying I wasn't too late to save my mom. Murray held out his hand, and I placed the micro files into his palm.

He offered a half-smile. "You can trust me, Rami."

I stood up straight, defiant. More determined than ever. "I'm going to stop Centurion."

"This isn't your fight, Rames," Finley said.

"It became my fight the minute they killed Kate!" Frustration seeped through my pores. Centurion had upended my life. "Kate left the files with me for a reason. You said I'm a pawn in their game, Finley. If you were in a chess match and one piece blocked you from the win, what would you do?"

"Remove the defender." Finley glanced from Officer Murray to me, tilting his head to the right. "A tactical chess move designed to distract the piece that's protecting the king. Stay three moves ahead of your competition. That's the winning strategy in chess. It means we remove whoever is defending Centurion's project."

I planted my feet in place and squared my jaw. "Officer Murray? Prepare to take down The Guard."

"You have no idea what you're saying, Rami." Murray's condescending tone returned. "Finley's right. Take out the defenders and eventually the king will fall. But The Resistance focuses on one layer at a time. They know what they're doing. You need to stay here until I tell you it's safe. Understand?"

I remained silent, holding his gaze as a plan formed in my head, knowing full well I would do anything in my power to save my mother.

CHAPTER 40

Wednesday, October 11

Darkness crept into the cabin as, one by one, each light flickered off. Across the room, Quince slept on the sofa with a pillow covering his head. From below the loft, Murray's light snoring created a rhythmic tone that should have lulled me to sleep, yet sleep evaded me.

Brannon and I sat shoulder to shoulder on the floor. He fiddled with the fringe on the woolen blanket draped over our legs and begged for an explanation. He listened, never interrupting, as I started from the beginning to finding Kate.

"My Aunt Kate worked for a tech company called Centurion, run by the Threats Division. She developed a tracking program for Allicio that—" I paused, gathering my thoughts. "Let's just say it's super creepy. Anyway, Kate saved the codes on a flash drive and my mom hid a SIM card in my house. The problem is, Centurion wants the files back."

Brannon's eyes went wide. "You have the files here? In the cabin? How did you manage that?"

"It's complicated."

"Whoa, Rami. No wonder they're after you." He leaned in close and for a second, I thought he wanted to kiss me. But he glanced over his shoulder and lowered his voice. "Did you make a copy?" I squirmed in my seat and tugged at my collar, unsure whether I should admit the truth. Brannon pulled me toward him until our bodies touched. "Hey? You can trust me. Okay?"

The unfamiliar sensation of our bodies colliding jolted me, making it impossible to think straight. My chest tightened as awareness flooded over me and my breaths became shallow. I rested my head against his chest, listening to his rapid heartbeat, unable to answer the question that hung in the air. *Could I trust Brannon?*

Brannon leaned in, his lips inches from mine. At first, his kiss felt soft and warm. When I responded, Brannon pressed against me, his body encompassing all of me until I was unaware of everything except for Brannon's lips. He kissed me deeply, longingly, leaving me breathless and desperate for more. He awakened a desire within me I didn't know existed. He pulled back and kissed my forehead, then stroked my arm. Goose bumps formed in quick succession as my skin prickled with desire.

I hadn't planned to kiss Brannon, but neither could I deny my attraction to him. The small nudge in my consciousness toyed with my emotions, forcing me to ask myself once again: Is Brannon trustworthy? I scoffed at the notion the instant the thought resurfaced. It was too late for that. I had already let down my guard. Fear crept its way into my thinking, and suddenly I needed to flee.

I untangled myself from his grasp and stood up. "I need to get some sleep."

"Wait." He grasped my waist, and I winced as pain shot through my injured ribcage.

I tapped my finger to my lips and pointed to Quince asleep on the couch across the room. I fell back to the floor, and Brannon threw the blanket over us and held me close. He closed his eyes and yawned. I felt I should leave. Everything in my brain told me to run, but my body stayed put. Never had I understood how strong a connection one might have to another human being, until now, when my brain and my body were at odds for control. Being with Brannon seemed right, as the hum of our heartbeats entwined in perfect rhythm.

Brannon's lips tickled my ear, his words almost inaudible. "How are you going to get your mom back?"

I debated my answer as my plan to overtake Centurion's headquarters seemed childish. How were a bunch of teens supposed to take down an expansive technology corporation whose tentacles interweaved throughout the government? And what would it cost my friends to follow me into such an attack?

"I'm going to raid Centurion's headquarters. I doubt Lela and Finley will join me, but I'm determined to make this work. Centurion's executives will never expect a kid to invade their data center and pull the plugs from their servers." I gave a slight chuckle. "Sounds ridiculous, right?"

When he didn't respond, I turned. Brannon was sound asleep.

CHAPTER 41

Thursday, October 12

A strong feeling of acceptance washed over me as I awoke to the rhythmic breathing of Brannon's body curled with mine on the loft floor. Someone whispered my name. A light flickered on, but I refused to open my eyes, wanting to hold on to this moment. Brannon stirred and pulled me close.

The voice grew louder. My eyes blinked open. Quince stood above me, mouth agape. Finley nestled against the door frame, his expression hard to read. *Anger? Jealousy?* When I jumped up, Brannon awoke and sat up straight. My eyes darted from Finley to Brannon, imagining how this must look. Before I could explain, Finley descended the stairs, leaving me to defend myself to Quince, who also retreated.

"Fin? Wait," I said, as the boom of the front door echoed in the loft. I opened my mouth to explain to Brannon, but the words lodged in my throat.

"Whatever, Rami," Brannon said, his voice holding a hint of defeat. "I thought we had something."

I bit my lower lip. "We do. I mean, I think we do. But Finley's my friend. I'm sorry. I need to talk to him."

Leaving Brannon alone in the loft, I climbed down the stairs, one painful step at a time, and walked outside. The sunrise cast a shadow on Freckles, who ignored me and scanned the yard. Blue glanced my way, clutched his weapon, then moved toward the woods. But my attention fell on Finley, hiding under a Boxelder maple whose low-hanging branches provided the perfect camouflage.

I edged closer, the crunch of fallen leaves alerting my arrival. "Fin?" He remained motionless. "It's not what you think."

Finley's lip twitched. "Really? Because that's not how it looked."

"I can explain." I heard the pleading in my voice, displaying a kind of weakness I thought I'd overcome.

Finley met me with a cold, hard stare. "I warned you about him. I told you I didn't trust him."

My shoulders slumped. "I know."

"And this is how you listen?" Finley clenched his jaw.

"Finley, let me explain. Nothing happened between Brannon and me."

He edged closer, one shoulder shifting upward. "It doesn't even matter at this point. You made your decision." I wrapped my arms around my waist to ward off the icy chill. "How much did you tell him?" When I didn't answer, Finley raised his voice. "Geez, Rami. Do you realize what you've done? You may have put us all in danger."

"I'm sorry." I choked back the words that threatened to drown me. "I like him."

Finley held my gaze as the tension hardened around the lines of his jaw. "Do you trust him?"

"Yes. I mean, I think so," I said, but there was no genuine conviction behind my words.

Finley gripped the tree until his knuckles turned white. "Think so or know so."

"I… I'm not sure."

"Well, too late now." Finley's enlarged pupils reflected the shame inside me. "You better hope you were right about him or we're all dead."

Slowly, I reached for Finley's arm. I needed his approval, longed for his acceptance, even if I didn't fully understand why. But he pulled away, creating a crevasse between us. "I didn't mean for things to happen this way. I didn't mean for *any* of this to happen." I squeezed my eyes shut, having a tough time forming the right words. "You didn't have to help me, you know."

Finley hesitated, appearing baffled, and a frigid expression emerged across his face. "No, Rames. I didn't *have* to. I did it *for* you." He turned without looking back.

What have I done? Just like my father, I'd broken trust and betrayed the one person who had helped me on his own accord. How would Finley understand what made little sense to me? My legs felt like stone pillars. I forced myself to return to the cabin where Brannon waited in the doorway.

"You're leaving?" I motioned to the bag thrown over his shoulder.

Brannon leaned forward and gently kissed my salty lips before wiping a tear from my cheek. "Finley hates me. Doesn't trust me."

My stomach tightened. "It's complicated."

"I don't want to come between you. Really, I don't."

I inhaled his earthy scent. "Where will you go?"

Brannon shrugged. "Wherever the RD hides me, I guess."

Murray turned on the ignition of his sedan and motioned for Brannon to join him. Quince gave Lela a parting hug and climbed into the front seat. Brannon slipped into the back, waved, and closed the door.

I crumpled onto the porch stairs and for once, Freckles didn't chase me away. She surveyed me, as if waiting for my daily question that had become our routine, but I couldn't bring myself to ask about Mom, whom Officer Murray suspected was being held hostage.

Lela breezed past me, returning with two steaming cups of coffee. She handed Freckles a mug before joining me on the stairs and slipping a mug into my tightly woven hands.

"Thank you," said Freckles.

A hint of a smile traced across her caramel skin, and her amber eyes glowed in the faint sunrise. In that slight gesture, I found a glimmer of hope. Hope that we'd be safe, that Centurion would keep my mother alive, and that I did the right thing by trusting Brannon with my plan.

I could trust Brannon, right? The thought surfaced, then faded as Finley's words erupted, threatening to explode inside me. *No, Rames, I didn't have to. I did it for you*, he'd said. But why? Then it hit me like a boulder tearing down a volcanic mountain. Lela had tried to explain, but I didn't listen. Perhaps I didn't want to because Brannon, whom I'd crushed on since ninth grade, liked me back, altering my perception of reality.

Three weeks ago, when my world turned upside down, it had been Finley who helped me when everyone else thought I'd gone crazy. Finley risked his life by hacking Connect Mobile. Finley did everything to keep me safe. Why hadn't I noticed?

I leaned my head against Lela and sighed. "Finley's in love with me, isn't he?" A rhetorical question, one that didn't require Lela's response. After all, no one in their right mind would risk their life for someone else unless they loved them.

Yet Lela answered anyway. "Rami. You're like a sister to me, but sometimes, you're as dense as they come. Your twelve-year-old brother figured it out before you did." I groaned, leaning heavily on her now. "Come on, let's go in. It's freezing out here."

We strode to the kitchen, where oatmeal simmered on the stove. When Finley spotted me lingering in the doorway, he turned away. Zac watched Finley busy himself with the silverware.

"Need help with breakfast?" I asked Zac.

Zac covered the oats with a lid before shifting closer. He pointed first to me, then to Finley. "Enough, you two. Rami, you screwed up. But if we're going to make it out of here alive, we need both of you. So, make up."

Zac had changed so much these past few weeks, I hardly recognized the boy in front of me. I considered my words. "Zac's right. I made a decision that seemed right in the moment, and my feelings for Brannon...well, that's not important. What matters is, um, I'm sorry. After all you guys have done for me." I blinked away tears that threatened to spill over. "I promise I won't let you down again."

CHAPTER 42

Thursday, October 12

The familiar crunch of gravel on the driveway drifted into the bedroom. Each evening, precisely at dusk, Donut and Muscolo arrived in an unmarked black SUV for the night shift and Freckles and Blue left the premises. Typically, the exchange was brief. One car entered; one car exited. The four rarely exchanged more than a few words. But tonight, muffled voices stood inches from my window. Muscolo, not known for his friendliness, appeared even more agitated than normal. His voice took on an edge that frightened me.

Pop! Then another. *Gunshots.*

Officer Murray assured me we'd be safe, that Dominic couldn't find us. Had Finley not hid his location as well as he thought?

Memories of the explosion came flooding back. My body tensed and my throat went dry. I wrapped my arms around my ribcage and crouched beneath the window, searching frantically for Blue and Freckles. Blue fired his weapon into the woods before racing behind the SUV, and Donut slid to the other side, using the vehicle's door as a shield. Muscolo motioned with his fingers and Donut raised his weapon, firing in the same direction. Chaos ensued, and I sat frozen, unable to move as Donut fell sideways, his head curving to the side. I suppressed a scream. *Someone help Donut*, I wanted to yell. The steady boom of bullets ricocheted off the cabin's tin roof. I covered my ears.

Muscolo shouted orders and raced in front of my window, firing a stream of bullets. He covered for Freckles as she sprinted to the SUV, where Donut lay motionless. Despite Freckles' athletic body and fast speed, the enemy was faster, and she didn't make it in time. I stared in horror as Freckles collapsed on the gravel driveway in a pool of blood five feet from Donut's lifeless body.

I bolted for the cabin door. "No, no, no."

But Finley blocked my path, holding my shaking body close to his. "You can't save her."

"I can't leave her to die all alone," I cried, pushing against him with every ounce of strength as the gunfire continued.

"You need to save Zac!" When I remained frozen, he cupped my face in his hands. "Rami? Get Zac!" He shoved me toward Zac's room, my legs propelling forward though my body longed to retreat.

I whispered Zac's name and heard a faint cry from beneath the twin bed. "Zac? Take my hand." I squatted below and reached for him. He remained flat on the carpet, his hands covering his head. "We need to go somewhere safe."

"This place was supposed to be safe! They call it a safe house!" he cried.

Zac was right, but that conversation would have to wait. I hadn't told him about our mother being held ransom in exchange for me because, like Zac, I thought we were safe from Dominic. The front window exploded, sending shards of shattered glass across the family room. Shrieks ripped through the cabin. *Lela. Is she safe? Where is she hiding?*

"Zac! Take my hand."

I yanked him from under the bed and bolted out of the room, across shattered glass, and down the narrow hallway until we reached a broom closet under the stairs. Zac slithered to the back corner, and I squeezed in next to him, crossing my legs underneath piles of musty papers.

I'd never given much thought to the connection between emotions and smells, but the longer I remained curled in a ball, the more I understood that fear contained a distinct scent—pungent, sour, and ripe—like that of spoiled fruit. It took my breath away, and I held a finger below my nose.

With my free arm, I pulled Zac against me, sheltering him from the shots that continued to erupt. The heartbeat in my chest pounded with such force, I was certain he felt it through my sweater. Then I prayed with all my might, begging God to let me live and keep Zac safe from harm. All my doubts about God suddenly disappeared in the heat of the moment, when all I could do was pray. Funny how my mind led me to believe that God didn't care. Because despite all I'd been through these past weeks, the fact that my mother might be alive was a miracle.

My mouth moved in silence as I repeated The Lord's Prayer and the twenty-third psalm, which Mom had encouraged me to memorize. By the end of the psalm, silence ensued, which felt both deafening and terrifying. The tension around Zac's lips softened, but I shook my head. Something didn't feel right.

Within seconds, muted voices within the cabin grew louder. Furniture overturned and slammed to the floor. Loud roars as each room turned up empty. Where were Lela and Finley? The pounding of my heartbeat intensified. I uttered another prayer, this time just above a whisper.

Above us, heavy footsteps climbed the loft stairs, and I pictured Battleship and Monopoly being strewn across the floor in a fit of rage as the cursing intensified. Someone pounded back down the stairs, then nothing. Not a sound, not a footstep. No banging, no shouting.

"Rami?" Zac whimpered.

My finger rose to my lips, silencing him. The acrid smell that filled the dark space made it difficult to breathe. My cramped body now swelled in pain, giving way to utter exhaustion. The day I'd run from Dominic Bell, after he threatened to kill Zac, marked the only other time I'd experienced panic, followed by the collapse of adrenaline. The memory sent chills down my spine, and the hairs on my arms stood on end.

He's here. I knew with certainty, just like I knew to search my horse trophy for the SIM card. My mother's presence surrounded me, and I realized she too must be praying because I was no longer afraid. A strong sense of peace flooded my veins. My only regret was I had failed to protect my brother.

"I'm sorry, Zac," I muttered, as a dim light illuminated the tiny enclosure.

A burly arm ripped me from Zac's grasp. His blood-curdling cry sounded like a wounded animal. I clawed at the intruder, digging my fingernails into his flesh until I drew blood. I screamed for Finley, Lela, and Zac, but I was no match for his strength.

"I've been waiting a long time for this, kid. Now, it's payback time," Dominic hissed as a foul-smelling cloth collided with my lips like poison. Dominic had silenced me. I resolved to remain strong, to stay the course and finish what I'd started. My eyelashes fluttered like my favorite butterfly. *So tired.* My head fell forward as darkness enveloped me.

Part III

"If we continue to develop our technology without wisdom or prudence, our servant may prove to be our executioner."

General Omar Bradley

CHAPTER 43

Friday, October 13

Flashing lights and high-pitched beeps tapped in rhythm. The pounding in my head intensified, and I blinked to clear my vision. I inhaled slowly, counting each breath one at a time. Anything to calm the fear. Across the room, a control board with dozens of monitors portrayed images of doors and hallways. Each picture flickered on the screen, followed by a green light, before flipping to the next.

Where was I? My thoughts turned to Zac. Was he alive?

Dizzy and lightheaded, I pushed myself upright and looked around. A massive warehouse appeared before me with endless rows of servers, their red and blue blinking lights illuminating the otherwise darkened space. I sat in a cold, gray metal chair on the second story of the warehouse. The complex was so large, I couldn't see the end of the building, as if it went on forever. A data center, similar to the one Finley discovered using GPS coordinates from Kate's coded messages, but with even greater capacity. Each computer stored millions of secrets.

Glass encased three walls of this second story office, which afforded a clear view of the large complex. The outside wall, made of concrete, contained no windows. I shifted backward, away from the metal chair where I'd awakened. My heel caught an open ledge. I looked behind me. The office sat thirty feet above the servers. A crane-like robot with an arm that extended to the second story caught my eye. Perhaps the robot used its arm to retrieve things from the servers and bring them up here. Had the doorway been left open intentionally?

A terrifying wave of dread washed over me as three dark figures encroached, surrounding me from all sides. My nightmare, the one that had hijacked my sleep for two years, began unfolding before my eyes. In the recurrent dream, I had no memory of how I arrived in an unfamiliar place. Each time, an evil presence encompassed me, suffocating me, until my only hope of escape became jumping from a ledge. I had witnessed this scene hundreds of times in my dreams. And I knew the ending.

I always awoke an instant before falling to my death.

What if it hadn't been a dream at all, but some sort of premonition or vision designed to warn me? To prepare me for this moment. Did I even believe in premonitions? Things like that didn't happen nowadays. *Did they?*

As the three men drew closer, I weighed my options. If I stepped back, I would fall from the ledge and likely not live to tell my story. If I darted forward, they would stop me before I could reach the metal stairs I'd spotted in the corner. The severity of my situation took root. Just like in my nightmare, they trapped me with no hope of escape.

One man took a slow, deliberate step toward me. My breath caught in my lungs. Dominic Bell's hand rested at his hip, clutching his weapon as if I were the real enemy. But my attention fell to the tall, dark figure in the center of the room.

His menacing eyes held my gaze. "Hello, Rami. We meet again." He lowered his immense frame into a chair across from me. "Sit. Please." His sharp eyes shot through me like arrows.

Unable to stop my body from shaking, I complied and sat across from the man who had held me captive at the Reinforcement precinct. The one the ROs claimed didn't exist. "You're not an Agent. So, who are you?" My voice held an unsteady tone.

His lips curved. "Malik Williams."

"You work for the Threats Division," I said.

"I *am* the Threats Division." His arms swept in every direction. "I built everything around you, achieving what others had only dreamed of accomplishing."

I wished I could come up with a clever comeback, but nothing came to mind. My silence must have amused him, because his laughter echoed throughout the building. "And here I thought you were going to stop me."

The men's mocking laughter fueled the fire raging within me. I resisted the urge to slap the smirks from their faces. Instead, I lunged forward and raced for a set of stairs tucked in the corner of the second-story office. My chair fell backward through the opening and crashed onto the robotic crane below, reverberating as metal clanged to metal. Williams grabbed me, swung me backward, and wrapped his arm around my throat, as if expecting my attempted escape. I scratched and clawed at his forearms, unable to breathe. My eyes widened at the realization that Williams could kill me.

When he released his grip, I dropped to my knees, coughing, sputtering, gasping for air. My lungs filled with oxygen, clearing my brain from a deep fog, and I muscled myself to a standing position, refusing to let him intimidate me.

"You realize if I wanted you dead, you wouldn't be standing here. Dominic's been wanting revenge for quite some time, but I held him off." Williams' voice bore an edge of arrogance. He kicked his chair toward me and hissed like a viper. "Now sit down."

Exhausted, I obeyed. *Why am I still alive?* Why kidnap me, bring me here, only to kill me when Dominic could have completed the job at the safe house?

"Are you aware of what the term Centurion means, Rami?" Williams said, not waiting for a response. "The Roman Empire was the greatest, most powerful empire of all time, spanning a thousand-year reign. The Centurion, or guards as they were often called, protected the empire at all costs. More importantly, they protected the emperor himself."

I rolled my eyes. "Thanks for the history lesson, but I really don't care. What do you want with me?"

"But you should care." Williams encircled me, his eyes never straying, as his guards kept watch.

My nightmare returned in real time. Each time the evil presence surrounded me in my dream, I froze, unable to react. But I was no longer that frightened little girl. I refused to let this man's god-like complex scare me into submission. While he continued his monologue, I scanned the platform, searching again for an escape.

"The Centurion enforced the rules handed down by the emperor to keep and maintain control. Law and order are essential to the success of a society. I founded Centurion Technologies to assist the Threats Division's efforts in monitoring citizens that could be dangerous. Keep a watchful eye on your citizens, and you prevent rebellion." He paused, as if waiting for me to respond. When I remained silent, he continued his annoying history lecture. "I loved history when I was your age. Couldn't read enough about world wars."

"So? What does ancient history have to do with me?" I controlled my words to sound indifferent while my heart thumped in my chest.

"After each world war, secret police became the most powerful and feared organization. They employed various tactics to keep and maintain their citizens." He lowered himself to eye level. "Here's the part that you and your band of teenage friends don't understand. We didn't need to arrest you or even harm you. All we had to do was socially paralyze you. Imply your father had something to do with your mother's disappearance. Ban certain social media posts for disinformation. Suggest on Allicio you threatened to harm STaR officials. Your peers now see you as unstable, untrustworthy. Dangerous. After all, you did plan to bomb your own school."

His words struck like a bolt of electricity pulsing through me. Anger spewed from my lips. "I haven't done any of those things and you know it."

"True, but it's not important what *I* believe. It's what *others* believe. Perception, Miss Carlton. The more a story goes viral on Allicio, the more it becomes truth. Whether the story is accurate at that point doesn't matter, because everyone's mind is already made up."

"Why are you telling me all this?" I said, my voice shallow and breathy.

Williams stood and shot me a half-smile, half-smirk. "I don't believe you're a bad person, Miss Carlton. But you and your friends need to be reminded now and then that STaR keeps you safe and offers you a good life. Young people don't remember how bad things got during the pandemic. STaR saved America from annihilation. STaR saved the world. My program is designed to remind young people of all the things STaR does for you." He learned over until we were eye to eye. "So you never forget."

Behind him, Dominic snickered, and I wondered if explaining the Allicio tracking program and what he planned to do with the information would be the last thing I heard.

But in one swift motion, Williams reached under my arm, forced me up, and placed his palm on the small of my back, leading me to the control board. Grasping my head with both hands, he swiveled it in every direction, forcing me to see the warehouse in its entirety. "Take a hard look around at the vast empire I built. With the help of your dear Aunt Kate—God rest her soul—I created the Bifurcation Tracking Analysis. The Threats Division can now watch everything you do on Allicio. From there, the TD determines whether you're a threat to STaR."

The mention of Kate's name made my blood boil, a purposeful slip intended to get under my skin and generate a reaction. The old me would have responded to Williams' manipulation, but not now. Not after what he'd just admitted.

I no longer had to wonder why Kate tried to stop the BTA program. Her suspicions were spot on. Centurion kept a file on anyone who disagreed with STaR, and The Resistance threatened their power.

But I wasn't part of The Resistance. There had to be a reason I was still alive. I had to keep Williams talking. The longer he talked, the greater my chances of survival. If I could get him to admit he worked for The Guard, I could pass this along to Murray.

I slapped on my poker face, hesitant to show my hand. "But surely someone above you gives the orders, right? I mean, you said so yourself. Centurion is simply a technology company."

Williams simply watched me, studied me, before throwing a glance at his watchdogs, as if deciding whether he should answer. I sensed the reality of my nightmare coming to fruition and fiddled with a ballpoint pen left near the keyboard, rolling its smooth edges between my fingers. I could stab Williams with the pen and make a run for it. But as quickly as the thought entered my mind, I shoved it away. I didn't hurt people. I wasn't like him. Besides, I wouldn't get past Dominic, who had been given the green light to kill me.

I had to change my approach. "Why pick on me and my family? I'm just a sixteen-year-old kid who prefers volleyball to social media."

"Kate," he said. "She was the best developer I've ever hired."

"Yet you murdered her," I muttered under my breath. His smile made me want to vomit.

"Kate didn't comprehend the seriousness of her betrayal," he said. "As for you, that depends."

"On what?" I asked, unsure whether I wanted the truth.

His face darkened, making him appear even more sinister. "Your mother is a traitor to her country. Just like her sister, Kate. But you,

Miss Carlton, are the future. STaR has done everything to protect you, to give you a good life. It would be a shame to throw that all away." Williams twisted a dial on the control board. A faint shriek escaped from my lips as images came to life.

Me at the Reinforcement precinct in the darkened interrogation room. Me at Connect Mobile attempting to fix my phone. Zac at the skateboard park. Zac in his room wearing an augmented reality headset. Me destroying my horse trophy.

"How..." I asked, mystified.

"You already know that STaR's Safety Division cameras are everywhere. Traffic lights, streetlamps, parking lots, buildings, even people's homes. It's really quite simple." Williams' face curved into a smile.

Chills trailed up and down my spine. Finley had commented about the military-grade surveillance cameras on the ceiling at the data center. But this was different. Centurion had access to *every* camera. They could hack and manipulate the images. I had never been safe. They'd been watching all along. I felt like Williams had placed a noose around my neck, just waiting to pull it tight.

"You can blame your own mother for your involvement. She took Kate's place. Your mother was a generous person, I'll give you that."

Was generous. Past tense. I was too late to save Mom. I pressed my lips together and swallowed the agony that threatened to overflow. Williams failed to get a reaction from me when he mentioned Kate, so this might be another attempt at manipulating my emotions.

"But you, Miss Carlton. You were the ticket to making your mother talk. All we had to do was threaten to harm you and Zac, and she spilled everything," Williams sneered.

"Liar," I shouted, gripping the ink pen until my knuckles turned white. With defiance blazing in my eyes, I faced him head-on. "My mother refused to talk, refused to give up Kate. That's why you used me and threatened to kill Zac."

Williams squatted in front of me. "The secret police understood human nature, that citizens would turn on each other to save themselves. By asking people to report suspicious activity on their neighbors, people guaranteed their own safety, and the safety of their family and friends. We use this same approach today, and thanks to Allicio, our informants can access information in real time. They see a controversial post, they report it. Sometimes it's taken down, sometimes it's stored in a file for later."

My mind tumbled like clothes in a dryer. "I don't understand."

"You were promised you'd be safe, right? So, how did I find you and your friends?"

Good question. How *did* he find us? There were only two people who knew about my plan to shut down this data center. Finley and Officer Murray. I had my doubts about Murray and repeatedly wondered if we could trust him. But Finley? He wouldn't betray me, would he? Then it hit me like a punch to the gut. There weren't two people who knew about my plan. There were three. And one of them hadn't really been asleep.

Bile climbed up my esophagus, threatening to overspill on the floor of the warehouse. The instant his name reached my tongue, I paled.

CHAPTER 44

Friday, October 13

Brannon Martinelli leaned against the stair rail in front of me, his once kind eyes holding an unreadable expression. *Conceit? Regret?* I believed the latter, if only to ease my own guilt. His self-assured gaze had vanished, and his shoulders slumped forward. In his blue eyes, the ones that had captivated me, I saw the painful truth.

Brannon Martinelli had betrayed me.

He inched forward until I caught a whiff of his familiar spicy scent. "For what it's worth, Rami, I'm sorry." His lower lip quivered, and I almost felt sorry for him.

Almost.

Brannon's words stung like a swarm of bees. I breathed hard to force down the anger that rose to the surface. "You're sorry? That's what you want to tell me? That you're sorry? I trusted you."

Even as I spoke, regret flooded through my veins. Trust had never come easily, but I'd wanted to trust Brannon. I'd wanted to believe he actually liked me, despite Finley's warning. Yet I'd endangered my brother and my friends with my reckless lack of judgment.

Brannon's face paled in the dim light, casting shadows under his eyes. "I...I needed the money. My dad's been out of work for almost a year. That's the real reason I work at Little Cone. One night after work, some guy offered me money to get close to you. He told me to find out where your mom hid something he wanted. Once he got it back, he said he'd pay me." Brannon's eyes shifted to Dominic. "But he lied. When you found the SIM card, I told them I wanted out."

"The bruise. Is it real or did you fake that, too?" I said.

"Yeah, it's real. That was my answer from Dominic when I wanted out." Brannon stroked his cheek, which now bore shades of deep violet. "Dominic instructed me to find the safe house. Only then would I be free from his control. When I told my parents the shooter from Finley's house attacked me, it was easy to get the RD to take me somewhere safe." Brannon lowered his head. "I swear I never thought it would come to this. I wanted to tell you..." His voice trailed off.

My face heated as rage spilled out. "People died, Brannon! And I'm not sure whether my brother and my best friends are alive!"

"I tried to save you," Brannon said, his voice pleading.

"Save *me*? No, Brannon. You tried to save yourself." Tears burned the insides of my eyes, but I refused to let them fall down my cheeks. I swallowed the anguish that clogged my throat. "The kiss? Was any of it real?"

Brannon's moist eyes met mine. "Yeah. It started out as a gig for money. But I fell for you, Rami Carlton. The kiss, the way I wanted you that night, how I had to make myself stop before things went too far...all of that...real."

I wasn't sure which hurt worse—the fact that he cared for me or that despite his feelings, he still chose betrayal.

Williams appeared behind Brannon and shoved him away like a discarded piece of trash. Just yesterday, I would have defended Brannon, but not this time.

"Well, this is a cute mini reunion, but all good things must end," said Williams.

One thug grabbed Brannon's arm. "Let's go, lover boy."

A sadness swept across Brannon's face. I got that his feelings for me were real, but his deceit overshadowed any feelings I once had for him.

"I really am sorry, Rami," Brannon called over his shoulder as the guard hauled down the steps.

Before I could process the betrayal, Williams narrowed his gaze like a panther ready to pounce. "You see, Rami, friends turn on friends if it means saving those they love. Or saving themselves."

I buried my face in my hands. "I wouldn't. I would never betray my friends."

"Don't be so sure," Williams said, his voice like that of a parent scolding a child. "Our capacity for self-preservation is far more intense than we realize. It makes us do things we never thought we'd do."

A lump formed in my throat. If I planned to stay alive, I needed to change my approach. I stared below at servers that once housed thousands of secrets just waiting to be exploited and forced a smile. "Mr. Williams, you seem like a brilliant guy. I mean, anyone who could build an airtight network to spy on citizens with the government's blessing must be smart. Why not use your intellect and clout for good? Seriously, you could develop a sustainable energy source with the time and effort you've spent on the BTA program."

A prideful expression shot across Williams' face and I wondered if I was getting through to him. Then he turned up his lip. "We're a little beyond bribery, Miss Carlton. Someone inside The Resistance made a copy of dear Aunt Kate's files. Perhaps Finley Drake made a copy and stored it on his laptop."

He shot a knowing look at Dominic, and for the first time, Dominic looked frightened. How did Dominic not find Finley's laptop when he attacked the safe house? Had Finley had time to hide it? *He thinks I have the copy or that I know where to find Finley's laptop.* It's the only explanation as to why I'm still alive.

My poker face proved effective earlier. Perhaps it would work again. "I have no idea what you're talking about."

Dominic stepped forward and whipped out a blade, the same one he'd shown me on the video. He brought it to my throat. "I warned you," he hissed as he made a slight incision. The cut burned my flesh and blood dripped down my neck. "Where is Finley's laptop?"

I refused to let the tears that formed in the corners of my eyes fall down my cheeks as I grasped my throat. "I don't know. I swear."

Dominic flung my hands away and sliced again, this time cutting deeper, but not enough to kill me. He knew how to inflict pain, to torture someone until he got the truth. I cried out in pain. "I swear I don't know anything about a copy, and I don't know where Finley put his laptop."

Williams' face darkened. "Remember what happened to Kate when she lied to me? You may want to rethink your answer, Miss

Carlton. Like I told you before, self-preservation is often far more intense than we realize."

He threw a towel at me, and I held it tight against the gashes on my neck to stop the blood. My eyes scanned the large space, again searching for an escape, while Williams turned back to the computer. He typed on the keyboard and multiple screens came to life, scrambling symbols together like a puzzle. "I had a feeling you might be unwilling to cooperate, so I came...prepared."

The way his tongue slithered on the word "prepared" made my skin turn cold. On the monitors, images of my mother and Zac, bound and gagged, came to life. I let out a gut-wrenching scream and grasped the desk with one hand to keep myself upright.

Williams wiggled his fingers at the two goons behind him, and suddenly my mother's shadowed silhouette appeared. My eyes searched in all directions, frantic to glimpse her. Then the shadow disappeared.

"Where is she, Williams?" I was through playing games and done with pleasantries.

Guards led Mom and Zac up the staircase, their mouths duct-taped shut and arms bound in front of their bodies. Mom's bones sunk into her face and her sharp green eyes held a deep sadness. The limp that she tried to conceal seemed more pronounced and painful, as evidenced by the wince that escaped when the guard shoved her up the last step.

"Mom!" I leaped forward, but Williams held me back. I pounded my fists on his chest, no longer caring that he'd broken me to the point of raw desperation. "She needs her medication. She has a chronic illness and will die without it! Please!" Frantic tears poured down my cheeks.

Mom stood wide-eyed, wiggling her bound fingers, and shook her head almost imperceptibly. The guard stepped aside, and Dominic gripped my mother's arm, forcing a yelp.

"Stop! You're hurting her," I screamed.

My attention turned to Zac, who shook his head, then dropped his chin downward and to the right. His desperate eyes held mine for an instant too long, then shifted down to the right again. I followed his gaze to my mother's bound hands. Her fingers moved in rapid succession over and over as if communicating in code.

Sign language.

On the morning of her disappearance, she signed to Zac and me. This wasn't a coincidence. With her hands upside down, the letters appeared backward, and I had to concentrate. Her fingers wiggled ever so slightly, signing one letter at a time.

R. I. G. H. T.

What did it mean?

Tears streaked down Zac's cheeks as he struggled to free himself. My heart broke. If I had trusted Officer Murray and the local ROs, Zac would have been safe.

My chin quivered. "I'm so sorry."

I stifled the last of my sobs and squared my shoulders. "Let them go, Williams. Please. I'll give you what you want."

Zac screamed and shook his head. Mom dropped her head and when she glanced back up, tears fell from her moistened eyes. Williams nodded to his guards and pulled Mom and Zac back down the stairs to a long hallway. I crumbled to my knees, dropping the bloody towel, as all the fight spirit within me drained with each drip of blood from my throat.

Williams yanked me up, grasping my chin, and forced me to face him. He pointed to the screen that showed Mom and Zac being led away. "We protect those we love. Even when we must betray others in exchange. I'll ask you one more time. Where is Finley Drake's laptop?"

Unable to form a reply, I pressed my lids together and allowed the tears to slowly trail down my face.

CHAPTER 45

Friday, October 13

My mind reeled, desperate for a way out of this bizarre situation. I didn't know where to find Finley's laptop, and even if I found it, Williams would still kill me.

I never wanted to be a part of The Resistance. My mother's ties to them had cost me everything. I had to make Williams believe I too hated The Resistance. My stomach clenched and heart pounded in my chest. But I steadied my voice to sound convincing.

"What if I agree to work for you? Finley trusts me. He'll tell me where to find the laptop. I could gather data for you to help you fight The Resistance. If I track Allicio the way Kate did, I could monitor the activity of certain individuals that you deem...fit for your program. Flush out teen resisters."

Williams paused, and for an instant, I wondered if he'd heard me. He typed a series of letters and numbers into the control board, waited until another sequence appeared, then entered more. *Code.* A much more sophisticated sequence of letters, numbers, and symbols than I could write.

Then it hit me like a tidal wave. I'd been recruited from the very beginning. They knew my mother was part of The Resistance and knew her connection to Kate. What they didn't know was how well I could write code. Until I showed them. *Stupid!* The whole thing was a setup. I had played right into the hands of Bald Eagle. He wanted me to find him.

Once they knew I could be an asset, their plan came together. They made sure I'd help them by threatening the people I loved. They knew I would do whatever it took to save Mom and Zac. I was a prisoner of the Threats Division.

Tension formed around Williams' jawline. "You've proven yourself valuable to the cause. Difficult but trainable." He turned to Dominic, who held the bloody blade ready to strike again, growling like an attack dog being held back. "You have three weeks to collect thousands of contacts. It will cost you greatly. Your friends, your reputation. And you might fail."

"And if I do?" My voice shook with fear.

He stepped so close his breath felt hot like that of a dragon, burning me from the inside out. "I'll kill Annie and Zac. And this time I won't hesitate."

The security images from the building suddenly vanished from the monitors. The codes scrolled rapidly, as if the computer recognized the algorithm Williams had typed moments ago. One by one, as each server lost power, the flashing lights in the warehouse disappeared, and the constant hum of noise ceased. The silence that ensued was deafening.

"Do you play chess, Miss Carlton?" When I didn't respond, an ominous smile appeared across Williams' face. "Ah, but your friend Finley Drake is quite the chess player, I understand. Every great chess player knows the secret to winning is to anticipate your opponent's next move." He paused, though whether for my sake or his, I couldn't be sure. "Self-preservation is a powerful weapon. You'll have to choose whether to save yourself and work for me, or save those you love."

With that, Williams locked eyes with me. The overhead lights flickered off. Fear turned to panic at the realization that I stood alone in utter darkness with Williams, Dominic, and the other guard equal in size and strength, with no way to defend myself. It took every ounce of courage not to leap from the ledge and fall to my death.

An alarm sounded, shrill and piercing. My ears rang and I could no longer decipher between the sound of the alert and the warning in my head telling me to run. Red lights swirled above door frames, illuminating exit signs, and a loud female voice aired through the speakers.

"Warning. Ten minutes to shutdown. Warning. Ten minutes to shutdown."

Smoke seeped from the computer board and a faint smell, bitter and cold, trickled into my throat. I glimpsed Williams fleeing down the steps, his trusty guards wedged on either side, as the smoke intensified. I coughed, my throat dry and constricted. *Gas.*

Williams watched me seal my fate. I would have to choose. Save myself and work for him or save my family. As always, he was one step ahead of me.

Dominic had dragged Mom and Zac down a long hallway. The darkness made it impossible to find my way, but my palms slid against the walls, feeling my way, until I reached another set of stairs. I raced down, clutching the railing to keep from falling. At least down here, I could breathe easier and the constant shrill of the alarm dissipated. I dashed quickly in and out of every room, shouting for Mom and Zac, but didn't see them. They could be anywhere by now, but I refused to give up hope.

My fingers fumbled with a doorknob at the end of the corridor. Locked, it wouldn't budge. I slammed my shoulder into the door, to no avail. Then I kicked it over and over as adrenaline fueled my strength. I bent over to catch my breath and tapped my neck. Blood continued to drip down my neck and onto my shirt. Despite my heavy breathing, I thought I heard muffled sounds in the distance. Had I searched the area too quickly?

I retraced my steps, covering my mouth with my shirt, and entered a room filled with boxes floor to ceiling. The thick air stuck to my lungs, and I had to stop several times to catch my breath. As I approached another closed door, the cries grew louder, more desperate. How had I missed this?

I opened a tiny closet and found Brannon bound and gagged on the floor. His eyes bulged, and he wiggled to show me both his hands and feet were bound. I loosened the gag around his mouth and his words gushed.

"Rami? Help me. Please," Brannon begged. Tears flowed down his cheeks. When I stood still, he repeated his pleas. "Rami? Please."

I stared at him, unable to respond as all the hurt and betrayal flashed to the surface. But no matter what Brannon had done, he didn't deserve this. I wasn't like Williams. I wouldn't leave Brannon here to die.

My body swung into action, tugging at the rope at his ankles. It moved, but not enough to free him. I searched the room and found a tiny scrap of metal on the windowsill, wedged it under the rope, and pulled until it loosened enough for Brannon to wiggle his legs free.

"Warning. Five minutes to shutdown," the voice above blared.

I had no idea what a shutdown involved, but neither did I want to be here when it happened. "Come on. I'll get your wrists later. We have to hurry."

I lifted him to his feet, and he followed me to the hall where gas oozed through the air vents. Brannon bent over in a coughing fit. We didn't have much time left.

I led him back to the locked door and tried to kick it open one more time. "I think my mom and brother are in there, but I can't get it open."

"Let me try." Brannon shoved the door with his shoulder, but nothing happened. He followed my example and kicked the door, alternating between kicks and shoves, but the door refused to dislodge. We were out of time.

Shouts sounded in the distance. Men with raised guns charged at me, one with an infrared laser pointed at my chest.

"Two minutes," the recording played.

"Rami?" one yelled. "Rami Carlton? Is that you?"

The smoke thickened the air, making it difficult to see who approached. My vision blurred as gas seeped into my lungs. Soon, I'd pass out from smoke inhalation. I didn't have long.

Through the coughs, I tried to say my name. The men lowered their weapons. "Come with us."

Three ROs dressed in standard navy uniforms tugged me toward the exit. I didn't know whether they wanted to rescue me or kill me. “My mom.” Cough. “Zac.” Cough. I pointed to the door.

One RO led Brannon away, while the others fired their weapons at the enclosure. The wooden frame splintered, and he kicked in the door.

“Clear. Clear,” they shouted. My eyes darted about, hoping, praying. “I’ve got two bodies. Coming out.”

My heart slammed in my chest as Mom and Zac appeared through a haze of gaseous fumes. I pulled Zac’s limp body into a bear hug. Mom’s arms flew around us like a mama bird protecting her young.

“Warning! This facility will shut down in one minute,” the recording rang.

“Go! Go!” they roared. “This place is going to blow.”

We followed the officers up the stairs, through the maze of servers that now resembled tombstones. A helicopter waited near the building with its propellers swirling smoke in all directions. Zac and I filed in, followed by Mom and the one RO. The other stayed on the ground and gave the word to the pilot. The bird spun its wings and took off. Brannon stood below, watching our copter before the officer who’d led him away shoved him into the RD vehicle. Although my hurt ran as deep as a canyon, at least Brannon was alive.

Smoke bellowed from the facility and, suddenly, the entire data center exploded. A mushroom cloud of smoke exploded near the copter, causing us to swivel side to side. Shards of metal flew in every direction.

I stared below until the burning building disappeared in the distance. My head felt like it would split open any minute and my lungs burned. I couldn't think straight. I just wanted to go home. The RO sat in the front seat next to the pilot and handed each of us a set of headphones. He motioned for us to put them on.

I pulled the microphone to my lips. "Why are you helping us?"

"You'll be debriefed when we land," he replied into the headset.

"And my friends? Are they alive?"

When neither the RO nor the pilot responded, I removed my headphones and turned in my seat. Tears filled my mother's eyes, but when she spotted me, she wiped them away and smiled. "You don't have to pretend for us," I shouted above the roaring engine. "They killed Kate, Mom. They planted a bomb in her car and blew her up like she meant nothing to them. I can see you're hurting, so please don't pretend anymore."

She nodded and allowed her emotions to flow freely, this time not stopping the sobs that followed. My mother, who had never let Zac and me see her in pain, wrapped her arms around her waist and heaved heavy sighs until her breaths ran out. Then she cried some more. Zac laid his head on her shoulder, and I held her weeping body. We stayed that way most of the ride home, unable to comfort each other with words.

Once Mom's tears dried, I broached the subject that had bothered me since before the fire. "The sign language from earlier. You signed the word *right*. What did it mean?" The rumble of the copter drowned my words and Mom had to lean in close to my ear.

Her concerned frown replaced the grief I'd seen moments before. "I've tried to teach you and Zac to do the right thing. To be strong and independent. But sometimes we're forced to make a choice." She paused and placed her hands in a praying position under her chin. "Rami? Never be afraid to stand up for what is right. But know there are always risks to our choices. Are you following what I'm saying?"

I hesitated, if only for a second, but enough to gather my thoughts. "Yes. I think so."

Mom held my gaze for a moment before replacing the headphones atop her head. I'd never been a good liar, and I sensed my mother could see straight through me. I doubted Williams would keep his end of the bargain since he expected me to be dead, but I would keep mine. Mom could never know what I'd done to negotiate her freedom. I would have done anything to save her, and given the choice, I would do it again.

CHAPTER 46

Friday, October 13

The instant we landed, the RO on board escorted us inside an airplane hangar at the edge of a runway. Officer Murray stood at a distance in full uniform with several ROs nearby. Although I thought I'd gotten past his gruffness, the edge in his voice said otherwise.

He'd told me he held a prominent position in internal intelligence and I didn't doubt his claims. He displayed complete control. He instructed the ROs to bring water and clean towels and no one questioned him. Another RO cleaned my wounds, attaching bandages on my neck. Murray stared at my mother and a slight flicker of recognition flashed across his face that the other ROs couldn't have possibly seen.

"Annie Carlton? I'm Officer Sam Murray from the Southeastern regional precinct. We've been looking for you for quite some time. Your disappearance caused quite a stir. Despite STaR's reminder that citizens are safe under President Young, some have questioned her methods." His eyes lingered on Mom longer than necessary, allowing the words to sink in. Mom remained silent and held his gaze. "Any citizen who poses a threat to this country becomes property of the Reinforcement Division. For the crime of treason, you, Annie Carlton, will be placed under house arrest until an official trial date is set."

My chest tightened. *Treason?* What was happening? Zac buried his face in his hands. I felt completely betrayed all over again. But my mother never flinched. She remained silent as Murray read her the rights she held under STaR. Mom worked for an attorney. Perhaps he could get her a fair trial. But I doubted it since most attorneys worked for STaR.

"You will remain inside your home during the designated time of day. If any camera catches you outside your residence except for assigned locations, you will be locked up at the precinct. Any questions?"

Mom held his gaze and didn't utter a word. I resisted the urge to strangle Officer Murray. He fiddled with his handheld reader and ordered an officer to take it to tech, claiming it appeared locked.

Then he yanked my mother out of her seat and whisked her outside, where a car waited. Zac and I raced to catch up, both of us baffled at the man who had once promised to help us.

He released the grip on my mother and lowered his voice to a mere whisper. "Listen to me and don't interrupt. Do not leave your house for any reason without me. I will come when it's safe. Do not speak about today or the past three weeks with anyone. Do not speak about any of this *inside* your home. Understood?" I nodded, and Mom and Zac did the same. "Good. I had to maintain my cover in there. I hope I didn't go overboard." His expression softened to a slight smile. "I'm glad you're safe."

"How did you know where to find us?" I said.

"Regina Jackson." When I burrowed my brows together, he said, "I think you know her as Freckles."

Regret flooded back as I pictured Freckles lying in a pool of blood with no one to help her. "Is she..." My voice trailed off.

"Severed shoulder, but she's going to make it. She's tough."

I swallowed. "And the others?"

Murray exhaled and shared the details of the brave men and women who had risked their lives to keep me safe. Mom squeezed my hand as one painful detail after another emerged. Donut passed away instantly. Blue went into the house to rescue me, but was too late. He died execution style, trying to save me. Muscolo rescued Freckles and took her to a friend who patched her wound. Their involvement exposed their secret—that they helped The Resistance—putting them on STaR's watchlist. They were no longer safe because of me.

"And my friends? Are they—"

"Safe and unharmed," he said. "I dropped all charges from the potential school bombing."

I bit my lower lip. "Why did the RD rescue us?"

"If they kill you, you become a martyr. By rescuing you, they ensure your loyalty. You become a spokesperson for STaR's safety efforts. Your rescue ensures the next generation understands STaR is needed to keep the country safe from terrorists like Dominic Bell."

"So, Dominic is a terrorist?"

Murray shrugged. "It's how President Young spun the story in her favor. If it got out that he worked for STaR, that would destroy everything she's built. Change the narrative and, well, you alter what people believe."

Williams had said something similar to me about altering perception. He'd said my generation needed to be reminded that STaR kept us safe. I gathered my thoughts. "Williams said his Allicio tracking program made sure the next generation would never *want* to rebel. They're turning kids against their parents. Kids become informants and it shuts down The Resistance," I said.

Officer Murray dropped his voice, so I had to strain to hear him. "You see why President Young needs you alive? She ordered the rescue herself. Her appearance on UNN was flawless. STaR keeps us safe. STaR rescues us. The crowd erupted in applause."

But my heart ached. Blue and Donut had lost their lives to save me. Why? I didn't deserve this kind of sacrifice. If I hadn't given Freckles the note, if Quince hadn't shared it with Brannon, Freckles wouldn't be in hiding and Donut and Blue would still be alive. How much tragedy had I brought to my family and friends? And how many more would suffer under STaR's leadership?

Murray pulled a miniature glass structure from his pocket. I recognized it immediately. Blown glass in the shape of an iridescent blue morpho butterfly. A man used to sit outside Marble Park and hand-blow glass into various shapes and sizes, creating incredible insects, animals, or flowers. Because of Marble Park's greenhouse, the blue morpho butterfly had survived in our region, and the artist claimed it was the most popular request. Lela had a matching glass butterfly, and apparently, so did Murray.

He raised his eyebrows. "I take it you are familiar with the blue morpho butterfly? They're able to hide in plain sight from the enemy." Then he shoved Mom, Zac, and me into the car and walked away.

CHAPTER 47

Wednesday, October 18

For the past five days, I questioned my dumb idea of working for Williams. Within hours of my rescue, I received another anonymous text message from an unknown number. It appeared and disappeared, just as the others had done, leaving no room for doubt as to the sender. Only this time I'd been smarter. I took a picture of the message before it vanished, wondering why I hadn't done that before. I opened my photos and reread the contents for the hundredth time.

Open the email in the next 24 hours or your family dies.

Williams gave me twenty-four hours to install Centurion's spyware on my friends' Allicio accounts, which would give him full access. In exchange, he promised to leave my mother and Zac alone. But clearly, this guy could not be trusted.

Returning home after seeing my house ransacked had been difficult. My things were spread out around the room in no particular order. I tried to assemble my bookshelves last night, placing picture frames where I once had them, but it seemed pointless. If Williams was going to kill me, why bother cleaning my room? Except that I needed something.

I rummaged through piles on the floor but came up empty until I reached for a small shoe box in the corner of my closet that contained memorabilia from my childhood. Stickers, award ribbons, and a small iridescent blue morpho butterfly. I placed the glass structure, no bigger than my middle finger, in my pocket and opened my bedroom door.

My stomach did flips as I stood at the top of the staircase, unsure whether I could face my friends at school. Mom had let me stay home for two days, but I couldn't avoid school forever. I took a deep breath and descended the stairs. The aroma of fresh pancakes made me nauseous, but I brushed it away because the smile on Mom's face reminded me of how I got into this mess to begin with. I couldn't let her down.

Nollie raced to my side, as if she had forgotten I lived here again. Only this time, she didn't growl. I crouched low and rubbed Nollie's floppy ear. "I think she missed me."

Mom piled hotcakes onto Zac's plate and turned to me. "Good morning, Rami. Do you want orange juice with your pancakes?"

"Sure." I offered a slight smile.

I set my backpack in the family room and peered out the wispy curtains to the front lawn where reporters had camped out for days desperate to talk to "Ghost Mom." UNN had a field day running stories about "Ghost Mom" returning from the dead. The stories angered me, but Mom took it with stride, saying how she was thankful to be alive. Although a few cars remained parked on the street, the lawn sat empty. It appeared most had given up on trying to get an exclusive.

"Looks like the reporters finally left," I said, joining Zac at the table.

Mom let out an exacerbated sigh. “Yes, and I hope they stay away.” She dropped three hotcakes onto my plate, then lowered herself into a chair, her voice becoming chirpy. “Officer Murray insisted on driving you and Zac to school today. The RD will keep you safe.”

Zac grunted something that sounded like “no way,” but with a mouth full of food, it was hard to tell.

I suspected Mom knew I’d agreed to work for Williams, and it pained me that I couldn’t confide in her. I lowered my voice. “What about you? Who’s going to protect you while we’re away?”

“The Reinforcement Division keeps everyone safe. We owe STaR our lives,” she said with such cheery enthusiasm, I almost believed her.

I caught the slight hesitation in her voice. Although Mom put up a good front, she understood that with Williams at large, we would never be truly safe. She would stand trial for treason unless Williams had her killed first.

“Anyway, I thought we could get a fresh tree for Christmas this year, as tall as the roof, and string popcorn like we did when you two were little,” Mom said, refilling Zac’s plate for the third time.

I shrugged and forced myself to swallow a few bites. “Sure, Mom. That would be fun.”

She stood over Zac and stared at the ceiling. “I... I wondered what you guys would think about, well, maybe we could invite your father and Olivia to join us for Christmas.”

Zac stopped chewing mid-bite and shot me a glance. “Uh...yeah, okay. That would be cool.”

I chose my words carefully, unsure how Mom wanted me to respond and knowing STaR was listening in. "Um, is that what *you* want?"

Weeks ago, my dad had begged for my forgiveness. After watching the way my friends stuck with me, even after I'd made terrible mistakes, I didn't see how I could refuse to forgive him.

Mom rubbed her neck with one hand while holding the spatula with the other. "I'm not sure what I want. Your father is a complicated man. But he was there for you when you needed him the most, and for that, I'll always be grateful."

I stood and wrapped my arm around Mom's shoulder. "After RD cleared Dad's name, I forgave him. It didn't wipe away the memories of the hurt he caused us, but I felt I had to do this. For me." I paused and reached for my mother's hand. "You know, Olivia is a lot like you. She's kind and giving, and well, she was good to Zac and me. I can kind of see why Dad likes her."

Mom's new phone buzzed, and she pulled away before I could gauge a response. "Well, we can talk more about this later. Sam is outside. I'll tell him to come inside and wait while you finish getting ready."

"Sam?" I questioned.

My mother flattened her hair. "Officer Murray. Silly me." Her words came out clipped and her voice rose an octave.

I raised an eyebrow but didn't say anything. After brushing my teeth and gathering my backpack, I joined Mom and Officer Murray in the family room. When Murray spotted me, he cleared his throat. I slung my backpack over one shoulder and edged toward the front door.

"Hey, uh, Rami?" Murray stepped close. "I, uh, got you something."

He handed me a Mason jar with four marbles of various colors swirling against the glass edges as if they were trapped. From his pocket, he retrieved a small clear bag of colored marbles and held it out to me. I pulled out a red and white swirled marble that reminded me of the red velvet cake with cream cheese frosting that my mother always made on Christmas Day.

"Anytime something good happens, you're supposed to place a marble in the jar," Murray explained. He pointed to the marble in my hand. "Red represents moments you feel loved. The yellow ones are for acts of kindness. Blue represents heroism. Well, the instructions are in the bag, so you can use it how you like."

I dropped the red marble back in the bag and set the jar on the coffee table, muttering a quiet thank you under my breath.

"You don't have to use it. I... I..."

"It's not that," I said. "It's just...never mind." I smiled. "Thank you. It's cool."

Murray's mouth twitched. "I, uh, got myself one too." He paused. "My wife passed away a few years ago. I hoped the marble jar would remind me of happier times."

We stood in an awkward silence, unsure what to do, until Mom spoke up. "Rami? Why don't you put a yellow marble in the jar for Sam's kindness?"

The mention of his first name didn't escape my notice. But instead of gold, I reached into my pocket and pulled out the glass butterfly in striking blue with streaks of black around the edges. I fingered it, then carefully placed it in the jar. A deep sadness washed over me as the nausea from this morning returned.

I swallowed hard and followed Officer Murray and Zac out the door.

Zac and I climbed into the back seat of Murray's RD-issued electric vehicle. He switched his screen off and powered down his handheld reader. Then, as if nothing had ever happened, he and Zac talked about augmented reality gaming. I stared out the window, mentally preparing myself for what I was about to do. I had confided in the last person I thought I would ever trust—Officer Sam Murray. But he had, after all, cleared my name from the school bombing, allowing me to return to the glorious Peachtree Park High, so I guess I ought to be thankful.

Murray dropped off Zac at the middle school before heading toward the high school. Murray's eyes darted from the road to me, as if I could escape my fate even if I wanted to. The wrinkles around his eyes had deepened and I could have sworn his once salt-and-pepper hair had now morphed into full-on gray.

"The marble jar was a nice touch," I said, avoiding eye contact.

"Glad you liked it." He sighed. "This isn't some game, Rami. You're toying with other people's lives."

"You think I don't know that?" My words came out sharper than I intended, so I dialed down my emotions. I needed him. I needed his help, his protection, and most of all, his trust. "Are you sure they understand what they agreed to?" I asked for the umpteenth time since returning home.

Murray neared the school but turned in the opposite direction to avoid detection. "It was Lela's idea," he answered.

He'd already told me this, yet I felt the weight of his words all over again. Lela, my best friend since I was twelve, choosing loyalty and faithfulness again. I didn't deserve her, much less the others. Although Lela's avoidance of me would go down as her best performance, I wasn't convinced Finley ignoring me would be an act. My pawn chain had collapsed, and now I faced the evil king all alone. I wasn't sure how Murray had convinced Finley to help, but I was grateful.

Murray pulled into a parking lot across from the school and put the car in park before turning around to face me. Sweat beads formed on the bald spots near his temples. "If, for one second, you suspect something's off, you stop. Understand me? And keep your location on at all times. No exceptions."

I nodded but remained silent, lost in my thoughts.

He dropped his gaze and exhaled in one long, forceful puff of air. When his eyes met mine, his expression bore a mixture of fear and admiration. "They believe in the cause, Rami. They believe in Project Blue. They believe in you. Don't let them down."

CHAPTER 48

Wednesday, October 18

It had been almost two weeks since I stepped foot inside Golden Heights High. The strange looks and the whispers behind my back made me edgy and irritable. My friends, loyal to a fault, put themselves in harm's way, even vouching for my innocence, making what I was about to do even more painful.

Williams led his employees to believe that his Bifurcation Tracking Analysis was necessary to ensure STaR's continued control. He even made it sound patriotic. But I had a choice.

I knew the harm that came from Centurion's program, yet I had agreed to work with the Threats Division. I was a traitor, a deceiver, and no matter what I told myself, I should have told Mom the truth.

At my locker, I pulled out my binder and stuffed it into my backpack. I needed the paper, and no one would think anything about me keeping my school-issued binder with me all day. As I weaved my way down the crowded hallway, Finley brushed against me, and I stopped. He glanced at me, then continued down the hall without a word. There was so much I needed to say, so much I wanted to tell him, but it would have to wait. Officer Murray's words weeks earlier repeated in my mind. *I hope you're worth it,*he'd said. Judging from Finley's reaction, I had my answer. *I wasn't worth it.*

Vomit shot up my esophagus, and I raced to the nearest bathroom. As my face smeared against the porcelain bowl, I let it all out. Not just the bile, but the sadness, the regret, and the guilt that weighed me down. I flushed it all down the toilet until I felt completely drained. I had made my choice and I couldn't turn back. I had to pull myself together.

Before leaving the bathroom, I rinsed out my mouth and splashed my face with cool water. Then, I forced myself to walk to class, one painful step at a time. I selected a seat in the back row of algebra, leaving my usual space in the front row between Lela and Finley empty. Mr. Tarito projected his computer screen onto the whiteboard and began the lesson on quadratic formulas.

"The solutions of a quadratic equation of the form ax squared plus bx plus c equals zero, where a is not equal to zero, are given in the following formula. X equals..." He glanced up from his computer, spotted me, and remarked, "Good to have you back, Miss Carlton."

Heat rose to my cheeks as twenty-nine sets of eyes turned to the rear of the room. I lowered myself into the chair, desperate to be invisible. Lela caught my eye and spun back around. Quince shook his head and refused to acknowledge me.

"Thank you," I said, my voice strained.

Mr. T nodded, then returned to the lesson, creating a barrage of complex problems that we were required to solve using the formula he'd given. I kept my head down until the bell sounded, then charged out the door.

By last period, I couldn't wait to get home. I walked into chemistry and glanced around for Theresa. I needed her to complete the next phase. The bell rang. Still no Theresa.

The teacher instructed us to move into our groups and complete the lab assignment. The same group I'd been in when Theresa covered for me. *Where is she*? The girl next to me helped Theresa with *The Grove*, but I didn't know her name. Suddenly I felt bad that I'd never spoken to her.

"Have you seen Theresa?" I asked.

She shrugged. "Not for a few days."

"A few *days*?"

Shock must have registered on my face because she said, "She just didn't show up one day and hasn't been seen since."

Chill bumps crept down my arms. I swallowed hard. "And her family?"

The girl shrugged again. "Gone. Their house is vacant."

My anger burned. Theresa had done nothing wrong. Except... I closed my eyes, remembering what Brannon had told me at the safe house. When everyone thought I tried to blow up our school, Theresa not only defended me, she vouched for me. She told the TD that I was with her that day. The rumors about people disappearing were true. STaR must have perceived Theresa's lie as a threat. If STaR sent Theresa away for a minor infraction, what would they do to me?

The girl picked up her backpack and pulled out a notebook. Theresa's notebook. The one she carried with her all the time. "Theresa said to give you this if you ever came back to school."

My heart sank. Like so many others, Theresa had trusted me, and I had failed her. I stuffed the notebook inside my shirt and asked to be excused.

I entered the same bathroom where earlier today I'd thrown up. It was one of the few places in the entire building without cameras. I opened the notebook and flipped through pages of blank paper until I came across a messy note in Theresa's handwriting. The words were sideways and messy, so unlike the Theresa I knew.

Rami. For what it's worth, I'm happy you're not with Brannon anymore. He told Vic you broke up with him and Vic told the whole lacrosse team, so now everyone knows. I don't blame you. I never liked him.

I glanced away from the paper. For all his faults, I had to give Brannon credit for preserving my reputation rather than saving his own. Despite my efforts to hate him, I just couldn't. Brannon had been in the wrong place at the wrong time and made some bad choices. Just like me. Perhaps we weren't that different.

But it was the last sentence that gave me pause. Like before, the handwriting was messy. But this time, I had to strain my eyes to read the letters. Had Theresa known the Threats Division was after her? I opened the flashlight on my phone, illuminating the faint pencil marks until three words became visible.

Never be afraid.

CHAPTER 49

Thursday, October 19

Seconds after receiving Williams' cryptic text message last week, an email appeared, outlining what he expected. One click on the link and the spyware downloaded to my laptop. Had I failed to open Williams' email within twenty-four hours, everyone I loved would be dead. After watching the callous way Kate died, I understood Williams would follow through on his threats.

Williams worked for the Threats Division and had founded Centurion, a front to execute the TD's tactics. But I suspected Williams was also a member of The Guard. Within the vast empire President Young had created were layers of corruption, deep and entrenched in every division of STaR. The Guard had moles at every level that reported resisters to the president. No one was really safe as long as STaR ruled our government.

Without Theresa's password, I couldn't access *The Grove's* users, unless I created backdoor access like I had with Allicio. After trying several passwords and failing, I wrote a sequence of codes and hacked the user database for my school's news app. My stomach did flips as I thought about Theresa and where the Threats Division had taken her. Were they monitoring the app and forcing her to work for them? Was she even alive? Tears burned the insides of my eyes, but I brushed them off. I had to stay focused.

Once I accessed the accounts associated with *The Grove*, I expanded my search to other unsuspecting kids. With a few simple commands, I installed Centurion's spyware. Every time someone accessed *The Grove*, I saved an encrypted file on that person, as Williams had instructed. Then I moved on to Allicio.

Thanks to the program Kate created, every Allicio user had a digital file stored at the Threats Division. Kate had spent years perfecting the program, giving the government full access to our lives. Allicio's tracking program made sure we would never *want* to rebel. They turned kids against their parents. Kids become informants and it shuts down The Resistance.

Lots of kids complained about STaR, but posting complaints on Allicio was deemed disinformation and was instantly removed. The user's file was then pulled by the TD and the person vanished. Just like Theresa and her family.

Within a few short days, I hacked nearly three thousand Allicio accounts from users ages eleven to eighteen. Centurion would store the encrypted file I created on each teenager in a database, which the Threats Division could access whenever needed. I remembered Williams saying it seemed too easy, and he was right. People put so much information on social media.

But I had a problem. In order to gain constant access to multiple accounts, my computer needed more memory, and I needed to convince Mom to take me to a big box retail store. I shut down my laptop and waited until the screen registered black before closing it. Since cash was black market currency, I could use the bills I'd stashed away tonight to prevent a digital record of the things I needed. I pulled the drawer of sweaters out as far as it would go, then reached to the back where I'd stored the wad of bills. Before closing the drawer, I placed my phone where the money had been hiding. I wouldn't need it tonight and didn't want the location to track me. If either Murray or Williams put a tracer out on me, my location would register as home.

After slipping the money in the front pocket of my jeans, I darted down the stairs and outside, where Mom and Zac waited in the car. Mom had received permission from the RD to leave the house, so we planned to eat at The Orient tonight, our favorite Chinese restaurant. Like ice cream, pizza, and candy, Chinese restaurants were permitted as long as they purchased their food from STaR. After days of macaroni and cheese with canned beans, I craved sustainable food. I dashed into the back seat and threw on a cheerful face. "Mom? Can you stop at the computer store on the way?"

"Why a computer store?" Zac asked as Mom closed the overhead garage door.

I let out a groan. "Since all my textbooks are online, my laptop is running slow. Sometimes I can't even complete my homework. I need more memory." A slight fabrication, but not exactly a lie.

"Sure. That's fine," Mom said and drove toward Technology Drive.

When we pulled into the parking lot, I glanced up at the streetlights. Several closest to the entrance had cameras. I slipped on the hood of my winter jacket and lowered my head. Once inside the big box store, the cost of everything surprised me, but within minutes, I selected an external hard drive with six terabytes of memory. Since it was all I could afford, it would have to do for now. I needed cash for the other items on my list.

Unable to come up with a reasonable explanation for what I planned to buy, I encouraged Zac to look for a new simulation game, and Mom followed along, still terrified of leaving Zac alone.

"Call me when you're ready," Mom said, as she followed Zac to another department.

"Actually, I left my phone at home," I said. Mom turned, lifted her brows, but didn't ask questions. "I'll find you after I check out."

Once they disappeared around the corner, I scoured the aisles and grabbed several micro flash drives and prepaid SIM cards before heading to check out. I kept my head low, pushing stands of hair in my face to avoid recognition. The young guy behind the counter didn't seem to notice and when he rang up the total, I asked for the cash price. His eyes widened, and he glanced over his shoulder. He held up double-digit fingers without speaking. I pulled out several bills, stuffed the contents of my purchase into my jacket pocket, and went to find Mom and Zac.

The sight of the Chinese restaurant renewed my appetite, and I realized I hadn't eaten all day. I ordered sesame chicken, my favorite, and Zac ordered Mongolian beef with fried rice. Mom selected Kung Pao shrimp. When our soup arrived, I devoured the egg drop and laughed at Zac when he turned up his nose and gave his portion to Mom. Like the soup, the familiar laughter warmed my soul, and I didn't remember why I had stopped talking to my mother. When our server delivered the fragrant dishes to the table, Mom took a minute to bless our food, grasping hands with Zac and me, before diving in.

After devouring our food, Mom suggested we go out for ice cream. Zac and I exchanged puzzled looks. *How could Mom afford ice cream*?

"Actually, can we order a large bag of fortune cookies to go? I've been craving them," I said.

Zac frowned. "Since when do you like fortune cookies?"

"Since we ate horrible food for eight days." I bit my lower lip as the lie came so easily.

"Ice cream sounds better," he said.

I smiled, struggling to keep up the façade. "What about a KitKat candy bar?"

A grin spread across Zac's face, then faded. "We don't have to go to Little Cone, Rames."

I hadn't seen Brannon since the rescue, but I had to face him sometime. I managed another smile. "No, it's not that. I just thought since we're celebrating, maybe we could get one little candy bar?"

Mom's mouth twitched. "Why don't we get all three? Fortune cookies, ice cream, and candy?"

Although I had no idea how Mom could pay for everything, I kept my mouth shut. I carried the cookies to the car and ate one with delight, as if it was the best food I'd tasted while secretly wishing I could spit it out the window. But I had to stick to the plan, and this was the only way.

Zac read aloud from the piece of paper rolled up in his cookie. "'Great things are in your future.'" He pounded his chest like a gorilla. "Yep. I know that's right. Rami? Read yours."

I swallowed one disgusting bite at a time of the cookie and turned over my slip of paper. I opened my mouth, but the words lodged in my throat, and I found myself unable to speak.

"Rami?" Mom darted her focus from the road to me.

"Yeah, uh, sorry," I stammered. "It says, 'Courage is not simply one of the virtues, but the form of every virtue at the testing point.'"

Mom stayed silent for so long, I wondered if she'd heard me. She reached across the seat and squeezed my hand as my stomach tightened. Did she know about the internal struggle I faced? I was going to need tremendous courage to pull this off.

Mom let go of my hand and parked outside of Little Cone. My stomach reached my throat, and I had to swallow the fear that overtook me.

Her soft whisper interrupted my musing. "You don't have to go in."

I reached for the door handle. "It's fine. We don't even know if he's here. And if he is..." My voice trailed off.

"Then we smile politely," Mom said.

Mom's ability to forgive knew no bounds. She'd forgiven Dad long before I had the strength. *Could I do the same?*

The three of us entered the brightly lit ice cream shop, with its sticky floors and multicolored painted walls. My body shivered, though whether from fear or the temperature of the room, I couldn't say. I dropped my head to my chest and wrapped my arms around my body to hold myself together.

Mom and Zac ordered small ice cream cones, and I selected a multi-pack of KitKat candy bars from the case. I didn't know how

Mom afforded the luxury of a restaurant plus ice cream and candy, but I didn't ask. Some things were better left unsaid.

"Rami?"

My eyes floated upward as Brannon rounded the corner. He shifted his feet uncomfortably on the linoleum floor. Brannon held my gaze, and I knew he expected a response, but I couldn't form the words. All the emotions from the past few weeks leaked to the surface, and I turned to leave before I made a fool of myself.

"Rami, wait. Please?" His voice trembled, mimicking my body's response.

Slowly, I faced him. "Hi."

"It's good to see you." Brannon's lip twitched, but I didn't reciprocate his sentiment. The room grew colder by the second as the ice between us refused to thaw.

I thought about what Theresa told me, and my frozen heart began to melt. Brannon could have saved face and told everyone that he'd broken up with me. I mean, everyone thought I tried to bomb our school, so he had just cause. But Brannon took the high road. I saved his life that day at the data center, and in return, he saved my reputation.

"Bitterness is like a cancer, Rami," Mom had explained when I refused to forgive my dad. Brannon may not have deserved my forgiveness, but I needed to forgive him. For me, so I could heal. Brannon's betrayal couldn't make me incapable of love unless I let it.

"Well...I should get back to work." He pointed to the growing line of antsy kids.

I took a step toward him and lowered my voice to a mere whisper so no one could possibly overhear. "Do you remember the day we walked in Marble Park watching the blue butterflies? Did you know they use sunlight reflected off their wings to temporarily blind predators?"

Before he could respond to my bizarre question, I raced out the door.

CHAPTER 50

Friday, October 20

After checking in with Rosemary and listening to STaR's usual report on my health, I pulled the health device off the wall and placed it upside down on the carpet, shielding the camera from viewing my activity. I double-checked the blinds on the windows to be sure they were closed before turning off my overhead light and switching on a small desk lamp. The clock next to my bed read 11:50. On my laptop, I closed my world history file folder and adjusted my headphones.

My favorite song from The Script rang through the headphones. But there was no way I'd ever be in anyone's hall of fame. What I was about to do haunted me. I wasn't sure I had the courage to see it through. Would anyone in the world know my name like the lyrics of the melody suggested?

Because President Young rescued me, she'd assumed my loyalty lay with STaR. She'd ensured my role as spokesperson for STaR's safety efforts. *Your rescue guarantees the next generation understands STaR is needed to keep the country safe*, Officer Murray had explained.

But President Young miscalculated.

Mom kept a collection of books from her youth in the attic's floorboard, hidden because STaR decided what we could and couldn't read. I'd spent hours in the stifling hot attic reading Mom's historical novels about women all over the world who served as spies and risked their lives to pass secrets back and forth. Their bravery saved countless lives. My mind flooded back to these heroic women, and I pictured them hovered over a lamp in the wee morning hours, risking everything for the cause.

I wiped my sweaty palms on my pajama pants and began unwrapping the fortune cookies, tossing everything into the trash can next to my desk except the tiny strips of paper inside. I gathered the fortunes into a pile. Tonight, I only need three, but there would be other nights.

I saved the papers in a sandwich-sized plastic baggie and ran my fingers across the seal to secure it. If anyone broke into my house, I doubted they'd rummage through my lingerie. I stashed the bag between a pink bra and a pair of white lacy panties and closed the drawer. Then I waited.

Connect Mobile updated its phones and computers at midnight for exactly six minutes. Six minutes to get in and get out undetected. If I failed...I shoved the thought away and stared at the bedside clock.

The instant the clock read midnight, I unfolded a paperclip and inserted one point into a tiny hole in the side of my phone. When the tray popped out, I removed the Connect Mobile SIM card with the iconic logo embossed on it—a red C encompassing a scarlet globe. I took out one of the prepaid SIM cards that I'd purchased from the computer store and tore open the cardboard packaging. Inside, a tiny gold and white rectangular card with the same red

C gleamed in the lamp's light. Careful not to switch the identical looking SIM cards, I placed the prepaid card on the tray and closed it. While I waited for it to load, I tore a piece of notebook paper from my binder and folded it three times until it was small enough to fit under the desk.

My computer had been running its spyware program for several hours, scouring hundreds if not thousands of Allicio accounts. It amazed me the things people posted all day and night. I had no idea what algorithm Williams had applied to the spyware, and I didn't care. If this was the way to rid myself of Centurion Technologies, then so be it. Everything automatically saved to the hard drive I'd purchased from the computer store. At the end of my three-week employment, I would hand over the hard drive and Finley's computer to Williams. *If* all went as planned.

Williams' emails contained specific instructions on how to save the data he wanted, including how to bring up the coding involved in the Bifurcation Tracking Analysis. I initiated the sequence as instructed until dozens of letters and numbers appeared in rapid succession. When the codes appeared on the screen, I was supposed to hit *Alternate-Control-Function-S* within a few seconds to save the sequence onto the computer's memory. But this time, I hesitated before activating the proper response.

Instead, I snapped dozens of pictures with my phone, unsure whether an alarm would sound, but I had to try. Ten seconds. That's how much time I allowed myself. I counted down from ten, each second more terrifying than the next. Sweat beads poured down my face.

When I reached one, I ran my fingers over the keys, cringing at each click. By the time I typed the letter *S*, I thought my heart would explode. But nothing happened. No alarm, no explosion. Just a blinking red light and the program resumed its search for questionable content.

I opened the camera app and saved the photos to the prepaid SIM. Then I placed the phone on my lap next to the folder sheet of paper and kept my legs under the desk. I opened each photo and copied the sequences onto the notebook paper. Writing in this position, keeping my legs pinned against the bottom of the desk to avoid any cameras, was awkward, but I wrote as fast as my clammy hand would allow until it nearly filled the paper. I opened the tray on my phone, took out the prepaid card, and reinserted my original SIM, popping the tray back in place. 12:05. I'd made it in under six minutes.

From the notebook paper, I transcribed the codes I'd copied onto three strips of fortune paper, again keeping the fortune paper buried on my lap under the desk. I breathed a sigh of relief and sat back in my chair, feeling braver than I had in a long time.

My backpack sat next to the desk, and I pulled out one KitKat candy bar, studying the sealed wrapper. With the help of a paring knife from the kitchen, I inserted a slit on the edge of one end to open the candy, careful not to tear the wrapper.

The candy contained four wafers wedged together by milk chocolate, and the grooves between the wafers provided the perfect hiding place. I carefully wound two fortunes into a tight cylinder and stuffed one into the left groove of the bar and the other on the right.

I wound the last fortune around the prepaid SIM card. I secured it in place with a piece of clear two-sided tape from the pink tin Olivia gave me. Using tweezers from Mom's makeup bag, I pinched the card and set it in the last groove of chocolate, pressing it with the tweezers until it stayed in place. Then I placed another sticky on the edges of the opening I had created. Virtually invisible at first glance, the adhesive surpassed my expectations. Satisfied it looked like any other KitKat bar, I placed it in the zipper pocket of my backpack before cleaning up my mess.

After ripping the notebook paper to shreds, I stuffed it, along with the cardboard packaging, cookies, and wrappers, into a paper grocery bag and packed the contents into my binder, pressing against the bag until it flattened. I set two alarms, one on my phone and the other on the vintage alarm clock plugged in by my bed. The instant my head hit the pillow, I fell into a deep sleep.

Five hours later, my mom dropped me off at school early. Thankfully, she didn't ask many questions. I headed to Coach Richard's homeroom near the gym, sure I'd be the first to arrive. But a boy I didn't recognize stood bent over a desk fiddling with a wooden box. I gritted my teeth. How would I get in and out without being seen?

I stepped back into a dark hallway that ran between the gymnasium and an outside exit. Seconds ticked by, but the boy showed no sign of leaving. He might be here for an actual help session, but if so, where was the teacher?

Minutes passed, and I tugged at my low-cut blouse attached to my skin by invisible tape. I never wore this kind of thing to school, but if anyone asked why I had the pink tin with me, I needed a reasonable explanation.

I glanced over my shoulder again, the sensation of being watched growing until it rolled up my spine. The hair on my arms stood on end. There didn't appear to be cameras in this part of the building, but I couldn't shake the feeling that someone was close by.

I wondered if the brave spies of old suffered this way when they embarked on a mission. Did they look over their shoulder or want to throw up before meeting a contact? I didn't know if I would survive today, much less years of spying as those women had done.

After what felt like hours, the boy appeared and walked toward me. *Gulp. Now what*? The pounding in my head intensified. I reached for my phone and pretended to read with great interest. I counted his steps and didn't dare move until he brushed past the hallway where I stood frozen against the tan cinder block wall. He paused at the entrance to the gym, and I panicked. *Did he see me?* I held my breath. But like me, he stood head down, glued to his phone, oblivious to my presence. When he entered the gym, I exhaled with such force, a tumbleweed of dust blew across the tile floor. I took one last look around, then hurried into the classroom.

After playing the game Battleship for days with Zac at the safe house, I memorized the coordinates on the grid. *C-3*. Three rows to the left; three seats back. I dropped into the chair and checked the underside of the metal desk. A microscopic X marked the location, and I slipped the KitKat bar into the desk, shoving it to the back. As I bolted out of the room, I nearly crashed into Finley and the boy I'd seen earlier, both carrying brown wooden boxes.

"Chess is a game of strategy to know your opponent's next move before they know it themselves," Finley told his new protégé.

"I prefer the game of Chinese checkers with bright blue marbles," I said. The boy gave me a quizzical look, but walked away, leaving Finley and me alone in the doorway. Then I lowered my voice to a mere whisper. "Did you know the underside of a blue morpho butterfly is actually boring brown? They fold their wings to camouflage their appearance and become undetectable."

Before Finley could respond, I raced toward the cafeteria, not bothering to look back. I rounded the corner and entered the food line, selecting a strawberry yogurt and two granola bars, the crunchy kind that came in bright green packaging. My stomach clenched as I sat alone in the back.

My appetite now squelched, I reached into my binder for the grocery bag of cookies and wrappers I'd collected last night. I tossed the bag and my yogurt into the trash can before sprinting to the nearest bathroom.

I dashed into the far stall and stood motionless for several seconds to be sure I was alone. When I sat on the toilet seat, I buried my head in my hands, amazed at how low I'd stooped. When no sounds floated from the stall next to mine, I reached into my backpack for the pink tin where I'd stuffed two pieces of invisible sticky tape, a metal nail file, and a micro flash drive. I took the nail file from the tin and pressed it against the seal of a granola bar. The green wrapper tore, leaving a gaping hole. Frustrated and out of time, I tossed it aside and selected the second granola bar package. This time, the sharp metal punctured a microscopic hole in the closure. I sawed back and forth with the nail file to create a half-inch opening.

Copying what I'd done earlier, I folded an adhesive around the flash drive and slid it between the two granola bars, pressing the bars together to ensure it wouldn't slide around in the packaging. With the second strip of tape, I secured the opening until it looked new again.

Then I waited.

Within minutes, the door opened and voices flooded the bathroom. I flushed the toilet and edged toward the sink, allowing the cool water to calm my nerves. Lela and Jess from our volleyball team checked the mirror and reapplied lip gloss. The way they stood six feet away made me think I had some contagious disease that spread through human contact.

Each time I opened my mouth to speak, my tongue stuck to the roof of my mouth as I tried to come up with a clever way to break the ice between Lela and me. Jess frowned at me in the mirror. I dried my hands and cleared my throat.

"Hey, Lela? Someone told me a few stray morpho butterflies survived. Surprising, since they normally only live for a couple of weeks. Anyway, want to go check it out with me?" My voice trembled.

Jess snickered. "Honestly, Rami. That seems really boring. Let's go, Lela. I've got to get to class."

"Oh, it's just that I wanted to see what all the buzz about their coloring is about. The technology district is swarming with plans to use their blue iridescence adaptation," I said.

Jess laughed, and I felt stupid. *What had I been thinking?*

While Lela zipped her purse, I held out the granola bar in the bright green package. "I got you your favorite from the cafeteria, so you'd have a snack before practice." I could hear the nervousness in my strained voice.

Lela hesitated, then tugged it out of my hand. "Thanks."

She followed Jess out the door, but before it closed, I heard Jess mutter, “What’s with Rami? She’s acting really weird.”

The door slammed, making it impossible to decipher between the thud of the door and the pounding in my chest.

CHAPTER 51

Saturday, October 21

The instant my dad dropped me off at Marble Park, the acid in my stomach churned. I clutched the heavy paper bag to my chest, but nothing could still my beating heart. The last time I came here, Brannon bought me coffee, and we talked about the shooting. He seemed concerned and offered to help, but it was all an act. Although his deceit overshadowed the feelings I'd once held for him, I was no different.

If the others hadn't agreed to help, I wouldn't have been able to finish this. I wasn't that courageous. Everything had come down to this moment. Without Officer Murray's protection, I felt exposed and vulnerable.

I avoided the fountain at the park's entrance that spilled water onto shiny marble rocks below. The mouth of the fountain in the shape of a lion contained a camera. The only camera in marble park. When the town's historical society restored the park years ago, they'd convinced the government that cameras weren't necessary in a location that promoted peace and rest, qualities the Safety Division valued as good for our health.

Instead of retracing the steps I'd taken with Brannon, I entered through a patch of glistening white marble at the entrance to The Path of Serenity. I pulled Finley's laptop and the hard drive I promised Williams from my paper bag and set them on a large, white rock. Whoever the TD sent to collect would spot the items in an instant. I kept my end of the bargain. I only prayed Williams would do the same.

I paused at the entrance to the greenhouse. By now, the butterflies had died off, their existence to be forgotten until next year. I refused to let that happen to Blue and Donut. Their death had to mean something.

I drew in a deep breath, pulled my hood down to cover my face, and continued walking in search of the famous sticker bench. For years, kids had placed stickers with catchy sayings on one bench in the park. Park maintenance scraped away the paper, yet the constant white residue lingered. When I spotted what appeared to be a new sticker from Little Cone, I sat down. My thumb trailed the edges of the silver metal square I'd stuck to the palm of my hand with tape before I left the house.

Birds chirped in the distance. A whiff of pine mixed with a floral scent blew in the light breeze. Everything around me made me want to relax, yet I felt edgy. Because of the absence of cameras, ROs and drones routinely patrolled the park. As an RO approached, I lowered my head and clasped my hands together with my elbows out wide in a meditation stance. In reality, I uttered a silent prayer, asking God for the courage I needed to complete this mission.

A drone flew overhead, its familiar buzzing causing my panic to swell. I kept my eyes closed and remained in my meditative state until the RO's handheld sounded. A female voice requested all units to report to an address in the technology district. The drone flew away, and silence ensued. Officer Murray had created a diversion, but it wouldn't take them long to figure out it was a false alarm.

My hands shook, so I tucked them under me. Squeezing my thin fingers between the small slats of the bench, I placed the flash drive against the wooden grain until it stuck in place. The flash drive contained copies of everything I'd given to Williams. The Resistance would have the proof they needed to expose the corruption at Centurion Technologies. Satisfied the flash drive was safe, I stood and retraced my steps.

Something in the distance caught my eye. I glanced over my shoulder. My eyes darted about, searching. Coming up empty, I couldn't shake the sensation of being hunted. The hair on my arms prickled. I picked up the pace in a full-on sprint and raced toward the entrance, expecting the fountain to come into view. Each pathway appeared the same, each tree a clone of the one before. Had I gotten turned around? I should be there by now. The white marble rock sat empty. A bird landed on a feeder.

Then a sharp pain pierced my back. I had no time to react. I fell face first into a row of yellow mums, scratching and clawing to get up, but my palms sunk further into the ground. My assailant's foot pressed against my back and my mouth filled with black potting soil.

"Where is it?" my attacker hissed.

In my region, it was common to see opossums in the middle of the road, allowing their hard shell to protect them from oncoming traffic. With my face planted in the dirt, I played possum. To pretend to be dead. Or at least injured. My performance gave my assailant pause and after a few moments, he removed his foot.

It was all the space I needed to roll to the side and scissor-kick his legs. When he stumbled backward, I scrambled to my feet. My fingers folded into a fist, and I landed a left hook against his nose. Blood trailed down his face. My attacker bent my arm behind me in a painful twist. I cried out. He lunged forward and used his body to wedge me against a tall oak tree.

Once again, Dominic Bell had me cornered. His dark eyes, menacing and vindictive, bore holes straight through my soul. I never knew what terrified me about my nightmare until now. The realization took my breath away.

The evil presence had been Dominic. The unfamiliar woods, the sinister aura that surrounded me…it had been him all along. Every ounce of resolve melted away at the reality of my situation.

"I should have killed you the first time we met," Dominic seethed through gritted teeth. "Now, where is it?"

My words came out calm and precise, but a throbbing pain pulsated at my temple. "I left everything on the marble rock, exactly where the instructions said."

Without warning, Dominic reached into his jacket and drew out a pistol, pointing it at my head. Bile traveled up my esophagus. "That's not what I asked. You made copies of the data."

An almost imperceptible hum followed by a slight crunch of fallen leaves buzzed near my ear. *Had help arrived?*

"You recruited *me*, remember? For my amazing coding capabilities." My words sounded calm, but inside I trembled.

He plunged the barrel deeper into my skull. "We know you're helping The Resistance."

I lowered my head in defeat. Dominic had won. "I never wanted to be part of this, you know. The Threats Division thinks they can control citizens. The Resistance thinks they can stop STaR. Either way, I'm a pawn. All *I* ever wanted was for Zac to be safe and for my mom to return home alive."

A flicker of surprise flashed, but quickly dissipated. He pushed the barrel deeper into my head and switched the safety off. "I said—"

Gunshots rang out. I started to scream, then thought better of it. My hand slammed over my terrified mouth. Blood sprayed on my hand and soaked my clothing. Dropping to the ground, I covered my head. Dominic's pistol plummeted to the ground, and he dropped to his knees before his body slumped forward in my direction.

Forty-three days after Dominic threatened to kill Zac, shot several rounds into Finley's basement, and beat Brannon senseless, the nightmare ended.

Dominic Bell was dead.

The shooter and his partner wore black masks and night vision goggles. Facial recognition would be impossible. No camera within a hundred miles could detect who had shot and killed Dominic Bell.

The shooter touched my shoulder. The ringing in my ears made it impossible to hear his command. When I didn't move, he yanked me into a standing position and dragged me to a parked car waiting on a side street. He shoved me onto the floor of the back seat and covered me with a tan tarp that smelled of mildew.

My emotional roller coaster came to a screeching halt as I fought back tears that threatened to surface. Exhaustion took over, and I collapsed under the weight of the plastic covering. As the car raced away, I peeled a corner of the tarp away and stole a peek at my captors.

Muscolo and Freckles. *They came for me.*

Finley's laptop and the hard drive containing thousands of Allicio accounts sat on Freckles' lap. Her arm hung limp in a black sling and with her good hand, she clutched the micro flash drive I'd left under the sticker bench. The site of Muscolo at the safe house had inflicted fear, yet his enormous presence today made me feel safe. He tossed a towel to the back, and I wiped the blood from my hands and face. My sweatshirt remained stained with Dominic's blood, and the sight of it made me nauseous.

Muscolo sped through side streets, weaving in and out of traffic. He avoided the technology district where Murray had staged a crisis. "You are either really brave or really stupid," he said.

"Maybe a little of both." Relief filled my veins, and a slight smile tugged at the corners of my mouth. "Officer Murray said you two are friends. Who do you work for?"

For a second, Muscolo stayed silent, the space between us tense. "The less you know, the better."

My throat tightened. With spies at every level, it was hard to know whom to trust. Yet Muscolo and Freckles had protected me not once, but twice. He drove down the long driveway to the horse stables across from my home. Pecan trees swayed in the light afternoon breeze.

He pulled up next to the barn and motioned for me to exit. "This is as far as we go. You can walk home from here."

I pulled at the door handle and tilted my head to the side. "Will I see you again?"

Muscolo snickered. "When Murray asked me to watch out for you, he should have warned me what I was getting into. Take care of yourself, kid."

Freckles jumped out of the car and pulled me into an embrace. The sudden show of affection caught me off guard and I stumbled backward. She placed a sharp object in my hand. The point pierced my palm, drawing a drop of blood. She brushed her lips against my ear so no one could possibly overhear. "For Blue. Never be afraid."

She dropped her arms and climbed back into the car. Muscolo, the muscular man of few words, sped away, leaving me holding a blue morpho butterfly.

CHAPTER 52

Saturday, October 21

Everyone gathered around the television in our small family room. Zac, Mom, Dad, Olivia, and Detective Murray. Even Nollie stood at attention at UNN's breaking news alert. I scratched Nollie between the ears as the cameras captured a chaotic scene.

"Check it out!" Zac's expression held excitement, even hope.

"Despite opposition among the intelligence community, Reinforcement Division's National Agents brought CEO Malik Williams of Centurion Technologies in today for questions related to the kidnapping of Annie Carlton..."

As National Agents led Malik Williams away, he hung his head to avoid the barrage of camera flashes that followed him to the black SUV. I feigned an outburst, gasping louder than necessary. I'd never been a good actress, and I felt Mom's gaze land on me. My best attempts to hide my clandestine activities hadn't escaped my mother's notice. Mom had known about my espionage all along.

When Williams held me captive and attempted to educate me on history, I had played dumb. My favorite novels contained stories of double agents—those who spied for both their country and the enemy—and I'd memorized many of these stories, fascinated with how the characters played the game. I thought about the novels I'd read, and a grin spread across my cheeks. I'd also been listening when Finley taught Zac to play chess at the safe house, and this was my moment.

I softly uttered under my breath, "Checkmate."

Within seconds of UNN's announcement, my phone lit up with messages, which I sorted by importance. Allicio buzzed with activity, its usage increasing 165 percent. The constant ding of the tracker alerted me to over three thousand Allicio accounts.

It was eerie to know so much about total strangers. What posts they liked, where they shopped, where they ate, and even who their friends were, but I told myself I did it for them—for Mom and Zac—and when I'm honest, for myself; for the freedoms I'd taken for granted.

Murray motioned for me to step outside. The back door had been repaired and the shards from my horse trophy swept away. "President Young has asked to meet with you." He kept his voice low and controlled.

I repeated the words I'd spoken earlier to Dominic moments before his death. "I don't want any part of this."

Murray edged closer. "Like it or not, you are a part of it. You can't escape your fate, Rami."

"I don't believe in fate. Everyone has a choice," I said.

Murray rubbed the back of his head where Dominic had inflicted a nasty blow. "Then it's up to you to choose your side."

My skin tightened. President Young allowed us to live in a free country, and to come and go as we pleased, as long as we didn't speak out against STaR. The instant someone questioned STaR, consequences followed. Mom had been kidnapped. Kate had been murdered. Theresa and her family vanished. The reality that I would never be free sent chills up my spine.

I was a prisoner, just like every other citizen. If I chose to be the spokesperson for STaR's safety efforts, President Young decided my fate. If I became the butterfly symbol for The Resistance, they controlled me. I was a pawn for the Threats Division, or I was a pawn for The Resistance. Either way, I was being manipulated to fulfill a plan. A plan I wanted nothing to do with. I'd been thrust into this game with no hope of escape.

I took a moment to gather my thoughts. "How will this end?"

"Williams' arrest is all for show. They won't hold him. He's too powerful. But some of STaR's secrets are out in the open and they know it. They'll do whatever it takes to keep citizens believing the lie that we're safe under STaR's protection. Under President Young. She'll change the narrative and citizens will go on believing the lie that she orchestrated your release and that you are devoted to her. Unless we take her down first." He paused. "Thanks to your efforts, The Resistance has what they need to destroy Centurion's Bifurcation Tracking program, but it's only one piece. The Threats Division will rebuild the tracking program."

"And when they do?"

"We'll be ready to take them down, one piece at a time."

I bit my lower lip before responding. "Why do you do it? If it doesn't make a difference."

"Because eventually it will. Peel an onion's layers and eventually you get to the core. With your help, Rami, we'll expose all of STaR's secrets and take down President Young. But we must be patient."

"What will happen to you? And the others who rescued me?"

"We're going underground. We've always known it was a possibility. But your involvement sped up the timeline."

"I never wanted to be involved."

Detective Murray sighed. "You put a face to the cause, a belief that what we're doing matters for the next generation. That's why you must choose."

With that, he slipped out the backyard gate and disappeared without another word. As the news droned on, I excused myself and went to the small enclave Mom used as an office to search for a paperclip.

In the garage, I stuck the pointed side of the paperclip into the tiny hole of my phone to remove the SIM card, as I had done so many times over the past few days. Connect Mobile's logo—a red C encircling the globe—stared back at me. I had once believed in their motto, that they would keep me connected to others, yet safe from outside threats. But not anymore.

I rifled through a tool cabinet until I found a hammer. With both hands on the handle, I smashed the Connect Mobile SIM into a million pieces until there was nothing left but slivers of plastic on the concrete floor.

Satisfied, I walked to the kitchen, placed a drain stopper in the sink, and ran the cold water. I dropped my phone into the pool of water, flooding it to destroy Centurion's tracker before I smashed it with the hammer. I'd waited for this day, dreamed of it even, and now that it arrived, all I could think about were the lives lost.

As tiny air bubbles leaked from the crevices, the memory of Kate, Donut, Blue, and Theresa came flooding back. Kate risked her life to stop Centurion. Blue and Donut died protecting me.

And Theresa disappeared because she tried to help me find my mother. I crumpled to the floor, overcome with grief.

"Rami? Lela's here," Zac called from the other room.

But I stayed in my corner, unable to bring myself to my feet. Lela dashed into the room with such flair, my tears morphed into giggles. She curled up beside me, holding me until the tears ran dry.

"We did it, Rames," she said. An array of feelings rushed to the surface, and I didn't know which one to entertain. As if sensing my distress, Lela raised her brow. "Hey. We did it," she repeated. "You're safe now. We all are."

Her giddiness reminded me of the sixth-grade girl who had become my best friend. Loyal to a fault. But I knew I'd never be safe. My shoulders sagged beneath the weight of what we'd pulled off.

"Project Blue," I said, just above a whisper.

Project Blue formed in my mind the day of my rescue when I'd learned Blue had given his life for me. The marble jar from Officer Murray sat on the bookshelf where my horse trophy had once stood. He'd given me a message that day—four marbles representing the four friends who had agreed to risk their lives for our freedom—Finley, Lela, Quince, and Brannon. When I placed my butterfly in the jar, it solidified the plan.

Project Blue was a go.

From the beginning, my friends and I knew the risk. Never be afraid to stand up for what's right, my mother had said. Theresa had written the same thing in her notebook. And today, when Freckles handed me her blue morpho butterfly, she'd reiterated those words.

Yet I fought my fears every single day as I passed coded messages. Sometimes I handwrote the codes needed to shut down the Bifurcation Tracking program on fortune paper rolled into a KitKat bar and left inside a desk. Each day, Finley took his brown chess set to Coach Richard's homeroom, and when the bell rang, he placed the candy bar in the box.

Other times, I saved data onto a flash drive stuffed into the classic green packaging of a granola bar, which I bought daily from the school cafeteria. I stored files of those whose social media accounts were being tracked by the Threats Division and who made Centurion's watch list. I stored Centurion's algorithms so The Resistance could stop future threats against citizens.

Lela put the granola bars in her locker, and every few days, Quince stuffed them into his backpack. Since Lela and Quince were officially back together after their fake breakup, no one thought twice about Quince hanging out at her locker after school now and then.

Quince placed the notes, SIM cards, and flash drives into empty ice cream cone boxes left outside of Little Cone for Brannon to recycle. Brannon took the boxes to the recycle center, where Officer Murray waited. I supposed Brannon agreed to help because I'd saved his life at the data center, but we never spoke about that day.

Although I didn't see these transactions, I trusted my friends would do the right thing. And in the end, they did. The Little Cone sticker on the bench today marked the last drop, the last chance to flush Dominic out of hiding. But his rage surprised me. If Muscolo and Freckles had arrived any later... I shuddered at the thought. I was alive and Project Blue had been a success.

Lela nodded toward the house, where Finley lingered in the doorway. Finley ran a hand through his wavy hair, and I couldn't help but smile at the familiar habit I'd come to love. Lela gave me a gentle push. "Go talk to him."

A lump formed in my throat. *Did I have the courage to face Finley*? *Had he forgiven me*? I edged closer, one cautious step at a time, and followed him through the house to the front porch.

Finley shuffled his feet on the wood. "Hi."

"Hi." I bit my lower lip and swallowed hard. "Fin...I just wanted to say...I'm sorry. About everything."

"You should be. You caused a lot of problems." The upward tug of Finley's mouth gave him away. His soft eyes twinkled with mischief.

I had so much I wanted to say, so much I needed to tell him, yet the words stopped short. "I... I..."

We stood in an awkward silence for several seconds, neither of us sure what to do next. I tugged at a fingernail, ripping it until it tore loose. Finley fiddled with his phone before dropping it to the wooden slats on my porch. Without warning, he stomped on it over and over, crushing the glass screen beneath the weight of his force. I jumped back, surprised by the outburst, and gave a nervous laugh.

"I've been wanting to do that for a long time," he said, as if explaining his actions. "I've also been dying to do this." He closed the gap between us and ran a finger across my bottom lip. "I love how you bite your lip whenever you're nervous. And how you get a certain sparkle in your eye when you're determined to get your way."

He wrapped his arms around me. I rested my weary head on his beating heart, grateful for the warmth and comfort of his arms. I wanted to love him the way he loved me—without fear and without reservation.

My breath caught in my throat. "So, what now?"

"We fight, just like we always have. And we prepare the others." Finley lifted my chin. "Rames. Look at me." I looked up, frightened by what I'd see. But his warm eyes showed no hate, no bitterness, only acceptance. "None of this was your fault. You didn't start the battle for control." He held out his hand. "Come on. There's something I want to show you."

"Now?" My voice tensed. But his palm remained, and I stared at it, wondering why he still wanted to be with me. "Fin—"

He softly brushed his lips to mine and thousands of nerve endings fired from the top of my head to the tips of my toes. I wanted to stay like that, but he pulled away and touched one finger to my mouth. "Shh. Trust me."

Finley had given me every reason to trust him. I'd run to him for help when I should have gone home. I'd asked him to risk everything for me and he did it without reservation. He'd proven himself over and over. Now it was my turn.

I reached for his hand, and it fit with mine as if it had belonged there all along. My palm tingled as we walked past the pecan trees and down the gravel driveway leading to the stables where Musculo had dropped me off.

Finley let go and stopped. "Wait. Close your eyes." When I frowned, he cupped my cheeks. "Do you trust me?"

My face flushed under his gaze, and my stomach fluttered. Trust didn't come easy for me. But trust was about relinquishing control and believing in the other person. I intertwined my fingers with his and closed my eyes in surrender.

Finley guided me toward the scent of hay. "There. Now open."

Streaks of pink and auburn hues lit the evening sky as an enormous orange sphere descended above the pasture where the horses grazed. We watched until the sky turned gold and the sun disappeared behind the barn. The horses paid no attention to the sunset, and I realized they'd become comfortable with the confines of their fence. But I wasn't like them. After living through this nightmare, I knew I could never be complacent.

"I told Murray I didn't want to be part of The Resistance." My voice remained calm, but the familiar fear resurfaced.

He stayed silent for so long, I wondered if he'd heard me. "This is just the beginning. Williams didn't act alone."

I let the words sink in. "The Guard. They control everything and everyone." I considered my words for a moment. "I'll have to choose a side, Fin."

Finley pulled me into his arms. He kissed the top of my head. "I know, Rames. I've always known."

Acknowledgements

The idea for *The Text* came in 2016 while I was writing *Sour Lemon and Sweet Tea*. I drafted a rough outline, then put it away until the events of 2020 prompted me to begin again. So many have helped me along the way, and I hope to name everyone who played an enormous part in helping me become the writer I am today.

To my amazing editor, David Aretha, thank you for believing in me and this story! Your attention to detail and encouragement made the story what it is today. Thank you to the team at Infinite Teen Publishing for the countless hours and dedication to seeing this novel through to the end.

I'm thankful to be surrounded by a strong and supportive writing community. To my dear fellow writers and 209 critique partners...we've been together a long time. Thank you for the countless hours, suggestions, critiques, and words of encouragement. To my amazing launch team, you spread the word about *The Text* and made even the most reluctant teen reader want to pick up a copy. Thank you for your genuine support! To my Beta readers, thank you for reading through the rough parts and for making the story way better! To Abby, thank you for making sure the kids sounded like actual teens. Your suggestions were invaluable to me! To Katia, thank you for your guidance on

Brazilian culture and ensuring my Portuguese and Spanish were correct! I sincerely appreciate your help!

There are friends who stick as close as a sister and I am blessed to have such amazing women in my life who spur me on, challenge me, love me, and make me a better person. Thank you Michele Hall, Allison Powers, Kristin Kohrman, and Michelle Wilde for your special friendship!

My parents, Gordon and Janet, taught me to stand up for what is right. I think you can see how their example played out in this book. I love you Mom and Dad! My sisters, Kim and Tara, are truly my best friends. We never would have thought that could happen, but here we are. Thank you for your never-ending support and encouragement. To my sisters-in-law, Tammie and Bunnie, I'm blessed by your presence and thankful for two more sisters who love me no matter what!

To my boys, Connor and Bryson. Never be afraid to stand up for what is right. There are always risks, but I trust you'll do what is right. I will love you forever!

For Dusty, my husband, and tech support, thank you! Your faith in me and my writing never strayed. You kept me going when I wanted to give up. You read the chapters, offered suggestions, and constantly reminded me I could do this. My endless technology questions kept you on your toes and I'm thankful you patiently answered each question in easy-to-understand language. I love you with all my heart!

To the Lord Jesus Christ, who loves each of us unconditionally. I owe it all to You.

About the Author

Julane Fisher is the author of the award-winning Sour Lemon Series. *Sour Lemon and Sweet Tea* is a humorous portrayal of life before cell phones and social media, emphasizing positive family values. Julane lives in north Georgia with her husband, twin boys, and their two mischievous Labrador retrievers. Be the first to know when she releases a new novel by signing up for her newsletter.

www.JulaneFisher.com
Goodreads @JulaneFisher
Instagram @JulaneFisher.author
Facebook @JulaneFisherAuthor

Milton Keynes UK
Ingram Content Group UK Ltd.
UKHW012123210923
429156UK00014B/138/J